The
Answer
Key

A Romantic Suspense

Jane Carver

THE ANSWER KEY
Copyright © 2021 by Jane Carver

ISBN: 978-1-953735-65-2

Published by Satin Romance
An Imprint of Melange Books, LLC
White Bear Lake, MN 55110
www.satinromance.com

Published in the United States of America.

Cover Design by Ashley Redbird Designs

Dedicated to the medical personnel who tend the ill at personal risk, teachers who present lessons long distance, and scientists who search for the answer key to Covid-19. Life presented them with problems, and they're using what answers they have to learn more.

DIFFERENT DAY, SAME OL' STUFF

Time stands still. Has no meaning. Keeps on ticking no matter what happens to those who float through it. At least that's what Shannon Waller thought as she once again checked the thermometer outside the kitchen window. Beyond that stood the rusted 1905 Model T car and glass bulb gas pump that Waller Senior used back when this was a working farm.

Now the land was gone but for three acres and this hundred year old house that let in every Montana winter blast of frigid air. A dingy dull landscape lay hidden under a foot of snow. Even spring's blooming flowers wouldn't liven up the place that much.

Shannon's sigh escaped into the heated room despite the single-pane yellowed window glass. She dropped the heavy curtain that at least blocked the frigid air that poured insidiously off the panes. Her home resembled a mausoleum often times with its heavy drapes. But the warmth and light inside lifted her spirits when the outside world threatened to stomp all over her.

Like right now. Her 2000 Ford Escort, bought from a rental company back in the day, needed yet another repair. She'd already resigned herself to having no heater in the car for the rest of the winter.

The heating fuel cost for the house seemed to get higher each month, not to mention the rest of her bills. The quilts she sold online only managed to pay for the fabric for the next one or two. Her passion didn't exactly put her into another tax bracket. Quilting only kept her sane.

"Move over, Simon," Shannon told the orange tabby cat that lay on the pile of bills spread out on her small desk. Simon seemed quite comfortable, his tail wrapped around his paws, his front feet tucked under his chest and his nose almost touching the latest electric bill as he snoozed. Shannon ran her hand softly over the elderly cat's back, enjoying the rumbles that rose as her only companion allowed the caresses. His head lifted, and he let her scratch his chin.

"Sorry, old boy, but I've got to rob Peter to pay Paul," she said as she picked him up carefully and laid him on the corner of her bed. He resumed the same hunched up, tucked in position, and within minutes, his head once more drooped so his nose lay just above the quilt top.

Someday that poor cat's going to die, and I'll really be alone then, she mused as she shuffled papers, trying to figure out where she could pay a bare minimum on one bill in order to pay a full bill somewhere else. Other than the wind occasionally whistling as it rounded the corner of her bedroom, the house lay in late Saturday morning winter silence.

Brrrring! The phone rang, and Shannon jumped, her heart going into a pounding beat.

"Jesus, that scared me." She clutched her chest as she reached for the portable phone, once more wishing she could afford a cell phone. "Hello?"

"Mrs. Waller, the Washburn account is due first thing Monday morning. I don't like to disturb anyone on Sundays so request you come in for several hours this afternoon to get the order ready."

Mr. Leven, the owner of Waller lumber company, minced no words. He would pay a meager overtime for her coming in, but he had no compunction about finding another accountant if she didn't. He was a crusty eighty-two year old who expected his employees to jump when he said so. She might have been married to his nephew once but having the same last name as the company or being a distant relative meant nothing to him. Being as she needed the job, no matter the paltry pay, she agreed. He seldom asked her to come in on weekends, but he expected her there when he did.

"I may need a little more time than two hours, sir." Leven did not answer to anything but *sir*. Using his first name would probably get someone fired, so no one ever tried.

"I'll pay for two hours, Mrs. Waller. I expect the work to be finished by then."

"I understand, sir. I'll be there at 2:00."

Without a word of thanks, her boss hung up.

"Shit." She wanted to cry but knew tears were useless. Her boss said come, and she would go, like it or not. Still a shuddering dry sob escaped, but she quickly shut down the emotion. "Sorry, Simon. Our movie date's gonna have to wait a few hours. I'll be home in time to feed you though."

She turned and gave the cat a few caresses before heading to the closet to find warmer clothes.

Dressed in heavy outerwear and snow boots, she trudged past the old Model T parked not far from the house—that was where it ran out of gas decades ago—and tugged to crack the frost on the Escort's door handle. Having to park outside in winter sucked. But the barn wasn't in any shape to keep the car warm though it would keep it dry. Still walking a hundred feet back to it just for her car was stupid. So she parked it right beside the kitchen door and prayed the car would start each time she needed it.

———

At 4:00 Shannon shut down her computer, wrapped up in her cold weather gear, and locked the office. She'd called Mr. Leven first and told him the order was ready, and she was leaving.

"Very good, Mrs. Waller," was all the old man said.

"You're welcome," Shannon said to the company cell phone after she hit the END button. "Ungrateful old bastard."

One more time her car almost refused to start, but the engine finally turned over, and she made her way home through a light snowfall, financial and weather worries eating at her the whole way.

"This is pretty sad, isn't it, Simon," she said as she and the cat snuggled among the covers on her bed. "A cat as my date. Wish Jacob was here." That was an old refrain. Fifteen years old. The past was past even if it was still a mystery. "Nothing we can do about it now, is there, old boy?" She pulled the cat up against her, gave him a tiny piece of bologna from her sandwich, and let him lick a little salt off her finger from her chips. With a click of the remote, the TV turned on, and the movie started playing. The cat probably didn't remember her husband, but Shannon remembered how snuggling in bed with a handsome hunk of a man beat settling down in cold sheets with a tired old cat. "Where's the love, huh, Simon?" To which the cat simply rumbled beneath her fingers.

———

"Emily, how's it going?" Shannon whipped up pancakes to go with her scrambled eggs and the last bit of sausage. Her breakfast for lunch.

"I'm so tired of cold, but the sun off the snow from last night is gorgeous." Emily Zimmer always provided a glimmer of sunshine on the dullest days.

Shannon heated oil for the pancakes with her portable phone tucked into the curve of her neck and head bent over to keep it still. "I'm looking forward to the flowers blooming in the garden. It always amazes me how they survive in these temperatures." The sizzle of batter hitting oil was loud enough that Emily heard it.

"Pancakes? Yum!"

"You and Todd come over and share some." Shannon enjoyed the couple with their optimistic outlook on life.

"Wish I could. We haven't visited since that last blizzard blew through, but Todd's brother and his family are headed over. They're coming from Emerson Junction."

"We don't live so far apart, so I'll catch you when you're free." Shannon moved two pancakes to a plate. "But you're going to miss some awesome pancakes and light as air scrambled eggs." Emily loved to eat, and Shannon enjoyed teasing her.

"Aw, now that's not fair, Shannon." At Emily's end of the line, a scuffling sounded. Her dogs. A doorbell rang. "Gotta go. Catch you later. Company's here."

"Enjoy!" Shannon waited for Emily to click off, then hung up the portable.

Simon wove in and out of Shannon's legs, begging for some sausage.

"Only if you let me enjoy my breakfast…and the view." She moved the plate and cup of coffee to the kitchen table but sat so she could see out the window. "Humm, as usual, Emily was right. It is a pretty day. Cold but pretty." As the rest of Sunday passed, Shannon had a lighter heart.

———

Monday morning dawned with no more snow forecasted. Sunlight glared off the white stuff and hurt the eyes despite the beauty. Employees came into the office shielding their eyes from the glow that they seldom saw during the winter months. Even into early April snow still slowed down work and stifled spring's arrival.

Morning, Shannon or *Good morning, Mrs. Waller* the men would say as they headed for the board where the job assignments hung. They always made a stop at the thirty-cup coffee pot that Mr. Leven started each morning. That was the only saving grace about her boss. He had the coffee ready when everyone showed up. Just the smell of fresh brewed coffee as she opened the door started the day off right no matter what else happened.

Shannon's desk sat to one side of the door, but she still

caught most of the drafts that came in when the door opened and shut. The heater beneath her desk ran eight months out of twelve. From her desk she could see straight into Mr. Leven's office.

"Good morning, beautiful." Charlie Hawkins entered the office, his tall broad, hulking body taking up most of the doorway as he came in.

When Shannon said nothing and continued to work on her computer, Charlie propped his hip on the corner of her desk and repeated his greeting. She remained silent and ignored him.

"Aw, come on, Shannon," he finally whined.

She continued to ignore him. Charlie considered himself as a lady's man and had come up with the idea years ago that she should go out with him because he was such a nice guy. He actually told her that. She informed him she was a married woman. When he said her husband wasn't in the picture anymore—ignoring the fact that Jacob Waller was never declared dead despite his disappearance—she blew up.

"I married Jacob and consider myself married until the day he shows up or someone finds his body. End of story," she informed him through tight lips.

Still, Charlie never stopped trying. This time he apparently decided to let the compliment go and get down to business. "Is the order for the Washburn account ready?" He fiddled with the things on her desk.

When she shot him a nasty look, he tucked his hands back around his coffee cup and gave her an innocent face.

"You happen to be sitting on the Washburn folder that I had to come in on Saturday and prepare," she informed him in an emotionless tone of voice. To show Charlie any kind of emotion only encouraged him to continue his insane idea that she might fall in love with him one day.

"Really?" Charlie jumped up and grabbed the folder that now wore a sharp crease from his buttocks. "Well, aren't you the clever one, getting this ready for me on a weekend."

Shannon bit her lip, so wanting to tell him that Leven ordered her to come in, but she refused to say any more to the man than necessary.

"Have a nice day, beautiful." Charlie puckered his lips and blew her an air kiss.

"Someday all that macho stuff is going to get you in trouble, Charlie." Todd Zimmer stood by the coffee pot, having seen the encounter. "She doesn't have to report it. Anyone can say something to the police about how you treat her."

"I treat her like a lady, Todd, and don't you forget it." Charlie's usual jolly-man attitude took a sharp 180* turn.

"If talking to her like that constitutes how a lady is treated, you need some lessons on modern day feminism. My wife tells me that guys like you get sued, go to court, and get fined or put in prison for doing just what you do all the time to Shannon. I'd think about it, is all I'm saying." Todd saluted a stunned Charlie with his coffee cup before slipping out the door, headed to his delivery truck.

Shannon grinned at her computer during Todd's impromptu set-down. She refused to glance Charlie's way. Her smile might infuriate the big man, and everyone knew he had something of a short fuse in the anger management department.

Charlie Hawkins and the boss were the only real blights in Shannon's life. Well, that and bills and a vanished husband. People like Todd Zimmer and her many friends in

Cut Bank helped balance things out most days though, at least where her emotions were concerned.

———

By the end of the week, Shannon's last quilt was in the mail to a customer in Atlanta. She'd packed it after taking photos. The quilt was one of her best, and she was justifiably proud of it. She'd paid her bills but only the bare amounts she could afford. Her Escort went into the shop Wednesday afternoon, and Todd graciously gave her a ride home, promising to pick her up Thursday and Friday if necessary, then take her by the garage to pick up her car when the repairs were finished.

By the time he dropped her off at her front door Friday evening—still without her car—snow fell in wet sloppy sheets, and she feared for his safety.

"You be careful, Todd. Emily will never forgive me if you get hurt." She half joked though Todd knew she was serious.

"This big ol' truck will take me home okay, Shannon. Not to worry."

"Call me when you get there, will you? That way I won't worry."

"Will do." With a salute off the bill of his cap he closed the power window and drove off.

His call twenty minutes later assured her that he was home and safe with his wife.

Once more Shannon saw a long weekend stretch ahead with nothing to do but some sewing and watching a few TV shows. With no companion of her choice other than an old cat.

———

"The lumberyard is closed today, Mrs. Waller. This storm makes the roads impassable. The highway department has advised everyone who can to stay home. The blizzard should blow over by this evening. Please call the employees, and let them know I expect them tomorrow as usual."

"Yes, Mr. Leven."

"What am I? An accountant or a secretary?" Shannon didn't bother laying the old phone down gently. She thumped it down good and proper. "Damn, it's gonna take a while to get hold of all these guys." Still, it was early yet, only 6:00. Giving the situation some thought, she decided to call the head of each work team, and that man could call his crew. With that idea in mind, she grabbed her employee list and used one finger to go down the list of names and numbers, stopping at key personnel. In less time than she imagined, she made contact with four employees who promised to contact their particular crew members. She asked Todd Zimmer to call Charlie Hawkins. 6:15 any morning was just too darn early to talk to that man.

Why did I never think of that before, she asked herself as she hung up a short fifteen minutes later.

Getting to work the next morning would have been impossible in her Escort—if she even had it. But Todd picked her up once again in his truck and later at lunch took her to pick up her car. By then much of the snow was slush, and she rode home in her own vehicle. The day was looking up even as the sun was going down, she realized.

———

Spring crept in, bringing fresher warm days and fields of flowers. Nothing changed at work. Mr. Leven was still a crusty old man. Charlie was still a determined wanna-be suitor, and home seemed lonelier than ever, with only Simon to greet her each evening. Friends visiting and calls between Shannon and girl-friends were fine but didn't make up for a long, lonely night.

After a particularly demanding day when several unhappy customers entered the office and dumped their complaints on her rather than wait for the sales manager… When Mr. Leven chewed her out for a missed important message he thought she forgot to give him only to discover the message went to his home and *he* missed it… When he never actually apologized for his nasty manner… Shannon came home in her dilapidated vehicle, put her head down on the steering wheel, and cried.

Hard sobs with flowing eyes and dripping nose. Sobs for a life that went sideways too soon. Sobs for all the dreams she'd given up of husband and family.

By the time she entered the house, the only things she had to show for her emotional outburst were a red swollen face, a snotty nose and a deep desire to hug her cat, the only remaining thing left from happier days.

She stopped by the bathroom first and washed her face. Simon would be asleep somewhere. His hearing wasn't as good as it used to be so he probably had no idea she was even in the house. Wrapped in a light sweater, she scanned the front room, then the kitchen.

"Simon, where are you?"

She entered the bedroom and smiled. "There you are. Asleep in the sunshine as usual."

When the weather was warm, she left the blind pulled up

and the curtains pulled back. The window ledges in the old house were wide, and the cat loved to snooze in the sunshine streaming in through the south window of Shannon's bedroom.

There he lay, his front feet tucked up under his chest, his tail wrapped around his body, ending under his chin which drooped almost to the window ledge. Sound asleep.

Shannon picked up the small digital camera she kept for taking photos of her quilts and snapped a few shots of Simon. She hated to wake him, but she really wanted to pet him a little and perhaps see if he'd curl up in her lap while she had some hot tea.

She moved to the window and ran her fingers softly over his head and along his back. When his rumbling purr didn't start up like some rusty old machine, she moved her hand over his back again. No purr. Nothing.

A sudden fear took hold of her, and she bent down to look at the cat's face. She hadn't noticed before, but now she saw…his tongue stuck out a bit, and his gums showed where his lips had pulled back.

"Oh, Simon." Tears rolled down her cheeks anew, her heart breaking. "Poor old guy." Her legs gave way, and she sat hard on the corner of the bed, her gaze on her last connection to Jacob. "Remember when Jacob brought you home? You were so little. We thought you might die, but you didn't." She reached out and stroked his back once more, knowing he didn't feel her touch anymore.

Now there was no family but an aging uncle in upstate New York. While she lived in Cut Bank, Montana, her godparents lived in Great Falls over a hundred miles away. Not a quick drive. But her best friend Immajean lived in Shelby just twenty-five miles away. She'd get hold of

Immajean as soon as she did right by Simon. Tonight she needed someone who cared deeply.

Moving as if the air in the house was molasses, she found an appropriate sized box, then went to her sewing cabinet. Inside she found what quilters call *orphan blocks*—quilt blocks she'd made when testing a new pattern but never put into an actual quilt. She pulled out a dozen and lined the box bottom and up the sides with the soft quilted material.

Dreading to move the dead cat but knowing it was necessary, she placed the box on the floor, then slid her hands under Simon's belly. To her surprise he was still in rigor. Probably died shortly before she got home. Carefully she placed him in the box in the same position she'd found him. Blinded by tears, she rubbed his head once more, then resolutely closed the lid. Finding packing tape in a desk drawer, she taped the box closed, a horrifying thought coming that she might drop the box on the way out to the big oak in the back corner of the property and out Simon would tumble. She preferred remembering him as he was now, not all ruffled up and weird looking.

Passing through the kitchen, she picked up a wooden outline of a cat that Jacob had made years earlier. Simon's name showed in faded paint, the wooden piece was so old.

Out the back door she went, stopping by the barn for a shovel.

"Here we are, Simon. There's Trip over there. You remember him. He liked to lick you when you were little. He seemed to think he was your mother or something. He wasn't around long after you came. But he's waiting for you, old boy."

Talking softly to the cat—really to comfort herself—

Shannon put her back into digging a nice hole next to the place where she and Jacob buried his old yellow Lab just months after Simon came into their lives. Like Simon, the dog died of old age, well-loved and buried with dignity. The three acres lay covered in close-cropped soft grass. That was one thing Shannon insisted on, that the place not look desolate with weeds covering it.

She knelt down to place the box in the hole but held it for a second or two, memories flooding her heart and mind. Memories of the cat, her, and Jacob. All lost to her now. With loving hands she covered the grave. Long ago they'd piled way more rocks on Trip's grave than probably necessary to keep wild animals from bothering the body.

"Trip doesn't need all these anymore, but you do," she said as she pulled rocks from around the other grave and covered the smaller one. Finally, she pulled the wooden cat figure out of her pocket and settled it among the rocks at the head of the grave. Beside her, Trip's wooden dog figure nestled a bit sideways among the rocks of his grave, his name long faded but not forgotten.

She wanted to say something meaningful, but the words seemed to get stuck in her throat. So she sat for awhile between the two graves and let twilight fall around her. Assuring the two pets that they'd never be forgotten, she returned home, more alone than ever before in her entire life.

CHANGES

"Immajean, I need to talk a bit. You free? It's not too late?" Shannon sat on the edge of her bed with the portable phone.

"Sure, I'm always free for you. It's not late. Danny's bowling, and Larry is at ball practice. Girl talk?" Immajean giggled in anticipation of Shannon visiting.

"No, just talk. Simon died today."

"Oh, Shannon, I'm so sorry. I know how much you loved that cat."

"Yeah, well, it's just me now, and I really want to be with someone who cares."

"You know I do. Come on, and I'll let the wine breathe."

"You're such a good friend." Shannon's voice caught for a second. "No, I'm not going to cry. I've done that. Now I just need to sit and—"

"Yeah, I know…talk. Come on. Drive safely."

"See you in about thirty minutes."

———

Shannon fell into Immajean Adams' arms and bawled like a baby for a good five minutes, soaking the other woman's shoulder. When she pulled away and saw the blotchy wet spot she opened her mouth to apologize.

"Don't you dare say you're sorry." Immajean hugged Shannon hard, then tugged her toward the living room where two chairs sat close to each other, an end table with wine and glasses between and a blaze going in the fireplace. "Come on. It might be spring, but for us in Montana that doesn't mean a thing. A fire still feels good."

"You bet." Shannon took the wad of tissues Immajean handed her and mopped her eyes.

"You ready for something to drink? I put out some cheese, crackers, and sliced apples too. I figured you took care of Simon and forgot to eat. If you're driving home tonight, then I'll limit the wine to these small glasses and only two apiece for each of us." She settled Shannon in a chair, poured wine in both glasses and handed over one.

"Eat, then sip," ordered Immajean.

"Yes, Mother," Shannon sniped with affection.

Both women gathered a cracker, added cheese, then added a thin slice of apple. Saluting each other with their concoctions, they crunched the cracker combo, then washed it down with a sip of white wine.

Another sip for Shannon and she relaxed into the soft texture of the wing chair. "I needed this. I'm…lost tonight. Not sure what to do next." She pulled her sweater closer over her chest and slumped in the chair.

Unlike some who might jump in at that point with a suggestion or question, Immajean remained quiet.

Shannon sat up a bit straighter, gathered more food and sipped again. "I wasn't born in Montana, you know." Immajean nodded. "My parents moved here from Texas. Mom was from Galveston down on the coast, but Dad was from Great Falls. His job took him all over the place, the last one being here where he opened an insurance business. Mom found a job as a nurse at the high school. I don't remember Texas. I was too young when we left. So Cut Bank is all I've ever known. I met you, then Jacob in elementary school, and we stuck together like glue."

"I remember those days. We thought nothing of being a trio. At least until Jacob realized he loved you, then he not so subtly asked me not to tag along."

Both women laughed. Jacob was a plain spoken man even at the age of fourteen. No doubting what he intended. He as much as told Shannon that he planned on marrying her and having a houseful of kids. His daddy said he'd help build them a house when they got married.

A sigh passed between the two. They sat quiet, somber until Shannon started bringing up more memories.

"Remember Trip, Jacob's Lab? That was one loving dog. He was our third wheel. Where Jacob went, Trip went." Shannon wiped an unexpected tear off her face, the memory too fresh after being beside the dog's grave.

"You guys were good together—you and Jacob. Too bad he disappeared. That's a mystery I'd like to see solved one day." Immajean pointed into the air as she finished off yet another cracker combo. "I really dislike mysteries."

"That's just it...he *disappeared*." A bit of frustration filled her voice as Immajean refilled Shannon's glass. "He left home in that VW his dad let him borrow and headed to Bismarck. That's over six hundred miles. He planned on stopping in Billings for the night but never made it. We called the hotel that he booked. It's like...like he vanished off the face of the earth between Cut Bank and Billings. Dead of winter and all. The police searched then and later in the spring."

"I remember those days. With Jacob's mom gone for years, his dad relied on Jacob for all kinds of things. Broke that man's heart. Literally." Immajean stared into the fire, her fingers curled around her wine glass. "I was working an ER shift when Mr. Waller came in. But it was too late. He'd waited to call 9-1-1, thinking the chest pain was stress over Jacob. Everyone thought the world of that man. You could have heard a pin drop when Doctor Laman called the time of death." Immajean sat with one hand over her mouth, her eyes fixed on the fire as if reliving those moments.

"He gave us the old house when we married, promising to build that new one for us, but..." Shannon shrugged her shoulders. "We know how that played out."

"You and Jacob used to talk about a home and a ton of kids to fill it. I think that man was crazy about kids. That went south too." Immajean leaned over to poke the fire with a long iron, flames leaping, then dying like Shannon's dreams.

"Yep," Shannon said. "And now Simon is gone, died in his sleep apparently in a sunny spot on the window ledge. Could you ask for a more peaceful perfect way to go?"

Immajean reached out a hand, and Shannon grabbed it. "We should all be so lucky."

"True, but, Immajean, that leaves me with nobody."

"You have a ton of friends."

"True, but that's not family."

"Don't you have that uncle you visit each year? He lives...?"

"In New York State. Yes, but it's not the same."

Shannon's friend opened her mouth to object.

"Wait, I have Uncle Leon, you, Emily Zimmer and a dozen other people I care about, but no one will be home at the end of the day. No matter what folks do during the day, they look forward to coming through the door at home and being greeted, in my case, by a cat at least. And Jacob found Simon…gave that darn cat to me."

She choked again. Too many words bottled up over the years tried to rush out all at one time. Wasn't going to happen. Too many memories flashed through her mind. Too much time alone from now on.

———

Shannon wasn't hung over the next morning, just lacked conviction for getting out of bed and going to work one more time. If she wrote a book about her life, it would take up pages until the day Jacob disappeared. Then she could write the story of her life on one page using big handwriting. *Different day, same shit* pretty much described her now.

A full-length mirror hung in the bathroom. Normally Shannon ignored it. She was clean and presentable, and that's all that mattered as far as she was concerned. This morning though she took a solid look at the woman staring back.

"Too thin," she pointed out as she turned sideways, noting she had no hips or butt to speak of. "Breasts almost non-existent." Her breasts lay like small bumps on her chest. "Feet too big though at five eight, I guess I need something that big to balance me out." She ran her hands up through her hair and gathered the shoulder length light brown hair in a twist on top of her head. "At least my ears lay flat. Geez, what if they stuck out! I'd look like Dumbo." A quick grin split her face. She leaned in and tilted her head one way then the other. "Narrow face, good bones. And green eyes. Okay in that department." She sighed and dropped the heavy hair. "Jacob would say I need a sandwich…or two. Maybe three." She stuck her tongue out at the reflection that mimicked her. "It is what it is." A chuckle sounded in the house as she left the mirror and dressed.

Customers in and out of the office and foremen as well as salesmen kept Shannon busy. Most wanted invoices, orders…the sort of things that came through her.

Charlie Hawkins put in an appearance just before lunch. "Hello, gorgeous."

Shannon ignored him.

"How about having lunch with me today?"

"No thanks. I have other plans."

"Oh? Like what?"

"Well, they're *my* plans, Charlie. Not *yours*."

While Shannon frantically searched for an idea for lunch without Charlie, Fate opened the door and flew to her desk.

"Shannon! You're coming to lunch with me to celebrate my graduation!" Helen Bass raced around the desk, pulled Shannon up, and hugged her so hard she almost choked the poor woman.

"Ooph! Congratulations, Helen. That's wonderful. I'm so proud of you." Shannon accepted the hug because she knew how hard Helen had worked on the two-year course. "I bet Victor is bragging."

"Don't you know it! In fact, he's buying us lunch, and we're almost late. Grab your purse, and we'll take my car. If we use yours, we might not make lunch at all."

"Hey, now that's just wrong," Shannon said as she

grabbed her purse and locked the desk drawers. She gave Charlie a finger wave as she sailed past him, her arm through her friend's.

They barely cleared the parking lot when Helen broke into a fully belly laugh. "That was priceless—that look on Charlie's face as you zipped by him and did that ta-ta thing with your fingers. I thought he'd blow up."

"That *was* sort of nasty, but he'd just asked me out to lunch. I was trying to figure out how to get out of going without causing a major flap when in you came. Thank you sooo much for saving me."

"You do know that man is crazy about you, don't you?" Helen pulled into the restaurant parking lot, set the brake, then shot Shannon a hard glare. But mischief played at the sides of her mouth.

"Correction—that man is just plain crazy. Ever since Jacob left he thinks I ought to be his personal woman." Shannon shuddered as she reached for the door handle. "I can barely stand being around him at the office. Can you imagine what it would be like to sit right next to him or worse to have him kiss you? Yuck!"

"So you owe me, huh?" Helen giggled as she locked the car and waved to her husband who waited for them at the door.

"Yes," Shannon said with an exaggerated sigh. "I know how you get when I owe you. I usually come out on the short end of the stick in terms of fair shakes."

"Tell you what, just because I'm in such a good mood, when you find something that you think settles the debt, then you let me know," Helen said before passing Victor.

"Agreed." Shannon followed, thankful she got off so lightly.

"Now if I can find a job, Victor and I can finally look for a house and maybe…start a family," Helen said, hope filling her voice.

"That would be lovely." Shannon saluted her friend's hopes but wished life had given her that opportunity.

———

A knock at the door about 6:30 that evening surprised—and alarmed—Shannon. No one had called saying they were coming. Salesmen didn't come because of the sign at the beginning of the drive, saying *We're not buying, so don't bother coming further*. That was her father-in-law's idea. It worked—until just now.

Glad she'd locked the house down when she got home, she called out, "Who is it?"

"Me—Charlie Hawkins. I thought we might have a chat and a night cap here at your place since you don't seem to feel comfortable going anywhere else."

Is he serious? Shannon knew some men just didn't read body language or take subtle hints. He wasn't coming inside at any time for any reason. She had to get rid of him. But first she had to get the portable phone—just in case.

"Charlie, go home. You're not coming in, and I'm not coming out."

"Aw, Shannon, you're no fun. I just want to talk, that's all." For a big man with an attitude, Charlie sounded a lot like a whiny kid.

"Go away, Charlie. I don't want anything to do with you." She stood near the front door but not next to it. She couldn't imagine Charlie being stupid enough to try to break in, but if he lost his temper he might try something.

"Why not? I'm handsome, educated, financially secure. I'm everything you could want in a husband."

"Go away. I'm married and not interested in anyone else."

"You're as good as a widow, Shannon. Admit it. Jacob is gone. Dead as a door knob."

"Get out now! Off my property. I'm calling the sheriff right now." Shannon wasn't one to bluff. She started dialing 9-1-1.

"You can't do that!"

"I'm doing it."

"Really?"

"The line is connecting. If you want me to tell the sheriff department that this was a mistake you better do something right now."

"Okay, okay. I'm leaving."

"9-1-1, what is your emergency?"

"Off my porch and away from here now or I'll tell her what you did."

"I'm gone." Charlie jumped off the porch steps and trotted to his truck.

She heard the sound of his feet hitting the wooden steps and the thud of his truck door as he slammed it shut. The engine started immediately and the truck moved out.

"9-1-1, please state the nature of your emergency. Do you need assistance?"

As the truck tail lights faded, Shannon spoke to the lady at dispatch. "I'm sorry. But a fellow worker tried to talk his way into my home. I'm married, but he thinks I'd like to be his girlfriend. When he realized I really was calling the sheriff, he left."

"Will he be back, ma'am?"

"I don't think so."

"May I have your name and information and his?"

"Do I have to give you his name? He left."

"Ma'am, if anything happens to you by accident or on purpose in the future, we'll have a record of this man bothering you. We won't pursue the issue today if you don't file a complaint, but it's best to get this business on record."

"Yes, yes, you're right. I don't think he's stupid enough to try anything else, but enough has happened in my life that I want backup if needed."

"Could you explain that, ma'am? That might help if added to this information."

Shannon pulled out a kitchen chair, sat, and gave the dispatcher all the information she asked for about herself and Charlie Hawkins. Then she added what she knew—which was darn little—about Jacob's disappearance fifteen years earlier. "I suppose that's the real reason this man thinks he can put himself into my life." Her story finished, she slumped against the hand propping up her chin.

"I'll file this, and if he ever bothers you again, we'll have it handy as background."

"Thank you for your help," Shannon said and hung up. "Geez, what a goof ball that Charlie is," she groused as she double-checked all the door and window locks again.

———

"You didn't really call the sheriff, did you?" Charlie whispered as he leaned over Shannon's desk the next morning.

"Yes, I did."

"Did you file a complaint? Are they going to arrest me?"

"Charlie, if I'd filed a complaint against you for harassment, you'd be in jail by now."

"Harassment! Woman, I love you. Always have! I'd never hurt you!" Charlie looked and sounded thunderstruck, his jaw hanging and his eyes wide.

"Love? I never asked for that from you. And you have a darn funny way of showing any love you say you have for me. Go away, Charlie. Go find a woman who really thinks you're such a great catch." Shannon spoke softly, delivered her final words on the subject, then turned back to the open accounting file on her desk.

"I *am* a great catch," Charlie hissed as he swooped in once more, only this time his face was red with what she figured was embarrassment as well as anger.

Thinking it best to ignore him before he lost it there in the office and got both of them either hurt or fired or both, she didn't look up, but she also didn't turn her back on him.

Two men from the yard walked in for coffee refills, so Charlie snapped up straight, shot her a dirty look, and stomped out of the building. Both men gave him a surprised look, then shot their gaze to Shannon. She gave a shoulder shrug and one of those *no clue* looks.

I just made a bad enemy. Working here may have to take a back seat to my well-being.

That evening she walked to her car, scanning the parking lot for Charlie Hawkins. His truck was gone, so she felt safe enough to get home without his interference. Maybe calling the sheriff was a good idea after all, she consoled herself as she turned over the engine. Or tried to. All she got was a grinding sound that seemed to come from the rear end of the Escort.

"Damn!" Shannon banged her head a few times on the

hot steering wheel and wondered where she'd get the cash to fix the car this time.

"Need help, Shannon?"

Shannon jumped, startled, thinking no one was around. Her heart raced, and cold sweat burst out on her face. Thankfully, the face on the other side of her window glass was Todd and not Charlie.

"I think she's really given up the ghost this time, Todd. She's making a funny grinding sound and won't turn over."

"Slide out, and let me try." Todd waited until Shannon exited the car, then slid in and turned the key. All he got was the same grinding sound that Shannon described. "Come on. I'll drive you home and get you tomorrow. You want to call a tow truck?"

"Uh, no. I think this time I'll just let it sit for awhile," Shannon said, too embarrassed to admit she had no money for towing, much less repairs. A bad day had just gotten worse.

At home she waved Todd off, unlocked her door, entered, then locked the door behind her. This time when she plopped into a kitchen chair, she didn't even have tears to shed. Like her money, her tears were gone. Propping her chin on one fist, she prayed nothing else would happen like the house burning down around her ears.

First her husband, then the cat her husband gave her. No money and now no car. Something had to change, or she'd be up a creek without a paddle. And this time she felt like she was already in the canoe ready to push off into the creek of poverty, not to mention solitude. Not normally a downer type of person, Shannon saw no bright light at the end of her proverbial tunnel.

SO WHAT ELSE CAN HAPPEN?

When the phone rang that evening she saw the New York ID and reached for the phone wearing a smile. That was her uncle's phone number. She'd not heard from him in several months.

"Hello?"

"Shannon? This is Mrs. Krandowitz."

Mrs. Krandowitz was Uncle Leon's housekeeper, cook, and general jack of all trades. If she couldn't handle a problem, she knew whom to call.

"How are you, Mrs. K? Uncle Leon okay? He told me not to come this year until he called. Said he wasn't feeling well."

"That's why I'm calling, dear. Perhaps you should sit down."

"Mrs. K, what's wrong?" Shannon immediately suspected the worst so followed the older woman's advice and sat down gently on the sofa in the front room.

"I'm sorry to have to tell you, dear, but your uncle passed away in his sleep four nights ago."

"Four nights? Why didn't someone call me sooner?"

"We're following his instructions, Shannon. Soon enough a lawyer will come see you with all sorts of paper-work and a video from Leon himself."

"What about a funeral?" Despite her firm belief that she had no tears left, they rolled slowly down her cheeks. Truly alone now.

"No funeral. He was cremated, and his ashes laid to rest along the water's edge at Seneca Falls. He so loved that area around Auburn and Ithaca."

A bone deep sorrow threatened to swallow Shannon. Her last connection to family gone. Then she remembered this kind woman and what she must be feeling.

"Oh, Mrs. K, I'm so sorry. You were with him for years. I'm sure you must miss him too."

"I do, dear, but he took care of me not long ago. Now the other reason I called—besides telling you about Leon— is that you can expect someone from the law office of Beau-fort, Black and Brody to contact you. The offices are out of Auburn where Leon did his financial work."

Shannon never knew quite what her uncle did. While she had no money, he apparently did. He never elaborated, and she never asked. She'd only learned of him after her mom and dad died in a car accident when she was waiting to marry Jacob. A sad start to married life, a few acquaintances said. Well, a husband disappearing for fifteen years is a sad way to continue married life, she mused, and almost missed the rest of what Mrs. Krandowitz said.

"I'm sorry, Mrs. K, I zoned out for a second. You were saying?"

"One of their lawyers will meet with you there in Cut

Bank. You know how wills are, always paperwork to be signed and filed."

"What about the house? And what are you going to do now?"

"Oh, I'll retire now. I've already bought a small condo near my daughter. Leon saw to that. For the future, he always said. As for the house, the lawyer will tell you about that."

"I guess there's really no one left now, Mrs. K. Even the cat that Jacob gave me died not long ago."

"I am sorry that you're alone now, dear. And I'm sorry that I had to deliver sad news."

"Thanks, Mrs. K. It's sad news for both of us, I guess. Can I write to you?"

"Of course, dear. I'd like that very much."

The housekeeper gave Shannon her new address and expressed her condolences one last time before hanging up.

With the portable phone dangling from her hand, Shannon propped her head up on that fist once more and gave a hearty sigh. She'd never asked Leon for a dime, but he'd never offered to help either. Her uncle was—had been —an odd man, though he invited her to his home—which she adored—each summer during her one week vacation. Other than that they visited by phone and wrote letters. Leon enjoyed going to his mailbox and finding her letters, he often said. The same could be said of her. She enjoyed seeing Leon's letters in her mailbox far more than seeing bills.

With her very existence teetering on the brink of financial and vehicular collapse, she had just lost another piece of her life.

———

"Psst, Shannon."

Her thoughts deep in the account she was working on, Shannon heard the words, but they didn't faze her until she heard them again.

"Psst, Shannon. Come out here for a minute."

Looking around, all she saw was Mr. Leven in his office. No one at the coffee pot. The door stood cracked open a few inches, and she spotted Todd motioning her to come outside.

She couldn't imagine why all the secrecy, but she casually stood, brushed off her slacks, then walked out the door to meet Todd further down the long porch that ran across the front of the office. Todd stood on the end farthest from Leven's office.

"What's up?"

"Have you heard any weird rumors lately?"

"About what?" She'd heard nothing but could hardly wait to hear what he might say.

"A few of my crew were in Shelby the other night at a tavern, having a beer after work." Todd held up both hands, palms out. "They weren't drunk or anything. But they overheard these two guys talking behind them."

"Talking about what? Why all this cloak and dagger, Todd?"

"These guys represent a company that plans to buy Waller Lumberyard, rename it, and move it to Emerson Junction just north of Great Falls."

"What?" Shannon grabbed Todd by each arm. "Leven can't do that! What about the guys who work here? What about all the folks who buy lumber here? What are they going to do when they need wood or nails or fencing to repair things? That's almost a hundred miles away!"

"Yeah, tell me about it. Not like we can all get up and drive that distance each morning, then back each evening. We'll all be out of work!" Todd turned white right in front of Shannon. She figured she was about as pale as him.

"Shit, not like life hasn't kicked me yet, now it wants to kill me," she moaned.

"I don't know what we'll do if Leven sells off this place." Todd paced the small area, his hands stuffed in his pockets.

"It's a rumor right now though, didn't you say?"

"Shannon, I hate to break it to you, but I think it's long past the *rumor* stage. These guys talked like it might be a done deal." Todd gave her a sharp look. "Have you done any different book work lately?"

Shannon only had to think a minute about that. "As a matter of fact, Leven asked me to pull up the financial records for the past year and create a document for him to look at. I did that about a month ago. I didn't think much about it other than he's the boss, and what he asks for he gets or you get canned."

"Yep, that's always been his way. Like he's got tons of folks to draw from if he has to fire someone." Todd took off his cap and ran his hand through his short hair, pacing up and down a few more feet, then turning to pace some more.

Using a post to support herself, Shannon wondered if life could sap much more from her. But this time she wouldn't be the only one to suffer.

"What's Emily say about this?"

"At least she's got a job teaching. I can find something, I reckon. But you know yourself that most of these guys have worked here for years and don't…" Todd lowered his voice, "have much of an education or anything to fall back on."

"A good bunch of guys but yeah, you're right. I can't imagine what they'll have to do to stay afloat." She jumped when Todd slapped the post near her.

"Damn that old man. He could do better by this bunch. I don't know about you, but we barely make it from paycheck to paycheck. Now he's thrown us all out in the cold."

Her hand up, Shannon said, "Add me to that paycheck to paycheck thing. See that old Escort over there? I don't have the dough to get it towed to the garage much less pay for any repairs, no matter how minor. *Broke* is my middle name."

"Sorry to hear that, Shannon. I can't help wondering what this might have been like if Jacob had taken over after his dad's death."

"I hoped life here would be better than it is at the moment, you can bet on that."

Both of them stood in silence, leaning against a porch rail that might not be theirs to lean on pretty soon.

"So what do we do now?" Todd whispered.

"I've never been one to let things get out of control…if I can help it. Mr. Leven's problem is that he's only thinking of himself and not his crews. I think…" she stopped speaking and did some quick thinking.

"You have a plan?"

"Not sure, but the first thing we have to do is find out if this rumor is true or not. I had a teacher once that said if you hear a rumor, go to the source, and find out the truth. So first thing tomorrow I'll ask Mr. Leven for the truth. After that…"

"Once we know if the place is closing, then we let the

guys know and see if we can get together to find everyone a job. I wonder how much time we have left?"

"I'll ask Leven that as well. Anything else I need to ask him?"

"Yeah, ask him if he'll help find jobs for us too."

"Wow, you don't want a lot, do you?" Shannon tried to laugh but couldn't muster the humor.

"If the man is going to sell this place out from under our feet the least he can do as a human being is do right by the men who made the place what it is so that he *could* sell it," Todd said with passion.

"Good man. We'll push for what we can get. Maybe a week's severance pay or something. I'll see what the budget looks like. In fact I can tell you, the budget is healthy. The old bastard doesn't use it to pay us a decent salary, that's for sure."

"As soon as you know something, then pass the word to me. We may need to meet somewhere tomorrow with the men and see what we can get started."

"It's been nice weather. How about coming over to my place. We can meet under the trees in the back yard. I've got plenty of room for parking. We can meet right after the yard closes for the day."

"It's a plan." Todd and Shannon shook hands before heading back to their duties.

————

"Mr. Leven, I need to speak to you." Shannon had taken special care to look nice this morning, not that her boss would notice or even care, but the effort and results boosted her morale.

"I'm busy at the moment, Mrs. Waller. This can wait." Leven barely glanced up from the single folder on his desk.

Shannon worked with many such folders and, as a good accountant-slash-secretary, could read writing that lay upside down to her.

"Briggs and Layman—top lumbermen, sir. They must be the ones buying Waller Lumberyard." She stood with her hands folded in front of her, her eyes focused on the old man who suddenly closed the folder and shot her a somewhat surprised look.

"I have no idea what you're talking about," he said as he composed his features.

"Yes, sir. You do. That company is buying out Waller and moving it to Emerson Junction. I want to know—the crews want to know—how soon and what are you going to do to help these people find another job. Oh, and how much are you going to pay them as severance pay?" She spoke with a straight face as Leven's turned a dusky red, and he gurgled.

"Hog wash!" He almost shouted at her, but she raised one brow and kept her gaze focused in a hard glare on him.

"No, sir. This is not hog wash. It's a coward's way of making money, dodging out of town and leaving your workers high and dry with no idea what happened or what's going to become of them for the rest of their lives. You can be a nasty tempered old man at times, but you've never been cruel. I suppose..." She raised her hands and gave him a nonchalant smirk. "There's a first time for everything, but this..." She suddenly shot a finger at him, startling him with her boldness. "Is not that time. You do right by these folks. They've invested their time and effort into making this company good enough for you to sell right out from under them. Any less effort on their part and no one would give this place a second glance." Her hand cut the air as if punctuating her words.

"You can't force me to help these men," Leven sat back and rested clasped hands over his stomach.

"You're right, but we can certainly make your life miserable after you dump us all. Social media, sir, is a bitch. I doubt Briggs and Layman want to have that hanging over their heads, and you'll feel the effects of it all the way from church to the restaurant where you go for lunch."

For an older man, Leven was addicted to Facebook and all the other websites where those who followed him could see him as a company owner and all-around good man. And Shannon knew that.

"Are you resorting to blackmail, Mrs. Waller?"

"Call it what you will, but I happen to be the accountant around here, and I know that you have enough cash right now to do right by these men for the time they'll be out of work until...or if...they can find something local. No one can afford to drive to work at a new lumberyard a hundred miles away even if Briggs and Layman wanted the old crew."

Leven fidgeted in his chair but still looked like a stubborn mule.

"And you can help these men find another job. You've got contacts with hundreds of locals. I know...I keep the books, and I can give you a print out in five minutes of everyone who owns a business who comes in here for supplies. You can be a heel or a hero. Your choice."

"Let me think about this," Leven said, sitting forward and clasping his hands together on top of the folder.

"No, sir, I don't think so."

"You're being impertinent, Mrs. Waller."

"No, sir, I'm being pragmatic. This doesn't take any time for thought. All you have to do is say yes or no to helping these people. We'll deal with whatever you say, but if your answer is no, then you probably won't like the consequences." Shannon shrugged again with a *take it or leave it* expression on her face.

Truth be told, she was terrified. This was the boldest she'd ever been. She never made waves, caused a ruckus. Well, other than calling the law about Charlie Hawkins. Maybe that was the act of rebellion that made this move easier. Futures were on the line, and she knew she had the backing of the others, even if they didn't know it yet.

So she stood in front of his desk with a patient expression but not a fearful one. To show this crafty old businessman fear at this point would only give him an out. Better to keep him stirred up.

"Your answer?"

For a solid minute, they faced off. Shannon figured she'd have to resort to more drastic measures after all. She shifted her shoulders, ready to turn, and leave the old buzzard to his fate, but Leven stopped her.

"Wait. One week's pay per man here."

When she raised an eyebrow, it took him a good fifteen seconds to read her mind.

"A week's pay for each *person* here."

"And help with jobs? I can have that list to you quickly. The only thing this is going to cost you is some money out of the budget—which you can afford—and the time *you* spend on the phone in the next few days, seeking employment for all of us."

Leven seemed to deflate behind his desk. He waved a

hand to her as if motioning her to her computer. "All right. Pay and help finding jobs."

"How much time do we have?"

"Two weeks until the gates are locked and the company dismantled and moved."

"You weren't going to tell anyone, were you?" Shannon couldn't help the nasty tone that crept into her words. She stepped forward and placed one hand on the desk. "You planned on being conveniently out of town that day when we all arrived to find the gates locked and a notice of the new sale and relocation. You're a cold-hearted man."

She stepped to the door but turned back. "I'll have those names for you in a few minutes. Please call a meeting of your crew chiefs and sales personnel and relay the agreement we reached. Oh, wait. Wait until I type this up, and *you* sign and date it. *Then* you can tell them. No sense giving you a way to wiggle out of helping calm the chaos you'll create."

Within five minutes she laid a single sheet on Leven's desk. He read it, signed and dated it, and returned it to her. In turn, she handed him several sheets with customer names and numbers on it.

"You can call in the crew chiefs now, *then* start making those calls." She didn't say *sir* this time and never would again.

———

Charlie passed Shannon's desk without a word, a dazed look on his face, a bit of a shuffle in his step.

"Do we still need to meet at your house this evening,

Shannon?" Todd whispered when he left Leven's office fifteen minutes later.

"I think it might be best, Todd. That way everyone can voice an opinion, and we can help answer questions and try to reassure everyone that things could work out okay."

"I'll pass the word. And I'll pick you up after work."

"Make sure the guys call their wives, and let them know they'll be a little late getting home."

"Will do."

———

During the short ride to Shannon's house, she told Todd about the showdown she had with Leven.

"You got that old bastard to agree to the pay and job search things?" Todd whistled and tipped his cap back. "Well, I'll be."

They appeared to lead a caravan of cars and trucks from the lumberyard to her house. Shannon no sooner got out of the truck than vehicles began pulling in and parking on the grass in the front yard. Even Charlie showed up. He wasn't the first one there but not the last either. The other sales reps beat him to the meeting.

While the guys gathered, she opened the kitchen door and laid down her purse. Pulling a copy of Leven's agreement out of her purse, she returned to the group.

"It's cooler in the back yard, guys, and there're places to sit too. Come on around," she invited.

Todd led the men around. Some sat on the ground, in a few of the lawn chairs, and anywhere they could get comfortable. Charlie leaned against the corner fence post. Being the senior yard chief, Todd spoke first.

"Bobby and Jose actually heard the conversation that started all this. I'm glad they came to me and said something, otherwise we'd all be showing up for two more weeks until the day the gates are locked and no one around to explain a damn thing." The men hooted, clapped, and slapped Bobby and Jose on the back.

"I asked Shannon Waller about this yesterday morning first thing. Know what she did?"

"Now wait a minute, Todd. I didn't do anything that anyone else might have." Shannon objected to him making her out to be a heroine or something.

"But that's the point, Shannon. You did do something. Only four of us knew what the rumor was—unless those two blabbed it around when they got here."

Several men slapped Bobby and Jose again on the shoulders, teasing them about spreading rumors first thing in the morning before anyone even had a cup of coffee.

"She marched into Leven's office, and I don't know what she told him, but it must have been powerful. I'd have loved to been the fly on the wall for that conversation." Todd grinned and patted Shannon's shoulder.

Hot embarrassment flushed through her as the men hooted again.

"Anyway she got him to agree to the week's pay to help tide us over until we can get new jobs, and the old man's going to personally call all our customers and try to get us those jobs. Shannon's desk faces his office so she can keep an eye on him and keep an ear open for what he says. That office isn't *that* big."

"Don't I know it," Shannon groused with a laugh.

"Okay, so anyone got something to say? Questions?"

For the next thirty minutes, the men got the details as

Shannon knew them about the sale and relocation of the lumberyard. The men weren't happy about how Leven had planned on just locking the gates and leaving them to fend for themselves. The dialogue got a bit heated before Shannon figured it was time to step in, say a few words, then call it quits for the evening. When she stood, everyone got quiet.

"Look, life's not fair. That's the law. But this time we got a jump on life. With a lot of luck and that old man's help, you'll all walk away and have a job to go to the next day. We have two weeks. Waller Lumberyard has been the best business around here for decades. Let's not let it go down the toilet in its last two weeks. Come to work like you always do...like you have years there ahead of you. Give the job your best. And when the gates close, we'll have a beer together and wish each other luck. As for me, I can only say you're the best bunch of guys to work with. So say *good night* and *I'll see you in the morning*."

To her surprise, all the men including Charlie and Todd, wished each other good night and left. In ten minutes, the only sounds Shannon heard were crickets.

A shuddering sigh went through her as she sat on the kitchen steps. Chin on both fists propped up on her knees, she sat until the sun went down and the stars appeared, looking like crystals hung on black velvet. Only then did she rise and go inside, her mind not on bills or busted cars but on the small victory she secured for her fellow employees that day.

Like the others, she only had two weeks. Best she put in some phone time herself, looking for a job. Best to create a resume. Best not to think about maybe having to move in order to be close to whatever job she might find.

NEW DIRECTIONS

Tension floated just under the surface of the office the next morning. Men came for their assignments and coffee with little to say. While Shannon did her job, she kept one ear tuned to Mr. Leven. The old man called as he promised. As she forced him to do.

As if the tension wasn't enough, Charlie stepped into the office mid-morning minus his jolly suitor demeanor. He cut a quick glance toward Leven's office, but the old man was still on the phone. So he stepped in closer to Shannon's chair.

"You're too close, Charlie. Would you back up some?" she asked, his bulk hemming her in, with a wall beside her.

"I'm disappointed in you, Shannon. You were quite irrational, approaching Leven like that. That was unladylike of you to force that man into a deal. Ladies don't act like that."

She cut her eyes up at him, thinking he was joking, but the hard glint in his eyes and his tight lips said he wasn't. No way was she letting him loom over her, spewing out his opinion of her. She wanted to push him back enough so she could stand comfortably, but no way was she laying a hand on him.

"Step back, Charlie. Now!"

For a few breaths, he stood firm, but she gave him a level glare and raised one brow. Her hand eased to the company cell phone lying conveniently close.

Charlie might be conceited and a bit narcissistic, but he wasn't stupid. He took one large step back.

Shannon rose, wrapping as much dignity around her as possible. On her way up, she gathered the phone…just in case.

"You should have asked me to talk to the old man about the company closing. I could have gotten the same deal. Probably gotten a better one. Leven thinks a lot of me. We could have struck a man's deal."

"A man's deal? Really. And how would that have been better than the deal I came up with?" Shannon refused to glare again, cross her arms in disgust or raise her voice. Doing anything but talking in a level tone and remaining calm would incite Charlie's fury. She'd seen him ignite a few times in the years they'd worked together and knew she didn't want to be that close to him if he went ballistic.

"Well, I would have…" Charlie got stuck in his thought processes so tried again. "I would have…"

She gave him no time to spin words into fantasy.

"The time for deals is past. Go back to work, and do what you always do—the best for this company. Mark the calendar, and get a resume ready in case you don't like the new job the old man finds for you. This is a perfect time to relocate into a bigger city. You're a good salesman and would be a fine asset to any company." She refrained from saying that his moving would remove him from her sphere of living.

"You think you're so smart," Charlie hissed, then shot a glare at Leven's office. The old man hadn't noticed their exchange. "I'm a good salesman and a good man. I love you and want you. But you're blind to that. You're unladylike and disappointing, but that doesn't mean I care less. You're just playing hard to get. This time, though, Shannon, you'll be coming to me for help...and satisfaction."

A threat? Maybe. An insult? Definitely!

"You go too far. Get out of here. Don't come near me again, or I really will call the sheriff. This time for harassment."

When Charlie shot hot daggers at her, his eyes hard and dangerous, she raised the phone high enough for him to see through his red haze of anger.

"Don't make me do it. You know I will. Get out. Don't come in here again. Send someone else for your assignments, paperwork, and coffee. I never want to see you again." Her tone level and soft, Shannon held his gaze without flinching.

"Unladylike." Charlie spit the word at her and took a step back. He backed slowly to the door, never giving her his back. One hand eased the door open, and he backed out into daylight, letting the pneumatic door close by itself.

Shannon stayed upright for thirty seconds, then collapsed onto her chair, her legs too weak to support her one second more. "Oh, Lord, this is just too much. Something's gotta change."

"Waller Lumberyard," Shannon answered when the cell rang.

"May I speak to Mrs. Shannon Waller?"

"This is she. May I ask who's calling?"

"My name is Justin Black. I'm a lawyer with Beaufort, Black, and Brody Law Firm in Auburn, New York. I believe Mrs. Krandowitz called you, saying to expect a call from our firm."

"Yes, she did. What can I do for you, Mr. Black?"

"When Leon Jeffers passed away, he left papers to be signed by his only existing relative as well as a video he made explaining his actions regarding his will. As you are his last remaining relative, Mrs. Waller, I would like to bring these by and visit with you, then we can watch the video, and you can take care of the paperwork. I'll answer all your questions at that time."

"Oh, my! That sounds a bit overwhelming." Shannon gave a nervous laugh as she shuffled papers into a tidy pile before her.

"I'm sorry if it does. Frankly, Leon was an over-whelming person on a day-by-day basis. He and I were friends for many years. We shared common interests, and I miss him."

The man's voice dropped to a melancholy tone. Shannon realized he was a friend as well as Leon's attorney, so her uncle's death was probably more personal for Justin Black than her.

"The weather isn't good right now, Mr. Black. Where are you? If you're flying in, your flight may be delayed."

"Actually I'm in Emerson Junction headed up the highway toward Cut Bank. I tried to time my call so I'd arrive just after you got home from work."

"Oh, I see. Do you have a room somewhere for the night?"

"I think I can make it back to Shelby or perhaps Emerson Junction tonight."

"We'll have to play this by ear, Mr. Black. The weather here even in late April can be unpredictable. Similar to upstate New York from what Uncle Leon used to write about."

"Ah, I see. Okay by me. I'll be at your place about five-thirty then?"

"That'll work. See you then."

Shannon hit END on the cell, once more wishing she had access at home to technology like this business cell and computer. Her life style lacked the money to support such things, but at least she knew how to use the devices and make life easier at work.

Work—shutting down the company in the last few days left to them was harder than she anticipated. All the accounts had to be closed and transferred to the new company. She finally got a date from Leven...the last day... so she could prepare severance pay for the employees. All but four had new jobs lined up. She was one of the four who didn't. Surprisingly, Charlie was another. She hadn't asked about him or any job offers he might have gotten. She had enough worries of her own without taking on someone else's.

Not that offers hadn't come in, but they were all far enough away that she'd have to move. Her home was Cut Bank, and though she knew she could give up the town, she wasn't sure about leaving her home, selling it to strangers who might not love it as much as she did. While the salary offers so far worked for living expenses, the businesses didn't offer enough up front to cover moving or rent. She'd never paid rent and had no savings to fall back on. At the moment she didn't even have a car. Todd had lent her his brother's old truck, but it was only a fraction more reliable than her old Escort which Todd had pulled to the house for her. The old car now sat next to the rusted Model T near the glass gas pump, another reminder for Shannon that life was slipping away, and she had nothing to show for it.

Should she have called Leon? Asked him for money? He had more than she did—at least she thought so. But he'd never spoken about his life or business and had never asked about hers. For all she had known, he was as poor as she was with a finer home to show for it. Shannon had toyed with the idea of calling Leon despite the fact he wasn't feeling well. But she had no intentions of throwing her worries onto an elderly sick person even if she were about out of options.

And then Mrs. Krandowitz had called to say Leon died. That put the squash on borrowing money from him. But with whatever inheritance he was sending her way through this lawyer, she might be able to afford a better car and a cheap apartment somewhere in a new city that offered her a job. The car being the most important thing at the moment.

In a few days she'd not have a job and no way to get to a new one. What more could bad luck throw at her?

———

She hustled to get home before five-thirty, wanting to wash her face and put on coffee to brew before Justin Black arrived. Just in case, she freshened the bed linens in the second bedroom and made sure the bathroom sparkled. Since no one used either room, she had little to do.

At five-thirty on the dot, a car pulled into her long driveway. The light was still good enough to see the rental insignia on the car's license plate. With clouds building, the wind beginning to blow snow, and the temperatures dropping with the setting sun, Shannon worried that Mr. Black might be in for the evening here at her home.

Justin Black approached the front door, rang the ancient doorbell, and stomped the snow off his shoes as he waited. Shannon didn't keep him out there long. Throwing the door open, she welcomed him and motioned him into the warmth, nervous at letting a stranger into her home.

"Good evening. I'm Shannon Waller. You're Justin Black. Nice to meet you." She introduced herself as she waved him into the living room where a heater created a homey atmosphere. "May I take your things and get you some coffee?"

"Thank you so much. It's colder out there than I anticipated." Black handed over his coat, hat, and gloves.

"Make yourself comfortable, and I'll be right back. Cream and sugar?" She started to leave but stopped. "Have you eaten? I've got some leftover chicken and some chocolate chip cookies?"

Justin gave her a studied glance, looked around the living room with its tired dated wallpaper, then gave an odd little sigh. "Frankly, that all sounds perfect. May I help?"

Shannon refused to be stunned by the man's easy acceptance of cold chicken, cookies, and hot coffee. Gratitude welled up in her, making her more comfortable with nothing to explain why. For some odd reason, the man gave off vibes of comfort and safety. She shook her head, surprised at the gut feeling.

"Your drive here must have been a challenge with this weather closing in. Warm up in here, and I won't be but a few minutes. The coffee just finished brewing, and I can put everything on a tray in a jiffy. Be right back."

The meeting she worried about turned into something of a living room picnic in the end. Justin—he insisted she call him that—turned out to be a man who was witty, charming, and modest. Becoming traits in anyone. He stood about six feet tall, was slender without looking too thin and a natural blond. In the course of enjoying their meal, then sipping coffee, Shannon realized one other thing about Justin Black. He was gay. Not openly or loudly, but subtly and quietly.

In the end, his orientation made no difference. She liked him. And made every attempt to make him feel at ease because she knew, sooner or later, they'd have to see that video from her uncle and discuss things like his will.

Perhaps she was stalling, this attempt to make the man feel at home. Perhaps she was putting off facing what she might have faced if the police all those years ago had come to her door with news that Jacob was dead. Whatever... eventually the meal ended, and both settled back across the small coffee table from each other, coffee cups in hand and a few bites of cookie left to eat.

"I have to tell you, Shannon, that you're exactly what Leon said you were. A warm gracious woman. An understanding, perceptive one," he added with a slight lift of the lips and a knowing eye cast in her direction.

A faint blush flushed Shannon. Such a compliment from her uncle and such perception on Justin's part. He knew that she knew about him.

"Before I turn on the video—which I've not seen by the way—and pull out that pile of papers Leon left to be signed, tell me how you met Leon. You were unaware you had family left, I believe?" Justin settled back into the plump but worn cushions on the sofa and waited.

"You're right. I had no idea I had an uncle. I honestly thought Mom and Dad were it. They died when I was in high school but old enough to live on my own without a guardian. Jacob Waller and I married a few years before his dad passed away. His mom was long gone. So when my husband disappeared I had no one."

"Disappeared?" Justin sat up straighter and placed his empty coffee cup on the small table. "He never showed up?"

"Uh, no. He's been missing for fifteen years now. He left for a trip and never arrived. It was wintertime. The police searched but found nothing. When spring came and rivers and ponds thawed, they searched again, but again found nothing. No body. Nor the small VW he drove. And no one reported seeing him either."

"No one declared him dead?"

"No, I refused to ask for a death certificate. There's still hope." She spoke with quiet defiance and stiffened her hands into fists.

"Of course. A mystery. So how did that tie in with Leon?"

"Leon contacted me about a year after Jacob disappeared. It seems he'd been looking for his sister—my mother—and discovered Mom and Dad were dead, and I was without my husband. At first I was skeptical. Mom never mentioned a brother. But Leon explained it all before we began writing to each other. Mom's family disowned Leon when he was a teen. Mom was just a little girl. She was old enough to remember a big brother but not really old enough to understand that he was leaving home never to return. Mom, of course, never told me any of this. Leon said their parents probably told her not to talk about a brother. He'd disgraced the family. Leon never told me what this *disgrace* was.

Apparently he wound up in New York of all places. A long way from Galveston, Texas. He took a number of jobs. He was, after all, still basically a kid, but back then kids worked even younger than thirteen. When he saved enough money, he worked in the investment business and eventually found and bought his home, Mon Coeur—my heart. He must have been good at the investment business. He made some money then retired, found me, and we both wound up happy. End of story.

"We wrote letters for years. I have to say he was good with words and descriptions. I enjoyed getting those letters. I've saved every one. He said he saved mine. Apparently, he never married and had kids. So like me, we were alone but for each other. Oh, I had a cat, but even he's gone now. Eventually we began the yearly meetings. Leon asked me to spend my week's vacation with him in Auburn. I admitted my salary didn't allow for air fare and vacations. I was more of a *stay-cation* type of person, anticipating working on my quilts while not at work for a week."

"You make quilts?" Justin perked up and sat forward.

"Yes, I make a few and sell them on Pinterest. I don't get a fortune for them, and frankly the money only pays for the making of one or two more and the postage to mail them. But I enjoy making them. Keeps me sane when my job and my life drive me batty." She ran a hand over the two quilts lying over the back of the tired looking sofa, giving them a loving pat before turning back to her guest.

"You're passionate about making them, I can tell. Good for you," Justin said as he sat back and gave an emphatic nod. "Someday I'll tell you how quilts influence my life," he said with a shy wink. "But for now, continue with your story." He gestured toward her, his hand waving her back into her story. "Please."

Shannon took a sip of cooling coffee, lifted her nose in distaste, and commented, "I'll refresh the cups in a few minutes." Putting down the cup, she continued with the story of her and Leon.

"Uncle Leon sent plane tickets and arranged a driver to pick me up at the Syracuse airport. I flew through Chicago but thankfully didn't have to change planes. *Overwhelmed* was a good word for the whole adventure. The driver took me along a gorgeous country road, then up a drive to a house I'd die to live in. Mon Coeur, a craftsman built in the 1920s in the manner of Frank Lloyd Wright. Leaded windowpanes, oak built-in bookcases and…oh, that house is beyond beautiful. Of course, you've probably seen it a number of times. I fell in love with it and my uncle. He was an oddball, don't get me wrong, but the most loving man, kind and funny. We never talked about work. I still have no idea what he did for a living. For that week each summer, we came and went wherever we wanted to go and did whatever we wanted to do. Always together. Mrs. Krandowitz took care of us as a mother would. For years, I looked forward to seeing Uncle, Mrs. K, and Mon Coeur again."

"Sounds like you loved it there."

"I did. I do. Mon Coeur and Uncle, even Mrs. K, were so different from life here and the people I know. Mind you,

I like the people I work with—well, most of them anyway. I have tons of wonderful friends here. My godparents live in Great Falls, so I don't see them often." Shannon blushed and admitted, "My car won't make it that far. Half the time it won't make it to and from work." She ended on a sigh of regret as one hand twirled a strand of hair.

"Leon loved having you. He talked of you often." Justin looked like a cat with canary feathers aside his mouth when he added, "And just so you know, Leon didn't *buy* Mon Coeur, no matter the impression he gave or what he told you. He bought the land and had the home *built* to his specifications."

"You're kidding!"

"Not at all. He had the money and wanted a place to live that suited him—down to the bone, as he always told me."

"I'll be danged. I suspected he had more money than I thought, but never knew he actually built his home. Way to go, Uncle Leon."

"You and Leon had similar tastes in many things, I think. No wonder I immediately felt comfortable coming here."

"Someone had to come, I suppose. I guess Uncle Leon couldn't just die without leaving paperwork behind, now could he?" She uncurled her legs from under her, took up both coffee cups, and gestured to the kitchen. "Want more coffee? Cookies?"

"May I help this time?"

"Sure. Come on."

They left the living room and entered the smaller kitchen.

"Help yourself. I want to see what's happening outside. You might be stuck for the evening."

Justin poured coffee into both cups. "Worse things could happen to me."

She thought he might be joking, but like Charlie, his expression said he was serious. Her sweater tucked around her, she flipped on the outside light and cracked open the door. Wind blew in, and sleet hit the side of the house like pellets against the old wood. Earlier snowfall now hung from the eve of the small porch roof as icicles.

"Justin, what do you think of sleeping in an old house under warm quilts?"

"Really?"

"Afraid so. Traveling anywhere tonight will be dangerous if not impossible." She closed the door, locked it, and turned off the outside light.

"Gee, let me think about that offer." Justin blinked once, laughed, and said, "Sounds like something too good to pass up!"

"Well, now that that's settled, let's get on with business. Frankly, I expect—"

Brrring!

"That's what I expected. Excuse me a minute." She picked up the handset and rolled her eyes, knowing exactly who was calling. "Hello." The conversation such as it was— rather one sided—lasted about thirty seconds. After hanging up, she finished her sentence. "I expected a call from my boss, asking me to let the employees know the lumberyard would be closed tomorrow but opened the next. I don't have a cell, so I'll use the phone here and join you in a few minutes back in the living room. How's that?"

"Works for me."

Five minutes later, Shannon appeared with her own cup of hot coffee. Justin had carried in his as well as a small plate of cookies. "Something to get me through the paper-work," he offered as an excuse.

"Guess we can sleep late tomorrow." Shannon put her cup down before sitting. "When's your plane leave?"

"The flight leaves Great Falls at noon, but I guess I'll have to reschedule. I can leave tomorrow late if things ease up, but I'll miss that particular flight. Not a big deal. Can we delay the paperwork and video for a few minutes while I make arrangements for a room and another flight?"

"Sure."

Justin spent a good fifteen minutes finding a room in Great Falls as well as rescheduling his flight back to Syracuse.

"I guess everyone else was thinking the same thing I was —time to get a room and rebook that plane," he sighed as he tossed his cell onto the coffee table. He'd abandoned his suit coat an hour earlier so sat in rolled-up shirt sleeves.

"No use putting this off any longer." Shannon pulled her sweater tighter, a defense mechanism. "Let's see what Uncle Leon has to say for himself."

Justin pulled a laptop from his briefcase and set it on the table. Shannon rounded the table and took a seat next to him. The laptop powered up, Justin paused before hitting the PLAY button.

"I know what's in the paperwork and suspect what's in the will, but I have no idea what's on this video. May I watch it with you?"

"Certainly."

Justin hit PLAY, and Leon Jeffers appeared on the screen.

"As they say in the movies, if you're watching this video, then I must be dead." Leon sits in a chair at his home, the leaded windows that Shannon admires visible beyond his shoulders.

Shannon hit PAUSE. A trembling hand came up to rest against her lips, holding back a sob and grief that threatened to overwhelm her. Tears watered her lashes though none fell. "He looks so bad. Thin. Weak. So sick." She turned a heartbroken gaze on Justin. "He shouldn't have been alone. It's so unfair."

Justin gave her a minute to calm down, then called her attention back to the screen.

"My dear Shannon, I lived a good life, albeit not the one my parents wanted. Nor millions of others who might see my lifestyle as abnormal…perverted, shall we say."

Shannon hit the PAUSE button. *Abnormal? Perverted?* "Uncle Leon was gay?" Her eyes must look like dinner plates they felt so large.

"Uh, humm, in a word, yes," Justin confirmed. "Is that going to be a problem?" The lines across his forehead and his hand brushing nervously against his pants leg told her that his question deserved a thoughtful and honest answer.

"No, no, I don't think so. No, I'm sure there's no problem. It's just that…I never realized…" She gave Justin a look that probably distressed him if the anxiety that flashed across his expression meant anything.

"That's okay. Some of us are better at hiding our proclivities than others." Justin looked disappointed now but nodded toward the laptop. "Shall we continue?" At Shannon's nod, he hit PLAY.

"Justin should be sitting with you right now, Shannon. God, I hope he is. He'll help you understand." Leon paused as if short of breath. His skin looked slightly paler. "I refused further medications, my dear. I found out about the pancreatic cancer just before you came last summer. I was already pretty far along. I tried radiation, but it made me sicker than just the bad feelings I already experienced, so I stopped the treatments. I know. I know..." He held up a hand as if warding off her objections. "You would have told me to fight. But I'm old, and I'm ready to go. I record this now before I take to my bed with morphine to stave off the final pain of passing.

I'm not afraid. Really I'm not. So many have gone before me. My parents disowned me when I was thirteen, when they discovered my boyfriend and me behind the house one evening. Father was livid. Mother acted as if I had the plague. They refused to let me say goodbye to your mother. She was about six, I think. I can't remember. Others have gone ahead...those few that I loved and cherished. But I left them eventually, fearing we'd grow too close, and someday I'd have to watch a person I love die." Leon dropped his head, then raised it, sighed, and stared off-camera for a few seconds. "I'm such a coward. Now it is I who am dying, and besides Mrs. K, a few close friends and you, I have no one left to call to my side. And you, young lady, were not called on purpose. You've suffered enough with your parents' deaths, that of your father-in-law and the disappearance of your husband. I'm just an old uncle, not really prominent on the family tree.

So I spared you. After all the letters we've shared, I can guess that you're furious—"

Shannon hit the PAUSE button so hard the laptop jumped. Justin grabbed it before she could slam it to the floor—if she were so inclined.

"Furious? You bet I'm furious! He was all I had left besides a damn cat!" Tears trickled in narrow bands across her thin cheeks. "That's not fair, making that kind of decision on my behalf. I would have come and stayed. At least he wouldn't have been alone."

Justin remained silent but hit PLAY. Leon's face wore a grin.

"I bet Justin's wondering what I got him into, sitting beside a ranting woman."

"Boy, he has you pegged," Justin said in wonder.

Shannon merely stuck her tongue out at the man on the screen.

"Get over it, Shannon. I'm gone and made the decision for you—you were to be told after I was dead. Period. So there you sit, watching this video with Justin. I'm not sure if you have questions or not. You haven't gotten to that pile of paperwork yet. I asked Justin to play the video first. Know this, dear niece, I loved you the first time I met you. Your letters sustained me during sunny days and dreary lonely nights. You're an accountant and work with numbers all day. I did too. Only my numbers turned into money. Lots of money. I never asked how you were doing out there in Montana. You never asked for help, so I

figured you, being a big girl, had it handled. If I was wrong, I'm sorry, but I'll make up for misjudging your situation if your life basically sucked."

A bubble of laughter caught Shannon by surprise. The merry sound didn't come from Justin…it came from her. Unexpected and so familiar, so like her uncle that she burst out laughing. "That was Uncle Leon's favorite word —*suck*."

"Yeah, I know. Every time we met, he used it prolifically."

"Justin will go over the paperwork related to my financial situation. It's all yours now. The will I left took care of Mrs. Krandowitz, but you know that already because I asked her to call you when it was over and let you know what happened."

Leon paused again, reached down to his side and pulled up an oxygen mask. For a few heartbeats, he held it to his face, each breath a raspy gasp. When he could speak evenly again, he laid the hissing mask on the table and finished his remarks.

"Everything I have in life goes to you, Shannon. It's a lot and will overwhelm you if you let it. With your head for numbers and your common sense, I think you'll accept the gift of my labors and do something good with it. Travel. Enjoy life away from Montana if you want. Give it all to charity. What happens to my estate is in your hands now."

Leon stopped and pulled his clasped hands off the table. They fell into his lap as his shoulders drooped. Such a deep sigh escaped him that Shannon wondered if the oxygen was for that very purpose.

He lifted his head, allowing Shannon and Justin to see just how sick and worn out he truly was. His facial muscles sagged, sallow, and thin. Bags bulged under his yellowed eyes.

"We won't meet in that place you call Heaven. There's no place there for people like me. So this is it—all you have left of me. I love you, sweet Shannon. Forgive me."

Leon reached out, pushed a button, and the screen went black.

For several seconds Shannon and Justin sat in silence, each lost in private thoughts. A delicate shuddering sob escaped Shannon. Justin reached for her hand and held it tight as she cried. Finally she managed to reduce the sobs to sighs.

"No matter what his lifestyle, he was my uncle and a good man. I loved him. He was so funny." A note of comic surprise filled her voice.

"Don't I know it."

For the next ten minutes they shared funny stories about Leon and his wickedly sharp sense of humor. Eventually silence fell, deep enough that they could hear sleet hitting the window panes.

"You'll be lucky to leave here tomorrow. Hope the sun comes out. At least all this will turn to slush." Shannon gently closed the laptop as she wished good weather for Justin's return.

"I hate to say it, Shannon, but we really have to get these papers signed, so I can explain your inheritance."

"You make it sound like I'm inheriting a fortune," Shannon joked as they pushed dirty dishes and the laptop to one side of the coffee table.

"Do you have any idea what sort of work Leon did?" Justin pulled papers from his briefcase as he asked.

"None whatsoever."

"I'll be darned. Then this is going to really knock your socks off."

"Seriously?"

"Dead on serious, sister. Leon wasn't *in* an investment business. He was an investor, plain and simple. He invested his money so wisely that he made money hand over fist. Similar to Midas, almost everything he touched turned to gold—well, money. He re-invested and lived off the interest if that tells you anything. He lived an extravagant life. Nothing second class for Leon Jeffers. He wasn't a fool or fanatical. He just loved the finer things in life so learned to use money to make more money. He had a gift for invest-ment...was a genius at picking the things that he sensed would be highly successful. Like you, he knew numbers, and he played the odds. He won those odds almost every time. Like him, you can live quite nicely off just the interest made on the money. What monies come in from investments he set up can be used, of course. But I seriously doubt you'll ever need or want to touch them."

Justin spread the papers out before them. "All these papers transfer his accounts and investments—all monies and claims to monies from said investments as well as prop-erties—to you. Lock, stock and barrel as they say."

Shannon sat so still she felt like she'd turned to concrete.

Her jaw sagged, her hands lay limp, her ears almost buzzed, this side of fainting dead away from shock. "All of his monies? Not obscene amounts surely." She swallowed, afraid her stomach might reject the coffee and cookies onto those papers. "How...how much are we talking about?"

Justin dived into the pile of papers, moved a few aside, and finally pulled up a page with a long list and numbers attached to the sides of each.

"Hang on to that word *obscene*, Shannon. With what Leon had in actual cash in banks, bonds, and such, including monies he invested and won't lose, that bottom number was his total worth at death." He passed the paper to Shannon and pointed to the last figure, one that had ten numbers separated by several commas.

A gasp escaped Shannon, and Justin's hand came out to hold her arm.

Probably to prevent me fainting onto the floor, her fuzzy brain reasoned. So many numbers. So many commas. That much...her mind refused to believe it. And then she realized...sadly...

"I'm disappointed in you, Justin. I didn't expect to be the butt of a joke." She handed the paper to him and stood, though wobbly. Even the *idea* of such a sum left her weak.

Justin looked up at her, a miserable expression on his face. Disappointment in her perhaps? "I'd say you're the one joking...but you're dead serious." His words made a statement, not a question. He shook his head and arranged the papers, the one with the staggering amount on top. He wrapped his hand gently around her wrist and gave a delicate tug. "Sit down, and understand neither Leon nor I are joking. That's really the number, and it's really all yours."

"That's a lot of money." She managed to speak but only

in a whisper, knowing those few words were a major under-statement. Bees still buzzed in her head. Her eyes kept blinking off and on like faulty lights, and butterflies the size of volleyballs bounced in her stomach. "That's more than a few million, isn't it?" She sank back down on the sofa and hunched over the paper, using one finger to count the numbers separated by those all-important commas.

Justin cleared his throat and confirmed, "Those ten numbers put you in the billionaire category."

"B...b...b..." The word simply wouldn't leave Shannon's mouth. The word had trouble even finding a landing place in her brain.

"That's not millions with an M, Shannon. That's billion with a B."

When Shannon swayed, Justin held her arm.

"Holy shit," she whispered. "What the hell do I do with that kind of money?" She gave him a stare that had to border on insane. "Is he serious?"

Justin held her as if she were glass, firm but gently. "It's a big thing, Shannon. I wasn't quite aware of his worth until I saw these figures. You can do this," he soothed. "You can handle this."

"This is crazy!" Shannon pulled her arm away from Justin and jumped up to almost run around the room, like a ping pong ball, practically bouncing off one wall, then another. "That's a B, Justin. Not a measly few thousand but a B, for God's sake!" She continued to bounce around the room, muttering, "How does a person who's about to lose her job, has no car or income become the owner of a b... b...?" Her mouth refused to say the B word. "...that much money?"

Suddenly she stopped in front of Justin, and her face

grew dangerous, her brows down, her eyes squinted. One hand shot out, a finger pointing at the man in front of her. "This is a joke, right? One of Leon's weirdly funny jokes. He's not really dead, is he? You guys made this up."

Justin shot off the couch and grabbed Shannon by her shoulders and shook her. "Leon Jeffers is dead. This is no joke. He loved you and left his inheritance to you. Snap out of it, and start acting like the sane person he knew you to be...the smart common sense woman he described to me." In a huff, he dropped his hands to his side.

Both stood face to face, puffing like bellows in a smithy.

"Justin?"

"Yes?"

"This isn't a dream or a joke, is it?" As Shannon spoke, her breathing slowed.

"This is no joke."

"Wow!" Slowly Shannon sank to the sofa behind her as Justin took up his original seat across the coffee table from her. "Wow. You must think I'm crazy," she whispered as she shook her head side to side. "I'm a numbers person. Logical, you know. This..." She waved her hand at the papers scattered on the coffee table, "defies logic!" Her breathing ramped up, and she huffed and puffed again. "Takes my breath away, you know?"

"Yeah. Sort of does, doesn't it?" Justin remained calm as he arranged papers in some kind of order and pulled out his fountain pen. "There's a lot of paperwork to go through. Are you calmer yet?" Shannon nodded but still looked shell shocked. "Ready?" He held up paper and pen.

"Huh? Oh, yeah, I guess. I mean...yes."

As if sleepwalking, she rounded the table and sat next to

him. Her hand trembled. The pen shook ever so slightly. She bit her lip and wished this was all a dream.

"Breathe, Shannon. Just breathe. You can do this," Justin assured her.

At her nod, they went through the paperwork, page by page, slowly and carefully. Justin left no page until Shannon could repeat what it meant. She initialed here and signed there. Initialed again and signed yet again. When they completed the final signature on the final page, Justin gathered the papers, put a bulldog clip on the entire lot, and slipped them back into his briefcase.

"That's it?" Shannon had resigned herself to her uncle's loss and the gain of his inheritance. She had yet to wrap her head around that row of numbers indicating just how big that inheritance was.

"Not quite yet. Sorry." Justin pulled out an envelope and handed it to Shannon. "Beaufort knows what's in Leon's will, but I don't. I was working on a big case when he wrote this years ago."

"Huh! You just handed me a video from Uncle Leon telling me about his life, then handed over a chunk of change in exchange for my initials and signature. What else is there?"

Justin shrugged and clasped his hands between his legs, his elbows leaning on his knees. "Might as well read Leon's will, and get the shocks over for the night."

"Shocks…you got that right. How the hell am I going to get any sleep tonight, huh? Answer me that one, Mr. Lawyer."

"I just deliver the paperwork. Getting sleep is your department." Justin held up his hands in surrender, a grin warming his face.

"Huh!" Shannon repeated as she eased the velum envelope flap open. She pulled out a single sheet, handwritten in Leon's tiny fussy handwriting. "The man had handwriting right out of the eighteen hundreds."

Last Will and Testament of Leon Maurice Jeffers

October 31, 2008
   Auburn, New York
   Witnessed by Troy Blantant and Jennifer Yates, their signatures below
   Notarized by Natalie Adam, secretary with Beaufort, Black and Brody Attorneys at Law

All my earthly goods go to my niece, Shannon Elizabeth Waller, my sole surviving heir. My financial goods now and in the future are hers. My entire estate, home and the acreage attached are hers as well. She loves Mon Coeur, my home, and will take good care of it. Mrs. Krandowitz receives a pension of fifty-thousand dollars for putting up with me for over thirty years. The condo I bought for her is hers alone and paid for. Beyond Mrs. K, there is no one else with whom I'll share my home or wealth. God bless you, Shannon, and best of luck. You know numbers. Use that skill to be happy, and make others happy if you want.

Signed in front of all,
   Leon Maurice Jeffers

Below Leon's name were the signatures of the witnesses as well as that of the notary and her stamp.

Shannon flipped the paper over, but the back was blank.

"That's it? With a paragraph that man turned over Mon Coeur to me? The car. The lake. That…what did he call it?"

"The folly?"

"Yeah, the folly in the middle of the lake?"

A nod confirmed the will and all she asked.

"But I live here, and Mon Coeur is in New York State." She spoke aloud while her gaze focused on the far wall, her mind racing in a million directions.

"I'd say you may not get much sleep tonight. You've got some thinking to do, decisions to make. *Do I stay, or do I go?*" Justin sang a familiar jingle from a TV commercial.

His silliness brought Shannon back to the moment with a laugh. "Boy, do I ever have decisions to make." A thought struck her, and she blushed.

"What? You look like a beet. You're blood red!" Justin reached out a long fingered hand and laid it against her forehead.

"I have an embarrassing question to ask considering my reaction to all this." She waved at his briefcase with one hand and playfully swatted his hand away from her face with the other.

"Ask away. Can't be any worse than what's happened so far."

"Well, I'm broke. The ol' *rob Peter to pay Paul* thing, if you know what I mean."

"Been there…in college."

"I don't even have a car right now. A friend has been picking me up and taking me back and forth to work. The company I work for is closing down in two days. I could take a job in other towns, but I'd have to move, and I don't have money to move or even repair my car..." She turned embarrassed eyes on Justin. "See where I'm headed?"

"You're so broke you can't pay attention as Leon used to say."

Shannon nodded.

"So you wonder how long before that B-money is available."

Another nod answered him.

Once again he dug into his briefcase.

"That thing resembles a pot of gold. Every time you dive in there, you come up with something awesome...like endless wealth." She breathed that last out in a tiny whisper. "So what have you got this time?"

"Cash...cold hard cash." Justin held a stiff envelope.

"Where'd that come from," Shannon whispered again as if he just produced money stolen from a bank robbery. Her hands remained at her side, afraid to reach out for immediate salvation.

"This is money to tide you over until I get back to Auburn and get these papers filed with the court and banks and investment firms. Leon wanted to talk to me specifically about something before he died, but apparently he was worse than even he realized because he never got around to telling me. He never left anything written either. Maybe that will come to light some day. In the meantime, I'll spend the next week running all over Auburn, Ithaca, and New York City with piles of death certificates and signed papers, transferring everything into your name. In the meantime, this advancement should take care of immediate concerns until you hear from me. Late in the week or early the next, I'd say, should do it. I'll call, and we can visit about any plans you might have as far as coming to Auburn and at least visiting Mon Coeur."

Justin handed Shannon a large leather envelope tied with an old fashioned hide thong.

When she sat staring at it without opening it, Justin chuckled and tapped the envelope. "Afraid to open it?"

"Wouldn't you be?"

"If I'd just gone through all the disclosures you've just been handed, I suppose I would hesitate too. But I happen to know how much is in there and know you can handle this amount."

"Easy for you to say," she said under her breath as she untied the leather thong and pulled the envelope open. Carefully she counted the money—fifties and hundred dollar bills.

"Ten thousand, right?"

"Correct. Enough to buy whatever you need."

"You're right."

"About what?"

"I handle monies like this at the lumber yard. So I'm not quite as freaked out, but then again, this money doesn't belong to Waller Lumberyard. It belongs to Shannon Waller."

"Now you're catching on."

———

"I made lists all night." Shannon showed Justin her yellow pad the next morning. He came into the kitchen just after seven, but she'd been there since five. "Coffee's hot, and I made some biscuits to go with the last of the deer sausage."

"Sounds good to me." He gathered breakfast and sat down across from her. "You make good coffee."

"Thanks. Jacob's dad taught me how."

"I'd like to hear about your list if you don't mind, but first I'd like to know how you're feeling this morning after all those revelations last night." Justin wrapped both hands around his cup and leaned his elbows on the table, prepared to hear what she had to say.

Shannon laid down her pencil and scooted her plate away before leaning back in her chair. One hand raked through her hair, and she blew out a big breath. "To be honest, I'm still having a hard time trusting all this." She held up her hand to ward off the anxious expression that crossed the man's face. "No, I believe. I trust Uncle Leon as well as you."

Justin's face broke into a relieved smile.

"It's just that life with good friends and a job doesn't make up for a having a home, husband, and relatives. And I'm down to just an old home if that tells you anything. I'm okay with all this if not majorly overwhelmed by the amount he entrusted to me. I'd have to work overtime to spend all the money he left me."

"You'd be surprised how easily some can." Justin saluted her with his cup and quirked an eyebrow. "There are plenty out there who can go through that much in less than two years. And that's being conservative."

"No kidding?"

"I kid you not. I've handled some cases out of New York City of family members versus family members who discovered their fortunes rested in multiple homes and cars, in trips around the world and jewelry. Nothing for a rainy day. Not even grocery money."

"Holy smokes." She pulled the list back in front of her and shook her head. "I can't even imagine."

"So what kind of lists did you come up with?" He gave her an inquiring look over his coffee cup. "Did you get any sleep at all?"

"If I slept, I don't remember." Shannon patted a yellow legal pad in front of her. "Things to do after Waller Lumberyard closes." One finger paused at the top of a lengthy list. "Research for a new car. One big enough to travel in comfortably and haul some of my stuff. I'm not big into flying. I like seeing the countryside."

"I like flying. Takes less time."

"Not really when you count getting to the airport so dang early, the time for the flight, then standing around waiting for luggage."

"True, but that beats days on the road."

"Po-ta-toes. Pooo Tat Oes." Shannon said, waggling her hand back and forth, meaning she had her opinion, and he was welcomed to his.

"So what's after that?"

"Research home improvements—new windows, siding, a new furnace, adding on a master bedroom and bath to the house as well as a double garage and enclosed breezeway between."

"Wow, you have been busy. But why the home improvements if you're not staying?"

"I know a really sweet couple here in town. He's got a good job, and she just landed a job in a local bank. Both have family here, so they're not looking to leave the area. But they want to buy a home and start a family. What if I rent the house to them? I know it's not the same as buying, but honestly I hate giving it up. What if Jacob suddenly returns? At least someone will be here that he knows and who knows where I am." She waved Justin off before his open mouth could say anything. "Yeah, I know. The odds of that are a zillion to one, but it could happen. Coincidence, you know?"

Justin quirked his brows, poured another cup of coffee for himself and refreshed Shannon's cup. "So you think they'll jump on this?"

"I'll charge five hundred a month with the provision that they keep the yard and acreage cleared. I've got two pets buried back there, and I don't want to see their graves overrun with weeds. So yes, I think they'll go for the idea. I'll talk to them in the next few days, but the house won't be ready for several months. Most of the improvements can be done simultaneously though. I hope."

"So you get a car and put someone in the house. Where will you go then?"

"Mon Coeur. I'll take what I want in tubs and suitcases in the car and take my time traveling. By early summer the weather will be perfect for cruising the highways."

"Can I offer a suggestion about the car?"

"Sure." Shannon broke open a warm biscuit and slathered it with butter.

"Don't get a car. Get a mid size SUV. Something with lots of room in the back when you lay down the seats. You're looking for something to use for hauling, not one for carrying people. So you really don't need things like DVD players on each seat back with built in headphones."

"Good suggestion. I never gave that a thought. I want all the standards like heat, AC, and all that plus the newer safety features. I also want comfort. If I'm going to travel by car, I want to get where I'm going without being cramped."

"Another suggestion?"

"Sure, you're batting five hundred now. Go ahead."

"Once I've got you set up with access to your money, you'll need a debit card as well as checks. There are a few times in life still today when you want a record of what you paid. As for the car or SUV or whatever you choose, go through the whole financing thing. Pay the monthly bill for —oh say, six or ten months—*then* pay off the vehicle. That way you build up a credit rating. Right now with the little you have and no plastic, you have no rating at all. Right?"

"True." She scribbled some notes on the pad and looked up, her pen poised over the paper. "Any other suggestions?"

"You'll meet Raymond and Clauster when you come to Auburn. They are—were—Leon's financial advisors. Now they're yours. They can answer more of your questions."

"Do you trust them?"

"I do, based on what Leon has told me over the years. He trusted them. We researched so many of those firms together that I thought I'd go nuts. He'd been with another group but grew leery of them. That's how I met him."

"You're the Black in Beaufort, Black, and Brody. But you're so young!" Shannon blurted that as she remembered just who Justin was though he had told her as much when he came in. The heat of embarrassment flushed her face.

"Young? Hardly." Then Justin gave her a second look. "You're serious?"

When she nodded, he sat in what looked like stunned, then delighted surprise. "Just how old do you think I am?"

Shannon knew she'd put her foot in it this time, as Jacob's dad used to say. She'd embarrassed herself and made Justin uncomfortable. However, he sat waiting for an answer, so she couldn't pass off her own statement, no matter how blunt it was.

"Uh, I figured you're about my age—mid thirties."

A grin spread across Justin's face. "Wait until I tell my husband. His name is Phillip, by the way. You'll meet him when you get to Mon Coeur."

"How far off am I?" Shannon cringed, afraid she might have alienated a new friend.

"Oh, a good decade and a half at least." That smile now told her Justin was enjoying this.

"Just how old are you?"

"Fifty-one."

"No way!" Shannon's hand slapped her mouth. She'd blurted out another embarrassing statement. "I want to know your secret for looking so young."

"Phillip's fifty-three and looks just as young. I'd say it's due to clean living, but we both know that's not true." That smile slipped a little as Justin turned rapt attention to his meal.

"Justin, I'm sorry for being so blunt and…and…and downright rude. I'm impressed. That's all I'm going to say."

"Forgiven. You erred on the side of the angels. But Phillip is so going to love you."

———

The snow day meant that the last day for Waller Lumberyard came sooner than expected. Everyone showed up during the morning to collect final paychecks. Every man of them opened the envelope and checked the amount. Shannon knew the checks would support the employees for at least two weeks if necessary, but everyone had a job now, even Charlie.

Todd drifted in just before lunch. "You set to close down?"

"Desk is cleared. Mr. Leven took all his things home last week. He's been working off just whatever he could lay on his desk. I'll miss my cell phone and computer. Oh!"

"What?"

"Oh, nothing serious. I just happened to think of something to add to a list I'm making. I completely forgot about a cell and laptop."

"Won't you have those things wherever you're going next?"

"How about I explain that over lunch? Call Emily, and ask if she can meet us at the Shoo Fly Inn cafe about noon. Maybe take her lunch and conference period together. Okay?"

"Sure. Are we even coming back after lunch?"

"You know, I have no idea. Let me go ask ol' sourpuss, uh, I mean Mr. Leven. Be right back."

The conversation with Leven was a short one as usual.

"What'd he say?"

"He said he and I have to be here until a rep from Briggs and Layman shows up to collect the last bit of paperwork and keys. The men can leave at lunch time."

"Bet he didn't plan on telling them that, did he?"

"I doubt it."

"He probably planned on them hanging around until three when he would magnanimously announce that Waller Lumberyard was closed for good. I'll let the guys know." He winked like a conspirator. "Sorry ol' bastard." Todd shot a sour glance at Leven's office as Shannon handed him his paycheck envelope.

"True. So what about lunch?"

"You can ride with me. I'll call Emily."

———

Shannon couldn't tell her friends just *how* much money Leon left her, but she could tell them she'd received an inheritance. One big enough to allow her to buy a new car and make some home improvements. And big enough to allow her to travel to New York to settle his estate.

Todd sat in stunned silence, his plate of food neglected, a sign of how much her news shocked him.

Emily recovered faster than her husband did. Short of getting up and hugging her friend in a crowded restaurant, she grabbed Shannon's hand and squeezed it hard. "I'm so glad for you." While Shannon blushed and avoided her friend's gaze, Emily added, "You've had a hard time for years now—your parents, Jacob, your car. Heck, even your pet. And now, thanks to your uncle, you can live a little. Breathe a little easier." Emily gave one last squeeze, then settled her hands in her lap. "I'm happy for you, Shannon."

Todd came out of his stupor enough to nod. A few deep breaths and he seemed to find words. "Wow, that's some news. Talk about a lucky break." At Shannon's wide-eyed expression, he realized how that sounded. "Sorry. I didn't mean that your uncle dying was lucky. Just that he loved you enough to take care of you so well."

"True. I'll miss him." She explained something even as she laughed. "He was what you'd call a *character*, Todd. Feisty and funny. Warm and cozy one minute, then all puffy the next. But I loved him, and he loved me. But I'm as shocked as you two, to be honest."

"So the house gets a face lift. Good for you. Oh, and a good—new—car too. That's really something." Todd congratulated her before diving back into his plate of home cooking.

"So when and where do you start?"

"Oh, Emily, I don't know. I've gone to work for decades, and tomorrow I won't have to." She shrugged and finished the last of her Coke. "I guess I'll do some research into SUVs. Justin—Justin Black, the lawyer who delivered all the paperwork night before last—suggested a mid-sized SUV for its hauling capacity. He reminded me that I've driven a car for years. Driving one of those big SUVs like a Suburban might be like driving a tank to me. But I'm going to check out them all. And find a contractor for home improvements."

"You're going to be a busy girl, Shannon." Todd motioned for the check. "Wish I were free to help with the improvements. I'd love to be involved."

"You can be my guide, Todd. Help me keep everything on the straight and narrow. Keep 'em honest, as Jacob used to say."

"I can hardly wait to see what you do with the place." Emily finally got a chance to hug Shannon when they stood to leave.

"Yeah, me too." Shannon giggled and tucked her hands into first Todd's, then Emily's arms.

———

Shannon returned after a long lunch to an eerie scene. No one in the lumber yard. The trucks parked when they should have been on the road. No cars or trucks in the employee parking area. No noises. No voices shouting. She unlocked the office door and entered but stopped when Leven pulled his car right up next to the steps. She refused to speak to him though she would be polite and answer if he spoke first.

Leven appeared to be of a similar mind because he entered the office without speaking to her.

She took up her position at her desk, and he entered his office, the same as every other day. He had a collection of files on his desk which made her wonder why she was even there. However it wasn't beyond the man to require her being there just to aggravate her. Just to have something to do, she checked her desk drawers once more and the filing cabinet behind her. She opened the coat closet, but all were empty. Returning to her chair she pulled out her key ring. She had three keys, one to this office, one to her house, and one for the rattle-trap of a vehicle she drove. Soon to be replaced, she reminded herself. She dared not smile even at her private thoughts. Leven might take it the wrong way, and the last thing she wanted was a confrontation with the man.

At two-forty-five, a car pulled up, and two men got out. They entered the office, nodded to her and entered Leven's office. Though they left the door open, the conversation was short and too quiet to hear. She waited, frustrated by being there when she had other things she could be doing.

One of the men came out of the office first and walked over to her desk. Leven and the other man—the folders in his arms—came out behind the first.

"May I have the last key, Mrs. Waller? Once I have this,

Leven, the deal is final, and no one may enter this property again. Understood?"

Leven nodded, while Shannon worked the office key off the ring and handed it over to the man who never introduced himself. He gestured Shannon and Leven out the door, turned, and used her key to seal the place and the deal.

She got into the truck she was using and turned it on. Pulling out of the lot ahead of Leven and the other two, she pulled the truck into a driveway leading to a ranch a mile back from the road. The other cars passed her while the truck idled.

"No more job. Turning over that key made that final. If I hadn't inherited Uncle Leon's estate, I'd be crying right now." She put the truck in reverse, checked the road both ways, and pulled back onto the pavement. "Huh, never knew how important a key could be," she commented to no one.

———

The problem with having choices and money to pay for them is that you have no idea where to start. By late that week, information about vehicles, home construction and improvements, even the current price of concrete per square foot, threatened to overwhelm Shannon.

She needed a break. Time to visit her godparents in Great Falls. The only problem was—she had no reliable transportation. Time to call on her best friend, Immajean. Besides, Immajean deserved to know what was going on. Not the whole truth—that much money was impossible to comprehend, much less explain.

Billions of bucks weren't just sitting in a bank vault, she

knew. Most of it was tied up in investments. But the interest alone was enough to keep her happy.

Before she could phone Immajean, her phone rang.

"Well, we know it isn't Leven calling for my services," she quipped as she answered. "Waller residence."

"Shannon."

"Justin, how nice to hear from you." He'd called several times since leaving, and she discovered she had a new friend, one that offered comfort as well as words of advice. She took the hand-held portion of the phone to the kitchen and poured a cup of coffee. Eight o'clock a.m. her time was ten for him. "What's the news?"

"All the paperwork has been changed into your name. Bank accounts are ready for your signature. I persuaded the bank to order checks. They'll be here by the time you arrive." He paused a second. "You *are* coming to New York, right?"

"Of course." She didn't expand on that because she knew several months would go by before she could come. "Uh, Justin, can I go by my bank and sign papers for the Auburn bank, or can they send them to me to sign?"

"What are you saying, Shannon?"

"I want to do that remodeling I told you about, but even with construction going on simultaneously, the whole project probably won't be completed for six to eight weeks." Silence on the other end prompted her to cringe a little.

"Only if you can go to the same bank in Montana."

"Humm, that might be a problem. Can they mail the papers to me?"

"The easiest thing to do, Shannon, if you're crunched for time, is fly here, let me pick you up, take you by the banks and investment companies for signatures, share lunch with me, then fly home. Everything can be done in a day's time."

A hefty sigh escaped Shannon, wafting over the phone's receiver. "Yeah, that would be best, I suppose. Can you arrange the flight for me?" She sat her cup down with a clink. "Oh, Justin, that sounded awful! I'm sorry. I could probably make arrangements myself, but I'm not sure how to go about it. Uncle Leon always made arrangements for my flights."

"Not to worry. I'll contact the travel agency he used. I use them too. They'll mail the tickets to you. Still don't have a lap top or cell?"

"No, and it's frustrating. At least at work I could use those things if needed. Now I feel like I've stepped back into the nineteen-fifties."

Justin's laugh brightened her spirits. "I can't even imagine. Okay, so here's what we'll do. I'll arrange for tickets to be sent within the next forty-eight hours from…where?"

"Make them from Great Falls. I'm preparing to visit my godparents. A friend will take me. Martha and Wallace will take me to the airport. After that—when I've finally got some major finances—I'll get some new wheels and return home. Oh, and I'll pick up the latest and greatest in technology while in Great Falls too. I'll get these remodel projects going, and when they're done, then I'll head to Auburn. Let me give you the address and phone number."

"Keep in touch?"

"Silly man. Of course. I now consider you not just my lawyer but a friend. Okay with that?"

"Suits me just fine."

Shannon could hear real pleasure in his voice and imagined his bright smile. "Oh, and Justin?"

"Yes?"

"Can Phillip come to lunch with us?" She could swear she heard Justin's grin over the phone if that sort of thing were possible. "I'd love to meet him."

"Absolutely! I'll let you know when to expect the ticket. Until then be safe. Be happy."

"And you. Thanks for calling. Talk soon."

She cradled the phone and sat in the sunshine for a few more minutes. But lolling around wasn't going to get things done. She needed to phone Immajean and ask for a ride. First though, she needed to contact Helen and Victor Bass. Would they accept her offer of the house? Probably but there was always that off-chance that they'd already made arrangements somewhere else in Cut Bank. Fearing that possibility, she dialed Helen's number at the bank.

"Stockman's Bank, Helen Bass speaking."

"Helen, it's Shannon. You have a few minutes?"

"Just a few, Shannon. I've got a customer waiting."

"Can you and Victor come to the house for dinner tonight? I've got something I want to pass by you, and it's important. For all three of us."

"Something wrong?"

"No! No! In fact, things are pretty awesome right now. But this is something that could benefit all of us."

"Okay then, if there's no crisis—"

"No crisis or emergency."

"Then we'll be there. Six too early?"

"Perfect. See you then."

With the phone off once again, Shannon moved to her tiny desk and picked up her yellow legal pad where she'd filled pages with information.

With a pencil she drew an arrow and labeled that as a

quick trip to Auburn to sign bank papers. Lunch with Justin/Phillip.

So many events crowded her timeline before she could get to Auburn and Mon Coeur. She penciled in dinner with Helen and Victor as a major moment. If they didn't want to rent the house, then she'd have to find the right person to love what she loved or else let it sit, and she wasn't ready to do that.

Long ago she decided she was the type of person who made lists, moved through life with practical details and liked schedules as well as peace and quiet. If adventure was to be part of her life, she wanted to be the one who said when and where.

With her list as ready as she could get it, she dialed Immajean.

"Hello?"

"Immajean, it's me, Shannon."

They visited a few minutes before Shannon asked her big favor. "I'm going to owe you big time for what I'm about to ask, but could you come here tomorrow? Maybe in the afternoon so we can talk? Big things have happened, and I need to explain, and ask you to drive me to Great Falls."

"Anything to do with Jacob?"

"Jacob? Oh no, no…nothing like that. But pretty big. Too much to explain over the phone. Not that I'd even try. It's all good. Just a game changer."

"You've certainly got my attention. I'll be there after lunch. How's that?"

"That'll work. See you then."

Her plans in action, she dressed and went out to the old truck Todd lent her. Cautiously—she never knew if or when the dang thing might leave her stranded—she made her way to the grocery store. Her basket filled with things for dinner that night, she paid in cash and felt the satisfaction of not having to worry about robbing some bill in order to pay this one.

———

"Holy cow, Shannon, I don't think I've ever eaten that well." Victor rubbed his stomach, innocently ignoring his wife's mortified expression.

"Lawrence Waller taught me how to grill those ribeye steaks."

"The mushrooms are the best though," Helen used the last of her garlic bread to sop up the juices still in her plate.

"Frankly, it was all good."

"I guess you're too full then to enjoy some dessert?" Shannon removed the plates but kept an eye on Victor's stricken face.

"Dessert too?"

"Yes, sir. If I'm going to propose something big tonight, I thought I'd butter you up with a knock-out meal. Dessert just seems the natural way to end a dinner like that."

"Well now, when you put it like that, then yes. I'd love some…?"

"How about some huckleberry scones with coffee?"

Victor groaned. "Only my favorite. My mouth is drooling already."

"Really, honey!" Helen swatted her husband's arm, while her face turned red.

"Don't kill him, Helen. Otherwise I'll have to force feed him."

"No need for forcing. That man could eat scones 'til he popped."

"No need for that. Here you go, Victor."

For a good ten minutes, the three savored the unusual dessert—scones in a state like Montana.

When they finally pushed back from the dining table, Shannon suggested, "Let's move to the living room. Bring your coffee. You want more, Helen?"

Their coffee cups full, the three moved to comfortable seating in Shannon's living room.

"So why are we here, Shannon? Besides sharing good company and a fabulous meal?" Helen teased her hostess even as she lifted her cup to salute Shannon.

"Here, here!" Victor added as soon as he could after swallowing a sip of hot coffee.

Shannon had given this proposal a lot of thought. So she didn't stammer in what she laid out for her friends.

"You're both working now, and Helen told me you're ready to settle into a home of your own and think about starting a family."

While Victor blushed a faint red, Helen nodded. Neither said anything. The floor belonged to Shannon at this point.

"You might recall my mother had a brother, Leon. We met after Mom and Dad were gone. Leon had been looking for his family…his sister. Instead of Mom, he found me. That was shortly after Jacob disappeared. We've been family to each other for years now. I wrote to him. He wrote back. We talked on the phone, and each summer I took my week's vacation in Auburn with Uncle Leon."

"Auburn? New York?"

"Yes."

"That's a far piece to go," Victor commented.

"True, and it looks nothing like Montana. But Leon and I loved each other and clung to each other as all the family we had left. Leon…" Shannon had to clear her throat before going on. "Leon died not long ago. Aggressive cancer that he didn't tell me about. He also forbid anyone else to tell me until after he was gone."

"I'm so sorry, Shannon. Victor only knew you had relatives to visit each year, but he didn't know the details about Leon like I did."

"Thank you. After Leon died, Mrs. Krandowitz, the housekeeper—she's a real jewel—called to tell me what happened and let me know a lawyer would show up here with papers to sign. Basically Leon left his estate to me." She sat back and watched the expressions chase across her friends' faces.

"That means?" Victor wanted a bit more detail.

"Leon had a gorgeous home in Auburn. Not overly fancy but it always suited me down to the bone. Well, I guess *fancy* means different things to different people. It's sort of a combo between Art Deco and Frank Lloyd Wright. Very open and natural."

"Sounds like around here. Open and natural," Victor quipped. "Montana is nothing if not open and natural."

Laughter helped ease Shannon's jitters for the rest of what she wanted to say.

"True. But Auburn's winters aren't quite as cold."

"A plus if ever I heard one," Helen said as she stared at Shannon. "You're leaving, aren't you? Going to Auburn and live in that lovely home forever."

"Well, I'm not sure about *forever*, but yes, I do plan on living there for at least a year just to see how things go. Actually, I want to travel to the Texas Gulf coast to where

Mom was born and raised. A place called Galveston. A city on an island south of Houston. Then I'll return to Auburn and see how life gets on."

"I'm happy for you, honestly I am, Shannon, but boy, am I going to miss you," Helen said with a smile watered ever so slightly by a tear that sat on the edge of her lashes.

"Weelll," Shannon drawled out the word because Helen gave her the *in* she had been looking for. An *in* into the proposal. "What if you stayed in touch with me quite a lot? As in I am your landlord?"

Helen and Victor looked confused.

"What are you saying?" Victor set his empty cup down with exaggerated care.

"Leon left enough money to take care of me for a very long time. I owe it to him to check out Auburn and his home. I want to travel a little. I can do that now. But I hate leaving my home here. This place…" She choked for a second, her gaze going over the ancient flowered wall paper and thin window panes. "This place means the world to me. Jacob was born here. We were married here. It's entirely possible that some day he may return. And this is the first place he'd come to. But I won't be here. That doesn't mean I want this house to sit empty. I want to update the place some." She left out just how much updating she planned. "Make it livable for a family—one I never had." She cleared her throat again and forged on. "I'd like to offer the house and land to you two, for a modest rental fee each month. I'd take care of needed up-keep and repairs, but the place would basically be yours. Maybe a few requests but all yours."

"Rent?" Victor looked like a kid trying to sort out all the gifts under the Christmas tree. "House? Repairs? Ours?

Requests? What requests?" At that, he squinted his eyes as if he expected something outrageous.

Poor Helen sat silent, with a numbed expression as if she wasn't sure she heard right. Her mouth hung open, and her coffee cup and saucer hung at the edge of her knees, an accident waiting to happen.

Never leaving her friend's stunned gaze, Shannon reached out, took the cup and saucer, and laid them on the coffee table.

"Uh, yes, a few requests. Nothing terrible I think, but that's up to you to decide."

"I'm all ears. Frankly, I'm waiting for the other shoe to fall—something that will prevent us from taking you up on this unbelievable offer," Victor said softly.

"No shoes. No gimmicks. Just a few personal things."

"Okay," Helen spoke at last. "What do you want?"

"Our—my—pets. They're buried out in the back of the property under that oak. Jacob's old Lab, Trip, and my cat, Simon. I'd like them to remain there. And the entire property always mowed so it looks nice." She stopped talking, waiting for them to respond.

"That's it? That's easy." Victor gave a hard nod.

"And the furniture…" Shannon rubbed her hand over the flowered chintz arm of the deep chair she sat in. "I'll leave it here, and you can replace it as you want. It's all old but still in good enough shape so you don't have to go out and buy an entire house of new furniture right off the bat."

"Done," Helen said.

"Leon's money allows me to fix up this place. Nothing fancy. All box store things but good quality so whoever lives here—you two, I hope," Shannon reached out and took Helen's hand even as her gaze vibrated back and forth between the man and woman. "never has to worry about the plumbing or electricity or god forbid, the furnace going out. I'm going to tear down that old barn and add a bedroom suite to the back of the house, replace all the windows and roof. Update the insides and add a garage. I think..." An image came to mind. "I'll keep the old gas pump out there with its glass bulb. That's part of the heritage of this home. All that work can be done in two months or less. Plenty of time before it gets cold. In fact, you should be able to celebrate the 4th here." Now that she'd said everything, she sat silent. Time for Helen and Victor Bass to decide.

"So you're going to update everything and let us rent the place as long as we take care of the pets and keep the place mowed? How much is the rent? After all those improvements, Shannon, we might not be able to afford the rent." Helen's voice carried a hint of desire but a lot more concern.

"I'm thinking five hundred a month. I mean, that's a pretty big chunk of money. You'll be carrying the insurance on the place. That's how rentals usually work. The money you'll pay to me rather than a bank. The good part is that you can live here as long as you want. I don't think..."

Something finally dawned on Shannon...something that had been hiding in the back of her mind ever since Justin left.

"I don't think I'll ever live here again. But the house is too good to just sit, not while a couple like you two can make a home with kids here. I think my heart would just about overflow to know you'll raise your kids here."

With a happy sigh, Shannon sat forward but remained silent. She'd said her piece. The decision rested with Helen and Victor now.

Helen opened her mouth—probably to say yes—but

Victor laid a hand on top of hers, silencing her. When she shot him a confused look, he patted her hand.

"Don't worry, honey. This offer is almost too good to pass up. But, Shannon, can you give us a few days to sort all this out in our minds? Think about what it means for our future? What if you change your mind?"

This time it was Shannon who laid a hand on both Victor and Helen's hands. "I won't. I promise. This place has been good to me, but I need to move on now. I want to move on. And I'll do that with a grateful heart if I know the people here are those I know and trust to love it as much as I do. But I'll never return and ask for the place back."

Like Victor, she patted their hands, bent to stack the cups and saucers and stood. "Take all the time you want. I'm going to get the remodel job started, so you've got plenty of time. And if for some reason you two don't want the house, I'll ask someone else, though I admit, I have my heart set on seeing your kids grow up here."

With that astonishing statement she made her way to the kitchen, a smile on her lips. The couple in the living room sat without a word.

"Uh, Shannon, we've got work tomorrow, so we're headed home. The dinner was great." Victor patted his stomach. "We'll let you know. I—we—just need to get all this sorted out," he repeated.

"I totally understand. If I were in your shoes I'd be talking to my parents and a good lawyer. If there's any concern, call, and we'll work out any issues. Until I hear from you, drive safe."

She walked them out into the fresh night air and hugged both before they got in their car and drove off into the darkness.

"That ought to keep them awake tonight," she told a firefly that flew past as she grinned and turned off the porch light.

———

"Immajean, I'm so glad to see you!" Shannon hugged her best friend's neck so hard and enthusiastically that Immajean almost choked.

"Whatever you want to tell me must be pretty damn good." She swatted Shannon off her. "Back off, would you? You're getting plumb silly."

"Sorry, but things are sooo different now!" Shannon pulled Immajean into the house and immediately pulled out left over scones, wine, cheese, and thin slices of prosciutto.

"Holy crap, where did you get this?" Immajean took up several slices of the cured ham and popped them in her mouth while waiting for Shannon's answer. "Holy Moses, and good wine too." She swirled the glass for a second or two, then took a small sip. "Oh man, now that's good stuff." Even as she took another sip, she cut her gaze at Shannon over the top of the wine glass. "What gives?"

"Come on, let's take all this *good stuff* to the living room, and I'll explain."

Immajean carried the wine glasses and tucked the wine bottle under her arm, while Shannon carried a heavily loaded tray to the living room. All things deposited on the small coffee table, the two sat next to each other.

"Salute." Immajean clinked glasses with Shannon, sipped the wine, and rolled her eyes as she hummed in pleasure.

After a second to savor the flavor and take up more

prosciutto and cheese, Immajean settled back into one corner of the sofa, facing Shannon while Shannon took up a similar pose at the opposite end.

"So what gives? This spread must have cost a fortune, and last I heard," Immajean cocked one eyebrow at her friend, "you have no job yet."

"Correct. But I had an uncle that died and left me a boatload of money."

Shannon tossed a kitchen towel to her friend, so she could mop up the wine that sputtered after that announcement.

"Damn, girl. Let's be subtle, why don't you?" Immajean mopped up a few splatters of red wine from the sofa back. "Sorry about that. Now you want to go over that again—minus the drama?"

Once again Shannon went through the story of Uncle Leon passing on and naming her as his sole beneficiary. As much as she loved Immajean—they'd grown up together and were best friends—there was no need to get specific about just how much money Leon had left. Besides, if Shannon who was an accountant used to dealing with thousands of dollars at the lumberyard still had trouble even saying the B word—billion—then she doubted anyone else would honestly believe her. That sort of thing was the stuff story writers loved to create. Inheriting boatloads of money never happened in real life—except it did. To her.

"Oh…my…god," Immajean whispered, the food in her hand forgotten, her wine glass in danger of tipping over.

Shannon motioned to it, then raised hers. "Salute?"

Immajean suddenly came to life, touched her glass to Shannon's, and shouted, "Damn straight!"

"I've got plans for remodeling the house. I'd like to ask

your husband to recommend someone as construction super-visor. Someone Danny trusts."

"That's a good call. That husband of mine has been around construction all his life. He'll know someone that will do right by you."

"There's a tight time line though."

"That could cost a fortune." Immajean held up a scone, and moved her fingers as if counting. "Oh yeah, lots of money—sorry! I forgot. No problem there." Her grin and laugh were purely wicked.

Her laugh made Shannon feel better.

"I'm going to New York to live in Uncle's house for a bit. Can you live without me for a while?"

At that announcement, Immajean set down the food and even the glass. "You're serious about leaving?" Shannon nodded. "It's been hard for you," Immajean conceded. "You've always told me how much you love Leon's house. And now that the lumberyard has closed, there's really no need to stay. Sooner or later you would have had to leave anyway. A new job would have been in a new town proba-bly. What are you going to do with the house?" Immajean might be a healthy eater and a bit of a joker, but her sharp mind came up with pertinent questions.

"I've offered the place to friends…to rent as long as they want. They're ready to have a home and raise a family. Maybe in the long run I'll just sell it to them, but for now I'll rent."

"You've offered, but they haven't accepted yet?"

"I just asked them about it last night. I wined and dined them pretty well before asking though."

"Smart woman." Immajean lifted her glass to Shannon once again.

"I suspect they'll accept. They love this place too."

"Can I ask who you asked?" A frown crossed Immajean's forehead. "Too much wine too fast—that sounded funky." She giggled but sat the glass down and started pulling off pieces of scone.

"Helen and Victor Bass."

"Oh, well done, Shannon!" That excited Immajean who clapped her hands, scattering crumbs over the sofa cushions.

"Dang, Immajean, I'm going to have to put the good stuff away and break out the coffee if you keep this up."

Together the women fell into each other's arms, laughing and giggling, amid a few tears.

"Can I come visit you in Auburn?" Immajean asked as they returned the tray, wine, and empty glasses to the kitchen.

While Shannon prepared coffee, she leaned against the counter. "I hope many of you will come visit. You and your family. Helen and Victor. Todd and Emily. Several others I consider dear friends. You're such close friends. I'll miss you all—"

"But it's time to break away and find yourself." Immajean finished her sentence as if reading Shannon's mind.

"That's not what I meant." Shannon protested but not loudly or with a great deal of enthusiasm.

"Yeah, it is. You've worked for years and lived in this old home, waiting for a man who for all we know has been dead fifteen years. You've never really established a life for yourself. Leon just gave you a perfect opportunity to get out and see the world. Maybe you'll see all that you want, then return. Oh, not to this house. You'd never take it away from the Bass'. Maybe you'll stay in Auburn in Leon's home. You always go on and on about it. You like driving, but I adore flying. I can fly to your home no matter where you decide to settle."

A heavy sigh escaped Shannon. "I suppose you're right. Maybe after I remodel the house it won't be so much…my house any more. I won't mind leaving."

"Hadn't thought about it like that, but I bet you're right. With a good remodel this old place will last another hundred years."

Her gaze moving over the outdated kitchen, Shannon imagined what the room would look like with newer cabinets, countertops, and appliances. "Maybe it'll look so good I won't want to leave."

"Huh! Now who needs that coffee! I see a new direction coming in your life, girl. Accept it, and run with it."

"Yeah." Shannon stood up, straightened her shoulders, put a hand on Immajean's, and gave her a hard squeeze. "I think you may be right." She poured the coffee just as she remembered. "Oh hey, can you drive me to Great Falls? I need to buy a car."

PREPARING

"Shannon!" Martha Ackerman held out her arms and embraced her god-daughter with a firm hold. "It's been ages."

"Not really, Martha," her husband Wallace said as he got in his own hug.

"It's so nice to see you both again. You remember Immajean Adams?"

"We do. Welcome." Martha pulled both women into the one-story home she and Wallace had lived in for thirty years.

"You are staying for the week, right, Shannon?" Wallace pulled out a chair for Martha at the dining table. Martha had told the girls to arrive in time for lunch.

"I am, though Immajean has to return this afternoon."

"Oh, that's too bad, dear. But we'll enjoy your company while we can," Martha said as she grasped her husband's hand, then reached for Shannon's. "Let's give thanks for this lovely meal and the good company, shall we?"

Three hours passed before Immajean insisted she had to

get on the road for home. She hugged Shannon especially hard. "Just practicing for when you leave," she whispered.

"That's not fair for you to say that, then leave." A tear trickled down Shannon's cheek.

"Truth hurts most times, girlfriend." Immajean planted a big kiss on Shannon's cheek, shook hands with Wallace, and hugged Martha. "I had a lovely time. Thank you."

Once Immajean's car was out of sight, Wallace, Martha and Shannon made their way to a bright back screened-in porch. Folks in Montana enjoyed the sunshine and warm weather whenever available, considering how cold and long winters that close to the Canadian border could get.

"So, Shannon, you said something about buying a car? Immajean brought you here, so I assume that lousy Escort finally died?" Wallace was a plain spoken man, never one to waste words.

Her Uncle Leon speech trimmed to bare minimum now, Shannon filled in her godparents on what had happened in the last month and what her immediate plans were.

"So Leon died. He broke his parents' hearts, but they got even with him when they refused to let him say goodbye or have any contact with your mom, Shannon. Frankly, I thought he died years ago and never gave him much thought."

Belatedly Shannon realized she'd rarely shared anything about Leon with Martha and Wallace. They were an older couple when her parents asked them to be their only child's godparents. Seldom does one truly expect parents to die and leave their child in that other couple's hands. Shannon was almost eighteen when her mom and dad died. While Wallace helped with the will and settled their estate, she never had to leave Cut Bank and come live with them.

"So you knew about Leon and his life style choice?"

"Life style? Oh no, dear. We just knew something awful came between your grandparents and their son. And your mom suffered as much or more than her mother and father. She and Leon were close." Martha resembled a lady of an earlier generation, knowing just the surface facts but not the details. And not wanting to know them either.

"Life style, huh. Well, I'll not ask. No sense in it now that the man is dead. And obviously he lived a long time and did good by you, sweetheart. So, I'm thankful he found you."

"Me too, Wallace. Now at least I can get a new car. And I plan on updating the house. Nothing fancy, just good solid work. Nothing custom. I think Lawrence Waller would turn over in his grave if I did. He never was one for fancy custom work if buying local could do the job just as well."

"Sounds like Lawrence. Too bad the lumberyard closed down. Now that you've got some money you're going to do what?"

"I'm going to get that new car, update the house, then go to Auburn in New York. Part of Leon's estate was his home Mon Coeur. That's French for *my heart*. And while I'm here, I'm taking a fast trip there to sign some bank papers. Flying. I'm waiting for the lawyer to get the flight information to me. Oh, and I need to get a computer and cell phone. Humm, where should I get my cell service? Here? Auburn?"

They spent a pleasant afternoon discussing cell phones, computers—Wallace was addicted to technology—and cars.

"I've done a ton of research at the library in the last few days about mileage, service, cargo space behind the front row." Shannon twirled a finger in the air. "Makes a body's head swim!"

"Did you decide on anything, dear?" Martha put a cold Coke can beside her and gave Wallace a Sprite.

"I'm going to look at a Subaru Forester. It gets great gas mileage, has four-wheel drive, and has over seventy cubic feet of space if I lay down the second row. I looked at some beauties online, but they had all kinds of entertainment on the rear side of the seats for passengers. I won't be hauling passengers but rather my luggage, sewing machine, and some of my fabric."

"I'm glad you're still quilting, sweetheart. I've enjoyed the quilt you made for me." Wallace patted her hand.

"That poor quilt is almost worn out, he's had it so long, and I've washed it so much."

"Time for a new one, Shannon?" Wallace gave her a sly wink and hopeful smile.

"If I have time over the next year, Wallace, I'll make one for you."

"Thank you, sweetheart. I'd like that."

Brrring!

Martha picked up her cell phone and answered, "Ackerman residence." She listened for a few seconds, then handed the phone to Shannon. "For you, dear. It's a lawyer."

"Justin?"

"Hi, Shannon. You ready to fly to Auburn?"

"Only if I must. I really don't like flying, you know."

"You told me, but this is necessary."

"I know. So when?"

"Day after tomorrow. Uh, I had to get a private flight for you here and back."

"How come?"

"There are limited flights out of Great Falls, and they all make three or more stops before getting to Syracuse. You'd be all day just getting here, and I know you'd hate being on a plane that long."

"You got that right. Okay. By the way, who's footing the bill for this? I don't have that kind of money yet, do I?"

"True. So my firm is footing this bill. After Thursday, those bills are all on you."

She could almost hear a grin over the phone.

"Well, by then I might have a car. Or not. Seeing as I've never financed a car before I doubt I can get one. Oh wait, everything's in my name now except the bank and checks. Justin, I don't even have any credit cards. How am I going to buy a car when I don't have any money?"

"Guess you'll have to wait until we hook up Thursday and I pass along the two cards I have for you."

"Oh."

"That didn't sound enthusiastic. Everything okay?" His voice modulated to a softer concerned tone.

"Yeah, it's just that I've never had enough money to worry about credit cards and paying off a bill completely at the end of the month, much less buying a new car."

"Overwhelmed?"

"Not yet, but I bet I will be by the weekend."

Justin's laugh lifted her spirits, giving her a bit more courage.

"I'm used to being by myself and relying on myself. This is going to take some getting used to, Justin."

"I can imagine. I'm not rolling in the green stuff, but I'm comfortable. I've never really been at the bottom in the financial department."

"Let me tell you something—I have, and it ain't no picnic."

"So, do you have some paper handy so I can give you some information about that flight?"

"Hold on. Martha, do you have something I can write on?"

It was Wallace who passed over a pad of paper and a pen.

"Okay, shoot." She wrote down the information. Something popped into her mind before they could ring off. "We still on for lunch? Will your...husband...be there?"

"Lunch? You bet. And Phillip is dying to meet you."

"Keep lunch light. God knows, I don't want to throw up on the flight back."

"Oh, good Lord!"

"Bye, Justin."

"See you in Syracuse. I'll pick you up."

She hung up and smiled before seeing Martha and Wallace watching her like hawks, curiosity written all over their faces.

"He's a sweetheart, and his husband Phillip is having lunch with us after I sign all those papers at various places." With that, Shannon returned Martha's cell phone and excused herself to unpack.

"That ought to keep their minds busy for the evening," she grinned as she put her clothes into drawers.

———

"Oh damn, I really don't like this," Shannon whispered to the empty plane cabin as she pushed back in the luxuriously soft cushions aboard a private jet she met at the Great Falls airport early Thursday morning. Butterflies in her stomach felt like they wore Army boots. Her small breakfast sat like a rock among those gastric butterflies. After the small jet surged into the sky, she discovered the breath-taking beauty of being above clouds and seeing the sun rise ahead of her. Flying isn't so bad, she decided, several hours later after a silky smooth landing. "It's just the takeoff and landing that suck." She gave Justin her opinion when he met her at the Syracuse airport.

"On a private jet, you're up and down in a flash. The big planes are the ones that you'd really hate. Too many people even in first class," he told her as he held open the door on his Jeep Grand Cherokee.

She settled into a luxurious seat and quizzed him about their agenda as soon as he secured his seat belt.

"Off to New York City, or rather the outskirts, to three banks and two investment firms. Then to the last bank. It's in Auburn. LNB—that's Lyon National Bank. Been around since the mid-1800. Full service. You'll be meeting with Gerald Fergusson. He handled Leon's banking finances but not his investments. When we leave him, we'll stop by Raymond and Clauster, your financial advisors. They handled all the investments Leon put them on to."

Justin drove for several seconds without saying anything. Entering the city limits, he offered some information about the banker. "Gerald and Leon have been thick as thieves for decades. Fergusson's never married. He's very proper." Justin dragged out the word *proper* in the style of an English butler which set Shannon to laughing.

"I wonder if he knew about Leon's...life style?" She remembered at the last second that Leon and Justin shared the same kind of life. Never in the world would she hurt Justin nor tarnish Leon's memory with hasty hurtful words. "Humm, wonder how you hide that?"

"Oh well, as for Leon, it's not an issue anymore. You don't think Mr. Fergusson will think I'm like Leon, do you?"

"Certainly not! Leon made sure everyone knew you were married. He did say that your husband had disappeared, but you were hopeful he'd show up again. He neglected to say just how long Jacob Waller had been missing."

Shannon caught Justin's anxious glance. "I'll be all right with all these businessmen, Justin. No one's got anything to argue about with me."

"I suppose."

They dropped the subject and concentrated on other topics, Auburn in general, Mon Coeur, and lunch. They made the rounds of the financial institutions before heading back to Auburn for the last bank and investment firm.

"Frankly, I'm starving. I wasn't hungry when I got up, and the thought of flying put me off almost everything but a single cup of coffee. I'm surprised I don't have a caffeine withdrawal headache by now." Shannon admired the sights as they drove but rubbed her temple.

"I can at least get you a cup of coffee at the bank. For the money you've got there in multiple accounts they ought to serve you a twelve-course meal!"

"Seriously? I'd settle for something light but tasty, thank you."

On a wave of silliness they arrived at the bank on Genesee Street—Lyon's National Bank.

Justin parked and pointed to the innocuous bank front. "Don't let that innocent façade fool you. This bank's been around over a hundred years. They know banking!"

Once inside, he produced a hot cup of coffee for Shannon. They waited about three minutes…short by her standards. A pleasant woman ushered them into a comfortable office, rather than the glass front cubby holes so many banks currently used.

"Mrs. Waller, a pleasure to meet you." A handsome older man came forward and held out a hand. "I'm Gerald Fergusson. Leon and I were friends forever. I'm sorry for your loss."

"Pleased to meet you, Mr. Fergusson, and I return the sympathy…I am sorry for the loss of your friend."

Fergusson might be in his late seventies and had probably seen it all in his life, but Shannon managed to surprise him with that statement. "Uh, thank you. Won't you sit?" He gestured her to a set of chairs around a low table rather than the two chairs positioned before a large elegant desk. "Good to see you again, Black." Fergusson motioned Justin to a chair beside Shannon.

"Before we sign papers and get these checks made official, may I ask if you have any plans for the future, Mrs. Waller?"

"Please, call me Shannon. I understand you've handled Leon's local immediate financial affairs for decades. No sense us being on such formal terms if we're going forward together."

For some reason, Justin added, "Shannon is a top-notch accountant."

"Really? How…good for you, Shannon." Fergusson hesitated over his words.

Shannon picked up on that, as did Justin. She could tell from Justin's cocked brow when Fergusson looked the other way. A sneaky grin said he mentioned accounting on purpose. Did that mean the banker might try something shifty with her money? Having just met the man and knowing nothing but that Leon trusted him to manage his immediate funds, she decided to let the matter drop until later. Right now, she needed to answer the banker's question.

"Plans for the future? I can only tell you what I have in mind for the near future, sir." The banker nodded and waved a hand, indicating she should continue. "Now that I have access to my money, I plan to update my home in Montana. Nothing fancy but make it tighter and safer. Friends of mine are going to rent it while I do a bit of traveling. My mother was from the coast of Texas, and I'd like to see that area. She talked about it a lot. Then I want to live at least a year at Mon Coeur. I visited Leon every summer for years and fell in love with that place."

"Mon Coeur is a jewel, and I'm happy Leon left it to someone who cares. May I ask where in Texas you plan to visit?" He sat relaxed-looking, back in his chair, a leg crossed over the other, an arm stretched out over the arm of the chair. He looked much younger than what Justin told her, his blond hair still thick with few age lines on his face or sagging jowls. Gerald Fergusson could easily pass for a man of mid-fifties instead of mid-seventies.

"Mother was born and raised on Galveston Island, just south of Houston. I want to visit there and enjoy the warm climate for a change. I might travel down the coast to Corpus Christi, a place she visited often as a child. I think her parents must have lavished good times on her after Leon left. That's all hindsight, of course." She didn't elaborate in case the man knew nothing of Leon's habits.

"Hindsight is always more accurate once a person has all the details, is it not?" Fergusson sat up and leaned forward, one arm still resting on the chair's side. "Now that we know you don't plan on buying a dozen cars, go cruising around the world or getting crazy extravagant with your new-found wealth, but rather act like a sensible person, shall we get down to signing these papers and getting you set up with checks and your credit cards? I understand Mr. Black has those."

"Oh, sir, does buying a new car count as crazy extravagance?" Shannon took a slight dislike to Fergusson's attempt at humor. *His* version of humor at any rate. But he's an older man from a different time, she mused. His idea of extravagance aside, the man seemed nice enough.

"I believe buying one car isn't extravagant but necessary. And you'll turn the current one in for a down payment?" The words *down payment* seemed to stick in the man's throat.

"My current vehicle will be consigned to the junk yard in Cut Bank, Montana…if it will make it that far." Shannon spoke without a touch of humor. Let him make of that what he would.

Fergusson cleared his throat, looked momentarily nonplussed, then adjusted to the situation by reverting to business. "Shall we proceed?"

———

"Lord, he does seem a little bit of a stuffed shirt. But then again he's an older man and a banker. I learned from taking care of the lumberyard accounts that bankers often have a limited sense of humor and sometimes lack social skills as well. At least the ones in Cut Bank." Shannon disconnected her seatbelt as Justin turned off the ignition. He'd just pulled up in front of a building where they'd join Justin's husband, Phillip, for lunch.

"I imagine somewhere under all that properness a real live man hides."

"At least Mr. Raymond and Mr. Clauster were wonderful. They know their business and appear to be quite transparent about what they do. I hate that I'm not up to Leon's standards when it comes to investments, but if they keep me informed on the accounts and what the market is so I can give them the go-ahead or not, then we'll be all right. And what was that bit at the bank that you added about me being an accountant?" She asked that as Justin got out and headed around the front of the car to open her door. She wasn't even sure he heard her over the street noise.

"I thought it best to let Fergusson know that you're not stupid when it comes to finances. Leon, of course, was a mathematical genius and an investment guru. I think you may have inherited some of his genes in that department. Just a hunch, but best that Fergusson knows you can tell what's happening to your monies." He slammed the door behind her and hit the key button to lock the doors. With one hand behind her back, he escorted her toward a door painted gray with bars across the window.

"What?" She stopped so fast, he almost pushed her over. "This is a prison?" The name over the door was Prison City Pub and Brewery.

"Prison? Good Lord, Shannon, no. It's just a name. Great food. Too early in the day for the really expensive stuff, so Phillip and I decided to go casual and wine and dine you at a local brewery. Besides, the food is fabulous." He put his hand to her back again but waited for her to move forward.

"Oh well, when you put it like that…" She giggled and stepped through the door.

The place surprised her, the light wooden floors, the metal tables, and chairs. Stools pulled up to a long bar. A big BEER sign hung on the back wall. Nothing fancy but from the looks of those indulging in a variety of food, the place apparently served a good meal in a casual setting.

"This is cool," she said sideways to Justin as they stepped further into the room.

Justin, though, was busy looking for someone. He spotted another man and motioned Shannon toward the back of the pub.

Justin and a man she presumed was Phillip did a full man-hug thing rather than the more delicate hug she imagined them doing. Justin turned to her, a faint flush washing his smile.

"Shannon Waller, this is my husband, Phillip." He turned to Phillip and waved a hand, palm up, toward Shannon. "Phillip, this is Shannon."

They shook hands even as each grinned at the other. Phillip was taller than Justin, with sandy blond hair tied back in a ponytail. His pressed khaki slacks and turtle neck suited him, the sleeves pushed up to reveal nicely toned arms.

"Justin has babbled on and on about you, Shannon. If he didn't love me, I'd think he loved you." Phillip gave a wink so exaggerated that Shannon giggled, and Justin blushed. With calmer decorum, he motioned them to a table tucked near the wall, a bit of privacy more secured.

"Phillip! You're so embarrassing," Justin tried to protest, but Shannon cut him off.

"He is a dear, isn't he? He might have babbled on about

me to you, but he's told me nothing about you. Real tight lipped, he's been."

"And with good reason. He didn't want to tell you that I own a fabric shop and that I quilt."

Immediately the world faded away, and Shannon dived right into a conversation with a fellow quilter and fabric lover. "Do you fondle the fabric?"

"Oh brother!" Justin groaned. "That sounds so erotic, and I'd go nuts ordinarily, but unfortunately I know exactly what you mean. And yes, he does." He rolled his eyes up as if frustrated, but Shannon noticed he grinned.

"Darling, I adore fabric. I tour my little kingdom each morning before opening the doors, running my fingers lightly over the lovelies."

"Lord, now that just sounds queer, husband," Justin whispered with a groan. "How about we order, and you two talk about quilting and leave the erotic fabric touchy-feely stuff for when Shannon settles into Mon Coeur?"

She cut Justin some slack, seeing as they were in a public place and no one but a fellow quilter or seamstress would understand their enthusiasm for fabric. "What's good here?"

"Oh woman, you had to ask," Phillip groaned. "The problem is it's all good. I encourage you to sample a flight of beer. A selection of several different beers they have here. Sip them as you eat so we don't have to pour you onto that jet later."

From there, the meal was a blast as far as Shannon was concerned. Justin had quickly gone from being Leon's and her lawyer to a friend—a lovely man with a wicked sense of humor—adding spice to her life. A rather dull life, she decided, as she sampled the last brew in a small glass that resembled a whiskey sniffer.

To add to the fact that she'd found a jewel in Justin, Phillip his husband was a fellow quilter, fabric fondler and just as charismatic as his partner. More spice in her life. Shannon considered herself the luckiest of women in the friends department.

The waiter eventually brought the bill, though the three sat for another half hour, talking about life and Leon.

"Shannon, it's already three. Your flight leaves at four. Will your godfather pick you up, or will you get a taxi back to the Ackerman home?"

"No, Wallace will pick me up. I think I'll probably sleep on the way back. Not that flying is less stressful, but the beers took the edge off my concerns, I think."

The men laughed as they escorted her out to the sidewalk.

Phillip hugged her hard. "I'm so glad to finally meet you. We're going to have lovely times together when you get here. In the shop and out." He leaned over and kissed Justin full on the mouth. "I'll catch you later for lovely times."

"Phillip!" Justin blushed so hard that Shannon headed for the car in order to give him time to recover his composure.

"That man will be the death of me," Justin groused when he got them into the flow of afternoon traffic.

"Maybe, but there's no denying that he loves you, you silly man."

"Yeah, he does, doesn't he," Justin agreed with a grin and a wink. The grin lasted all the way to the airport.

Shannon hugged him, then waved from the jet's tiny door. The flight home passed without her worrying. She slept but woke to daydream about the car she'd buy the next day. A real car. Not something second hand or something that would leave her stranded on the side of the road. If that ever happened, she'd have the resources to get someone out for a quick pick-up and repairs. In the long run, having some money—she rolled her eyes at the word *some* she'd just mentally used—meant she could live a bit more comfortably. Again she rolled her eyes. A *bit*? Lord, another B word!

———

The only blip on Shannon's radar of good things came the day before she left her godparent's home. Martha called her from the bedroom to the living room.

"You have a visitor, dear. One of your co-workers. Nice man." Martha positively gushed as she escorted Shannon to the hallway outside the living room. "I'll just leave you two alone."

Shannon did a double take as Martha practically cooed over her and winked. Confused, she entered the living room, having no clue who might be waiting.

She came to an immediate halt when she saw Charlie Hawkins waiting for her.

He rushed over to her and wrapped her in an embrace that scared the crap out of her. Fighting him off, pushing him back, she brushed hair out of her face as she stepped away from him. "What's the matter with you? Are you nuts or something?"

"I'm so glad to see you! I missed you and knew you

were missing me." He stepped forward, and Shannon stepped back again.

She held up a hand and moved to the side of the room, putting a chair and side table between them.

"I have no idea what you're talking about, Charlie."

The smile on the man's face never changed, but his eyes squinted ever so slightly. He might not be aware of it, but he transmitted his displeasure plain enough for a child to see.

She'd always thought Leven, her former boss, was a narcissist. She even looked up information about the condition on her desk computer one day, but decided the description didn't fit him as well as it did this man. So, she practiced defending against him whenever she could. Basically, she didn't react. She wasn't about to play his game, get angry and act out. He'd love that. Silence would be her best defense against him no matter what he said to or about her.

"You always act like you hate me. I've never given you any reason to," Charlie began, a classic victim statement. "You make a big deal out of everything I do." He stood there calmly accusing her, as if he were totally innocent of harassing her at work, then coming to her house.

Despite his implication that *she* did something wrong, Shannon remained silent.

"Don't you see how perfect we will be together?"

"No," she answered, never breaking eye contact but not moving from behind the barrier she created for herself. From her reading she knew the word *no* could infuriate this kind of personality. Charlie wanted to control her. She'd lived too long as an independent woman to allow anyone to control her.

Charlie's face flushed a faint red as his lips pressed tighter.

She could see the anger building. She'd just put a target on her back.

"I just want to take care of you, Shannon. Love you and make you happy." Charlie spoke in the same whining voice he'd used before in the office.

"No."

"Dammit, woman, you have no idea what I can do for you." His eyes squinted, and he stuck his neck out, like a fighting rooster. "You have no idea what I can do *to* you," he amended softly.

"No."

If Charlie Hawkins were a volcano, his sides would be swelling from pent-up pressure, preparing to blow.

"You may leave now." Shannon moved to the side of the chair, her hand gesturing toward the front door. She spoke softly, giving him no reason to attack her. For she knew he would, if not physically, then verbally.

"Shannon, you have to come to reason. I want you. And I'll take care of you forever."

She refused to even give him her one-word answer. Again, she gestured toward the door.

When he stood planted like a huge oak tree in the middle of the living room, she reached into her pocket and pulled out the new cell phone she'd gotten only that morning. Calmly she showed him the phone's face as she held one finger over the Emergency button—the 9-1-1 button that would summon the police.

Charlie tightened his lips so hard that she wondered if he were biting his tongue. Without a word, he stalked to the front door, pulled it opened and slammed it shut behind him.

Her knees threatened to give way. Shannon collapsed into the chair that had provided meager protection. *Best I tell Martha and Wallace about this in case he comes back looking for me.* Another idea popped into her head as she stared at the 9-1-1 button. Best she let the police know what happened just in case. Best to protect her godparents from the nut that now lived in Great Falls.

"So you see, Charlie thinks he's the greatest thing ever and has this crush on me. I've told him over and over that I'm still married to Jacob, but he doesn't see it that way. I'm asking you to not let him in again after I'm gone. Don't even talk to him. Just tell him I'm gone, and you have no idea where I've gone. He'll believe that. No one but my closest friends in Cut Bank has any clue where I'll go next."

Martha cried, ashamed that Charlie's charm had seduced her, possibly putting Shannon in danger. Wallace comforted his wife with an arm around her shoulders.

"I'm going down town to the police station and ask them to do a little extra patrolling in the neighborhood for a few more days. I filed a report with the Cut Bank police, not for Charlie's arrest, but just letting them know in case something happened to me that they might want to question him."

A quick trip to the police station turned out to be three hours long. Without filing a complaint she had to wait to talk to an officer who could simply take her statement and confirm the same sort of incident with the Cut Bank police.

Once she'd done everything she could think of to keep herself and the Ackerman's safe, she began packing for the trip back to Cut Bank. Driving a brand new car. One she fell in love with as soon as she saw it—a red Subaru Forester. Just what she'd hoped for. She'd stop by Shelby first and visit with Immajean's husband Danny about remodeling the Waller home.

———

Not until she talked to the building supervisor that Danny Adams recommended did she realize her home wouldn't be fit to live in during the remodel.

"Simply too much going on all over the place." The supervisor David Joy told her that when they finished the walk-through. He'd agreed to doing all the remodels at the same time, though he informed her the cost would be staggering. When the winter finally released its grip on Montana, contractors became busy people. This job would require the services of a number of people, all at the same time. However, Shannon assured him she would pay in full when the job ended and pay for supplies as needed.

"I think this is crazy, Mrs. Waller, doing this all at one time, but I can understand wanting the remodel done in time for the new owners to move in and settle before bad weather sets in." The man scratched his head, threw his cap back on, and set to figuring what exactly he needed.

Immajean invited her to stay with them, but that was thirty miles away. Instead, Emily and Todd Zimmer invited her to camp out at their place until the house was ready.

Shannon wanted to watch the work each day. She told the supervisor as much. He groaned, but she assured him she'd just sit and watch. If there were any concerns, she'd come to him rather than jump on the workers.

"I've never been in the position of getting my butt chewed out in front of fellow workers and crew chiefs, but

I've seen it done at the place where I used to work. You won't know I'm anywhere around. I promise."

"Fair enough. As long as you don't butt into the work, you can watch."

They shook hands, and she said she trusted him because of Danny's recommendation. "Your husband was a good man, Mrs. Waller. I'm sorry no one ever found him. And your father...another good one. Lawrence Waller...now there was a man who knew and appreciated wood."

With that, the remodel of the Waller home place began with determination. Hammers thudded, saws buzzed, wood crashed as the old barn came down. Several men dug up the old gasoline tank—not a large one—disposed of that and stored the glass-bulb gas pump until the work was completed. The old Model T went into storage as well. Both would return as pieces of family history when the job was completed. Crews built forms for the garage and breezeway joining it to the house. Another crew set the foundation for the new bedroom suite. Meanwhile inside the house—where the supervisor wouldn't let her go—other crews were taking out the old walls in order for plumbers and electricians to rewire and plumb the house.

"I tell you, Emily, I never knew it took so many people to get this kind of work done." Shannon sat on a quilt under the tree in her front yard, sipping a Coke and finishing an apple after sharing a picnic lunch with Emily Zimmer.

"Normally one crew does the work, but it takes a long time to finish the job. You're just lucky you have enough bucks to get this all done at the same time. And you're fortunate to find a man who can supervise the whole thing and knows where to find all the workers," Emily pointed out as she picked up all the trash and put it in the hamper.

"True. If Jacob could see this now, he'd probably drop dead of amazement."

"It is pretty mind-blowing, isn't it?" Emily stood and arched her back. "Being pregnant ain't no picnic. But better to be this far along in the summer and the baby due in September than go all winter like this, stuck inside."

Shannon didn't look at her friend, her large belly sticking out just above Shannon's head. How she'd have loved to be in that kind of position. Her and Jacob having a child. But it never happened and probably never would.

"You got a sweet ride, Shannon. I like the color too. What do they call that?"

"Ruby. I thought I wanted a subtle color…you know, like gray or black. Something no one would notice, but then I saw this on the lot, and I decided it was time to get over being dull."

"Ruby, huh. It's not dull. That's for sure. And I love the smiley face ball on the back roof rack."

"Immajean's son figured out how to attach that ball so I can tell my car from others. This brand of SUV is popular, and so many looked so similar. At least I can find my car in a parking lot!"

They laughed as Emily stored the hamper in the back. She moved back to the front of the car and leaned back beside Shannon. "Sure is a lot of work going on." She pointed to three different crews. "And that's just the ones we can see out here!"

"Remember how much work we did getting my stuff out of the house before all this started?"

"Do I! I could only supervise, but I'd say we did good, cleaning out the whole house in one day."

"Helps when you don't have a lot to clear out, doesn't it?" Shannon added.

"Yeah, but it was all quality," Emily said sweetly.

"Oh yeah, right. Quality. Stuff older than me in that place and you know it." Shannon sighed and rubbed her cheek as she thought of all the things they'd unearthed. Photos and blankets. Clothes. Things she'd forgotten. "A lot of those things weren't even mine—or Jacob's."

Five years after Jacob went missing, she reluctantly and without making a production of it, took all her husband's clothes to Goodwill. His toiletries she threw out. If and when he returned, they'd buy new, she told herself. However, a few things still remained from their time together and even more lay hidden from her father-in-law's time there.

"What about your quilting stuff?"

"That all goes with me in the car. In totes. Fabric and notions and my machine. Besides suitcases."

"Where are you headed first?"

"I first thought I'd drive to Texas and see where Mom was born and raised, but I think it best if I go to Mon Coeur first. I want to settle in."

"But what about going to Texas? What will you do with the house then? You'll be in the same position as leaving this house."

"Humm, yeah, you're right. I have to talk to Justin and Phillip about that."

"You really like those two don't you?" Emily bumped Shannon's shoulder and grinned.

"Stop it. You know they're gay, right?"

"Yes, but you still like them. You smile every time you talk about them."

"They're so…" Shannon had to think a moment. Her gaze passed over the early summer lawn that the crew cleaned up every night before leaving. "They're just nice people. And they make me laugh. They're smart and down to earth, yet sophisticated. Comes from living so close to New York City."

Emily sighed. "I've never been out of Montana."

"Come visit me in Auburn. There's a standing invitation for you and Todd any time."

"Seriously?"

"You think I'd kid about something like that?"

Emily squealed and hugged Shannon so hard that the baby objected by bumping them.

"Oh, sorry, Scooter."

"You're really going to call your child Scooter?"

"Not if I can help it, but we have to call the little dude something until he or she arrives." Emily gave a *what the heck* shrug as she moved to the passenger side of the car.

"Lord, that poor child will probably go to the grave being called Scooter Zimmer."

"Like I said—"

"Yeah, I know—not if you can help it."

Laughter filled the car as they pulled out, headed to Emily's home.

"Did I tell you Phillip suggested that I make a detour through Pennsylvania to Lancaster county where all the Amish quilters and shops are?" Shannon drove carefully but couldn't keep excitement out of her voice.

"Oh my god, I can see you needing a bigger car to carry all that fabric with you to Mon Coeur."

"Not hardly. I can't afford it," Shannon said automatically.

"Humm," Emily cleared her throat delicately and gave her friend an eye-roll and a head shake. "How quickly they forget," she mourned in fun.

"Forget? Oh! Yeah, sorry. I did forget. Not quite used to having money yet." That ominous B-word flashed in her mind, and she swallowed hard. "Yeah, it takes getting used to."

"Wish I had enough of the green stuff to get used to like that."

For several minutes they dropped the subject of money and enjoyed the pleasant afternoon drive.

"You plan on leaving your things in storage or what?" Emily finally asked as they reached her house. She stepped out, closed the door, and joined Shannon at the rear of the car to retrieve the hamper.

"When my place is back in shape, before Helen and Victor move in, I'll go through all that mess in the storage unit and return the furniture and dishes, things like that. Personal stuff I'll just have to wade through. Some of it may go to my godparent's home in their basement. It's climate controlled."

"I think it's wonderful that the Bass' are moving in," Emily said.

"Me too. Like someone told me, by the time the place gets updated, it won't feel like home to me, so moving on won't be so hard. The hardest thing, I think, may be leaving Trip and Simon."

Emily put her hand through the crook of Shannon's elbow and eased closer so they stood touching. "Saying goodbye is hard, whether it's a person or a pet. And it never gets easier."

MOVING FORWARD

Three months to the day after the big remodel started, Shannon turned over the house keys to Helen who wept in her arms. Victor hugged Shannon so hard she thought he might break one of her ribs.

"Give me a minute, would you? I want to visit Trip and Simon before I go." Shannon disengaged from Helen and set her back a few feet. Both cried, but Shannon did so silently.

"Sure thing." Victor pulled his wife into his embrace so her tears of happiness over the house and sadness over Shannon's leaving would water his broad shoulders.

Instead of going out the kitchen door, she went out through the front door. Walking around the house, she admired the deep double car garage. One step up and she opened the door to the breezeway. Eight feet across and she stepped out of the opposite door leading to the back yard. The view to her right stood open—the old barn gone and the spot clean and mowed. Behind the garage, in a small fenced area, stood the old glass-bulb gas pump beside the Model T. Further back on the property under the sprawling oak she stopped beside two graves, each covered by soft summer grass. The rocks over each lay bleached, as faded as the name tags. This time Shannon left the tags tilted as they were.

"Bye, fellows. I'll be around, but I won't be here all the time. Helen and Victor will live here now. They'll take care of you." Words failed her for a second, and she had to put her head back, so the tears would slip down her throat instead of leaking out of her eyes. "I miss you both. Simon, I miss you at night and each afternoon. You were always there. Heaven is so lucky to have both of you. I love you."

Afraid she might break down and never leave, Shannon turned on a sharp heel and marched back to the house. In through the breezeway and straight into Helen's arms she went, her sobs heartbreaking to hear.

"Turning over that key makes me feel so strange, like being a traitor to Jacob." She noted the shocked expression Helen and Victor's faces and quickly amended that to a clearer meaning. "What I mean is that it's just odd leaving the house, but I'm leaving it in the best possible hands. I wouldn't have it any other way, and Jacob would agree if he were here." At the mention of his name and the thought of not living in the house, now not quite as familiar after the remodel, she teared up again, "I've got to go now, or I may never leave," she finally managed to say. "Take care. I love you both."

Practically running, she bolted out the door. Into her new car she climbed and turned over the ignition. All good-byes behind her now—she'd said farewell to Todd and Emily and other friends earlier in the day—she headed to Great Falls. Past Immajean's place. They'd said their goodbye the day before. Past her godparents' place and on to the hotel for the night. Her heart simply couldn't take another leave-taking.

―――――

Hotels were few and far between on the first leg of Shannon's trip from Great Falls to Glendive on the eastern border of Montana. Leaving the hotel in Great Falls at seven that morning, she drove over four hundred miles to the small town in about nine hours. She stopped several times to stretch her legs and once to gas up, then find lunch. Even if she finished her coffee and a Danish in the car, she had a trash bag. No way was she going to have a crappy looking vehicle like some of the lumberyard workers had.

Highway 94 went on forever, or so she thought that day. She checked into the hotel and fell into bed. She'd grabbed a snack in the late afternoon so wasn't hungry. She'd take care of a shower the next morning before breakfast. She'd never driven so far before, and her mind as well as her rear was tired.

After her shower the next day, she dressed and sat at the desk in her room. She made a few fast phone calls, assuring Immajean, Emily and Martha as well as three others that she was safe and about to get on the road again. She made a last fast call to Justin letting him know she was about to leave. He had her driving agenda so he could keep track of her journey.

Before she'd left her godparents in Great Falls she'd spent a few hours at a book store, going through the reading material and journals. Despite the fact she had a new Dell laptop that met all her needs, she still wanted to write by hand in a journal about her new life. So she added to the entries she'd already made about visiting Martha and Wallace in Great Falls, the incident with Charlie Hawkins and the weeks of watching the remodel.

This time she wrote about leaving the Waller home, saying goodbye to Helen and Victor in the house that really didn't resemble the old one anymore. Saying goodbye to her pets. If she wiped away a stray tear or two she didn't comment on it in her writing. She did comment on how hard it was to drive that far in one day though.

The trip that day would be a shorter one, from Glendive to Bismarck, North Dakota. That was about two hundred miles, taking about four hours.

Totes of fabric, her sewing machine, and suitcases filled the cargo area of the Subaru. She'd bought a cover to put over everything so nothing would tempt someone to break in. The only thing she had to do each day was make it to the next hotel before bedtime and pull out one suitcase.

She arrived in Bismarck early enough to catch a quiet lunch and walk off the stiffness of her drive in a beautiful green park near the hotel. Her journal updated that evening, she read a few hours, checked the weather and turned in. The next day would be about the same as this one... Bismarck to Fargo, North Dakota...another short drive along Highway 94 but in heavier traffic.

Heavy traffic became the norm for Shannon after leaving the relative open spaces of Montana and North Dakota. She left Fargo and headed to LaCrosse, Wisconsin in traffic, a long stressful day. From there she drove to the suburbs of Chicago, a five hour trip that turned into seven hours with an accident stalling traffic.

Her comment that night in her journal recorded she had a headache but was getting used to long days of driving and traffic. She included the wish that she could stay and see Chicago, but she'd save that for another day. According to the map on her cell, she could do that in two days, coming back from Auburn to Chicago. An easy trip compared to what she was doing now and planned on doing in the near future.

By the end of the next day in Parma, Ohio, she asked herself why she drove so long each day. She wrote the question and answer in the journal that evening. *I want to get to Mon Coeur as soon as I can.* That was her goal now. Her new home. Or at least she hoped she'd feel good about living there permanently.

Per Phillip's instructions, she planned a side trip with an extra day built in for shopping and just plain ol' sightseeing. Shannon didn't necessarily look forward to the almost four hundred mile trip from Parma near the shore of Lake Erie to the middle of Lancaster county, Pennsylvania, but she knew the next day of shopping and relaxing would be pure pleasure.

Once settled into the B&B that evening, she perused a map of Christiana, looking for the quilt shop Phillip liked to visit—The Quilt Ledger. She also checked out the location of some Amish shops nearby. Her plans included rising late, eating a sumptuous breakfast provided by the B&B owners who were kind enough to allow her a late meal. To walk would be the highlight of her day after a week on the road. She noted how far she was from Philadelphia, Baltimore, and Washington, DC. How she wanted to tour those places. But again, she put those on her list of places to visit later. With only one day of traveling left—from Christiana to Auburn, she wanted to enjoy the freedom of being outside in great weather.

Being with like-minded people lifted Shannon's spirits. She strolled through the quilt store, enjoyed visiting with ladies in the class that was taking a break for lunch and oohing and aahing over batiks, florals, solids, and patterns. Mindful of her limited traveling space for things like fabric, she restricted herself to three yards of several prints. She bought some fat quarter bundles in florals and one in batiks.

She did splurge though on patterns as well as threads and blades for her rotary cutter. The store had a special sale on cutting mats and wool ironing pads, so she got a new mat, ironing pad and two rulers. Texts flew between her and Phillip and occasionally from Justin when those two met for lunch. By the end of the day she sat on her bed in the B&B second floor bedroom and *fondled the fabric* as quilters like to say. Because all her totes were full, she left everything in the bags she got when she checked out.

All her purchase packed, her bill paid and goodbye said, Shannon left Christiana and drove through the breathtaking countryside of Pennsylvania to Auburn, a journey of about six hours. She arrived at the restaurant where Justin wanted to meet and parked. Her head bent over on the steering wheel, she sighed long and hard. Her first journey completed, she wanted to slip into bed and sleep for a week. A tap on the passenger window, however, woke her from the easy snooze she'd fallen into.

"Justin! Sorry, I guess I fell asleep." She apologized as she hugged him. "Phillip!" she called as the man approached them and got a hug as well. "That was such fun—going to the quilt shop. The place is so neat."

"Hey, before you two go off to fabric land, let's eat. I'm starving." Justin pulled each along, headed to the restaurant's front door.

"Yeah, me too. My butt's tired. Think they have padded chairs?"

"Only the best for the lady," Phillip quipped as Justin opened the door to a swank restaurant that thankfully had lush padded cushions.

———

"Oh…" Shannon sighed, as she stood in front of Mon Coeur. "It's just as I remembered it."

Beside her, Justin and his husband Phillip remained silent.

"I think…I think I'm ready to go in now," she said after a few times of swallowing hard. Memories of Leon and their summer weeks together over the years crowded in suddenly, making the sight more precious. "I wish Uncle Leon were here."

"But then you'd not be here for good," Justin said softly.

"True, but I'd rather visit one week a year and have an uncle than live here permanently with no family." She gave them a smile that felt less than real. "I guess I'll have to adopt you two and claim you as family."

Phillip stepped to her side and slid an arm over her shoulders. "At least you know what you're getting if you adopt us."

She couldn't help it. That was so like the man to make a small joke to help ease the tension. She'd noticed it in his texts and emails. And right now, she appreciated the presence of two friends. Facing Leon's house alone didn't seem so daunting when in company.

"You bet—only the best."

Phillip hugged her shoulder a bit tighter. He stepped aside until the three stood shoulder to shoulder.

They stood by Shannon's SUV, admiring the place. A craftsman-style two-and-a-half story home, in deep blue-gray with pristine white columns and porch rails, the home looked like a set of squares on top of each other, the second floor roof jutting out over the first floor and the tiny attic roof jutting over the second floor roof. Each window displayed multiple leaded panes in the manner of Frank Lloyd Wright, the famous architect of the late 1800s and early 1900s.

"Have you ever been inside, Phillip?" She knew Justin often visited Leon on business.

"Justin has, but I've never been inside."

"Come on. I'll give you the fifty cent tour. That'll help me get over the idea that Uncle Leon isn't lurking around somewhere and just hasn't put in an appearance yet." She gathered her purse and headed up the walk. "You have the key, Justin?"

"Right here." He handed over a ring with several keys. "One for the front and back doors. One to lock down the garage and storage shed out back. There's a third key, but I've never figured out what it's for. Maybe you know."

Shannon accepted the key ring and inserted the front door key. "I have no idea what that extra key might be for. Looks old though." As the lock turned, she thought of other keys. How important they'd been in her life up to this point —the lumber yard key…the Waller home key. And now the keys to Mon Coeur. A new beginning. Thanks to a man she only met a little over a decade ago.

Once the wide door swung open, she breathed the scent of polished wood. "You got someone in to clean. That's wonderful." She thanked Justin as she stepped into what was now her home. "Come on, guys." She gestured them into the front entryway.

"Uncle Leon built this home and put in all the things he loved about architecture and life. Wood everywhere. Nothing but nature, he always said. He loved the leaded glass of the Art Deco era, so the windows and glass doors feature spectacular work. To be honest, the first time I visited I felt like I was in a museum. Over time though you just take it for granted that life is this lovely. See these— built-in bookcases here at the entrance to the living room and even with the fireplace."

"There are enough windows so you almost don't need electricity." Phillip pointed to the wall of windows in the living room and along one wall of the dining room. Wooden chairs with footrests and rockers, deep sofas and square arm chairs sat on a bright flowered rug. "He believed in wood. It's everywhere!" The bookcases, floors, furniture, and arched room dividers featured polished cherry wood.

"Hey, Phillip, even the kitchen has leaded windows with designs over the sink and counter," Justin pointed out.

"Are those real Tiffany lamps?" Phillip leaned over to look at one sitting on a long table but kept both hands behind his back.

"Afraid to break it?" Shannon teased him but didn't touch the lamp.

"Aren't you?"

"Well, yes, but I got over that fear long ago. Uncle Leon said he broke one or two through the years and simply replaced it with an excellent reproduction if he couldn't find a similar one for sale."

"Big bucks and yet he went for a sale. Huh!" Justin leaned against the staircase banister.

"Leon was a garage sale junkie! He loved looking for bargains. The thing was, he seldom bought. He just found. That was like a treasure hunt to him." Shannon joined Justin at the staircase. She pointed out the windows set in the wall as they made their way up to the second floor. "Those are so beautiful with their rounded tops and the inset for sitting. I told Leon he needed to have a cushion in each window seat, and the next time I came I discovered he'd done just that. I spent several hours each afternoon reading there while he napped."

"Now when we get up here, you'll find four bedrooms— big ones—plus a library and Leon's study. One bedroom he said was mine. I'll use it and decide what to do with Leon's room later. Each room is so big that I can set up my sewing machine, store the fabric, and still have room to enjoy my desk and all the usual stuff in a bedroom. Each room has a walk-in closet and its own bathroom, too."

"Holy shit. No wonder you thought you were living in a museum." Phillip admired the long wide wood paneled hall-way. "Look at these pictures."

"Wait until you see the library and his office. Leon knew what he liked and enjoyed looking at it as often as he could."

Together the three strolled the hallway, Shannon pointing out various pictures. "This one of the fish jumping out of the bowl…Leon said it was pure joy." She laughed and pointed to a young woman holding a baby lamb. "Now this one he said gave him peace. Made him feel good." On the other side she showed them the autumn draped tree set against a roiling winter sky. "Leon told me nothing stays the same…everything changes." She cocked her head to one side. "Funny…when he said that he sounded…sad."

She opened a door, and they stepped into the library. Book shelves lined two of the fourteen foot tall walls, while windows filled the third wall. Against the fourth they saw chairs, lamps, a table, and a pile of books.

"I asked the cleaning lady not to disturb anything Leon might have left laying out. Those were the last things he was reading."

"Thanks, Justin. I'll take care of them." Picture frames adorned the wall next to the reading area. "Cardinals, irises —the garden is full of them—both the birds and flowers," she told Phillip. "He admired the paintings of Alphonse Mucha and Jose Royo."

"I like the way these colors flow through the paintings of the elephant and lion." Justin used one finger to follow the lines along the elephant's back. "I always did, and I told him so."

"Lady Di and Einstein?" Phillip stood near the corner of the room where a light shone softly on the two portraits. "That's quite a contrast in personalities."

"Not really. He admired them both for their strength. She took life and made it what she wanted though it cost her almost everything. Einstein dealt with the matter of reality. Both dealt with reality—just in their own distinct ways. If Leon could have loved a woman, she would have been Princess Diana."

"You're wrong there, Shannon. Leon loved your mother and you."

Shannon reached over and gave Justin's hand a soft squeeze. "Thank you. That means a lot." She motioned them out into the hall again. "Let me show you his bedroom. The view is magnificent."

Again she pointed out not only the view but Leon's choice of paintings. "He loved fractal pictures." Several hung in a grouping, the largest a spectacular one of deep blues and golds. "He loved the sea so had several photos of shells like this conch." A stylized painting of a phoenix hung over his bed. "Leon believed that the human spirit always rose up after being knocked down." Over his desk hung a quilted wall hanging featuring an abstract of light and dark. "That's what I made for Leon after I came several times. He asked for a quilt too. I suppose it's on his bed under the spread."

"That's quite a beauty," Phillip pointed out, letting his finger follow the stitched lines.

"Thank you. I figured you'd like that."

"He loved this style of picture, didn't he?" Justin pointed to a grouping, each featuring an object set against a dictionary page. One said TIME, while another said JOURNEY and BOOK.

"Wait until you see the ones in my bedroom. Come on, I'll show you."

In her room hung a similar grouping but these pertained to Shannon. SEW and SCISSORS as well as a second similar painting related to time, with several time pieces on it.

"He had a thing about time, didn't he?" Phillip walked over to the windows and gestured to the back yard. "I see about ten different colors of irises down there."

"I think as Leon got older, he realized time wasn't his friend, and he'd wasted a bunch of it. He always said these pictures spoke to him. I agreed with him. I can see my life reflected to some extent in many of them. We seemed to have similar tastes in our lives."

"Well, similar or not, you've now inherited his home and all that entails."

Shannon headed for the staircase, and the trio went down together.

"Let's get your stuff inside and your car in the garage before it gets dark. Okay?"

"Really? Wow, that would be wonderful. Thanks. I dreaded leaving it out here or even in the garage overnight, knowing sooner or later I'd have to drag all that stuff inside. At least Leon had an elevator squirreled away, so I don't have to literally drag the totes upstairs."

"For real? There's an elevator?" Phillip went nuts, turning this way and that.

"Oh, for goodness sakes. Boys and their toys." Shannon laughed as she led them through the kitchen to a set of back stairs. "Here you go, Phillip. Give it a whirl." She stopped beside a door that looked like a broom closet to one side of the kitchen.

She and Justin laughed themselves silly as Phillip rode the small elevator up, then back down twice.

"Now that's what I call sweet!"

"Come on, you two. Let's get this stuff inside before the sun goes down."

"Hey, how about pizza?"

"Here or there?" Shannon asked as she hit the Unlock button on her car fob.

"Your choice. You're the one who's been driving for days." Justin swung out a heavy tote and passed it to Phillip, awaiting her answer.

"What say we get at least half of this into the house, then

I'll call the nearest delivery place for pizza, and we can finish unloading while we wait. Then we can collapse and enjoy our meal without having that hanging over our heads."

"Works for me." They agreed as each one gathered a tote, and Shannon wheeled two suitcases up the walk.

An hour later the SUV sat snug in the locked garage, and the porch lights shone through the windows as the setting sun outlined the sugar oaks, pin oaks, and chestnut trees on the property.

"When I close all the drapes over these gazillion windows it's pretty snug in here." Shannon waved her hand to the multitude of windows as she sat in a square arm chair with her feet propped on a padded stool. Justin sat in the recliner, and Phillip sat in the rocker.

"You don't get pizzas like that in Cut Bank, let me tell you, guys," Shannon rested back against the cushion and balanced the empty paper plate on the chair's wide arm.

"That's New York style pizza, thank you very much." Phillip toasted her with the last bite.

"Heck, even the cheesecake was delicious."

"Also New York style," Justin specified.

"Well, excuse me." Shannon balled up her napkin and aimed for Justin.

He ducked and came up laughing. "I can't remember when we've had such a good time. Well, I mean besides just the two of us." He winked at Phillip who blushed.

"Here's to good friends." Shannon raised her drink cup. "May I find plenty more."

"Here, here!" the men seconded.

———

"You ought to see them, Immajean. They're so sweet," Shannon chatted as she clutched her cell phone in the crook of her neck and prepared spaghetti. She'd invited Justin and Phillip over for dinner. Later she wanted to run some ideas past them. "Yeah, the cleaning ladies. A grandmother—who worked for Leon way back in the day—her daughter and the granddaughter. They get here about eight and hit the ground running—cleaning, laundry...you name it. The place shines when they're finished. The grandmother was born in Canada and still speaks French when agitated. She's a naturalized citizen, but the rest of her family is American. She reminds me of the guys at the lumberyard. Busy all the time." Her sigh must have been louder than she thought. "Yeah, I miss the place. I miss the house. But this house is so...so...it's like a dream come true."

She moved the uncooked meatballs to a pan and set them in the 'frig. Meanwhile she kept an eye on the cast iron deep cooker with the sauce. That was something she learned from Waller Sr.—how to make flavorful sauce.

"What? You have to go? I understand. Oh, and tell Dan and Larry hello. Miss you. Love you." She hit END and carefully set the cell down using two fingers, her hands still dirty from handling the meat.

Down the back staircase came Beth, the granddaughter. She carried a pail with various cleaning bottles and rags. Behind her came her mother, Betty, a plain heavy-set woman who belied her pudgy looks and worked like a tornado in an apron. Thump by thump came the grandmother, Bettina.

"We be done for this week, miss. You need anything else?" Bettina asked as she stored the vacuum cleaner in the laundry room. Earlier Betty put all the sheets and towels into the washer. Sometime later, Beth put everything into the dryer. The trio worked like a well-oiled machine.

"The beds are made fresh, and the rooms vacuumed as well as dusted. The hall upstairs too. All the bathrooms are fresh." Betty ticked off each completed chore on her fingers. "We dusted down here and vacuumed. You're not a very messy person, Miss," she tossed in at the last minute.

"Never could afford to be messy, Mrs. Betty," Shannon said with a chuckle. "I lived alone after my husband went missing."

That was news to the ladies. "Missing? He come home?" Bettina asked in her broken English.

"Not yet. Maybe never. He's been gone a very long time. We have no idea what happened."

"Another woman?" Beth asked. Out of high school for the summer, her seventeen-year-old imagination immediately jumped to the worst possible scenario, short of Jacob being dead.

"Uh, no. He wasn't like that. Anyway," Shannon knew it was time to distract the youngest cleaning woman. "I've lived by myself for years and just never made much of a mess because...well, there wasn't anyone to pick up after me but...me!"

"Makes sense," Betty nodded as she untied her apron. "We're done for the week. Give us a call if you need us before next Friday."

"Will do, ladies." Shannon handed over an envelope with their money in it. "Thanks. Have a good weekend." She walked them to the porch and stood there as they drove off in a misty rain. The forecast called for summer showers off and on for the next few days.

A sense of peace settled over Shannon, listening to the

rain drip from the eaves. The trees beyond the drive looked greener than yesterday. Perhaps the rain washed off the summer dust. As much as she'd love to sit on the porch and read while sipping hot tea, she needed to return to the kitchen and get the meatballs cooking.

———

"You said you wanted to run some ideas past us." Justin settled with his coffee in the living room.

"I'm used to being on my own but also reporting to work each day, so someone would know if I were missing. Now that I'm truly not accountable to anyone, I think it's necessary to let someone in on my plans."

"What you need to do is get out and meet people. Come by the shop, and take some classes," Phillip suggested.

"You're right. And that leads into another plan I have. I don't care to live here alone."

Justin coughed. "Excuse me?"

"Oh, not what you think…I think." She grinned as she set her cup down on the lamp table and drew her bare feet up under her in the wide arm chair. "I'm going to travel here in the US. For sure to Texas, but maybe other places too. I'm not ready to go international and don't think I'd want to go alone there either. But this house—as wonderful as it is —is much bigger than the Waller home place. I positively rattle around in here. I was thinking of asking someone—a couple maybe—to live here. Rent a bedroom suite with access to the entire house. That way when I'm gone someone will be here, and if that couple travels, I'll be here. The house will never be alone as it's been since Leon's death."

"That's a tall order, Shannon. You'd have to vet these people carefully in order to know they'd not steal or allow others in who might."

"For sure. That's where you two would be a big help. You know people, and you know what I'd have to do to make sure good people moved in. The place is insured for gazillions of dollars, but that doesn't mean I want someone stealing or destroying things I love."

"How about you doing what Phillip suggested…get out and meet people. Let us take you to some parties, and hey, throw a party here. Sort of a housewarming party to meet our friends. Do you have time before you leave for Texas?"

"I think so. I want to go there in late September or early October when the weather isn't stifling hot. Or crowded. I understand after school starts most tourists only come to Galveston on the weekends. Things crank back up for the holiday season, so September or October will be best for me. I may be gone a month, probably less. I want to drive, of course, but I want to visit places as I go along. I know I don't want to live this close to DC without visiting there."

"What about New York City?" Phillip asked.

"I think it best if someone goes with me for that adventure."

The guys grinned at each other. "Unless you find some other handsome hunk to take you, we'll take you." Justin's grin accompanied a leer with wagging eyebrows.

"Thanks—I think," Shannon teased back.

"Okay, so live-in friends. What's next?"

"Let's see. I suppose it's the trip to Galveston. I want to drive down the coast too. Maybe look for a small piece of property that I can rent or maybe even buy in case I want to spend time each summer on the Gulf coast."

"I understand it's hot as blazes down there, and the mosquitoes are huge."

"Really, Justin, I want to at least think about it. I'll check in with a realtor maybe."

"And they have hurricanes too."

"Uh, I believe New York had Hurricane Sandy," she came back.

"Yeah, there's that," Phillip admitted as he stood and headed to the kitchen.

Justin followed. Shannon gave the living room a quick glance, making sure they'd not left any food or plates. Habits formed by years of living alone still kicked in.

"In the meantime, I want to drive around the area and learn my way around. Justin, did you say a gardener comes each week?"

"Yes, but he may be waiting to hear from you. You know, not sure if you want to keep him."

"Do I have his name and number here?"

"Leon should have it listed somewhere on his desk. He was so damn organized, he made my teeth hurt," Justin groused as he put his rinsed dishes in the dishwasher.

"Hey, I can do that," Shannon said as she manhandled Phillip's plate away from him.

"Oh, let him do it, Shannon. The rule at our house is everyone takes care of his own dishes and clothes. We take turns cleaning the kitchen, but the dishes must be in the dishwasher. We do the same with the laundry. All dirty clothes in the hamper, or they don't get washed."

"Oh, okay. Not a bad plan really." She returned the dirty plate to Phillip and followed Justin through the living room to the porch. By that time, the outside light was on as well as the security lights over the garage and around the house.

"Come by the shop Monday, and we'll set you up in some classes, Shannon." Phillip made his suggestion as he hugged her.

"When you leave there, come by the office, and meet my partners. Then we can meet for drinks at our favorite bar, and you can hang with some of our friends," Justin offered. "Oh, and it's not a gay bar, in case you're wondering. Bar slash food…everyone welcome. You'd be surprised who shows up there now and then."

"I'll do that, but this weekend I think I'll drive around and scope out the area. I got used to driving and miss it now. Well, my butt doesn't," she admitted with a laugh as Phillip closed his car door and started the engine.

"Take care, and call if you need anything. We'll be here in a flash." Justin leaned over Phillip's shoulder and assured her of their swift arrival if needed.

"Will do. I'm a safe driver. What could go wrong?"

———

"Uhhh," Shannon groaned. One hand went to her fore-head, while the other lay limp in her lap. Her hand came away with blood on it. "What happened?" Her voice sounded weak and scared. A white blob—the car's airbag—lay deflated against the steering wheel, sagging into her lap.

Steam rose in front of her as well as thick underbrush. The steam came from the engine of her poor SUV that stood crumpled in a thicket of greenery.

"Hello, Mrs. Waller, are you all right? StarLink—Subaru's SOS system—reports that your car has received damage," said a voice from…? Somewhere. Shannon's fuzzy mind wasn't processing this well. Damage? What happened?

"Mrs. Waller, can you answer?" The voice came across as calm but insistent.

"Yes, yes, I think so." Shannon replied, eyeing the emergency service button through groggy eyes. "I'm not sure how I got here. I'm not sure where I am even."

"We've got you located from the car's GPS and an ambulance and police are on the way. Is anyone else with you? Is there anyone you want us to contact?"

"Justin Black at Beaufort, Black, and Brody, attorneys in Auburn."

"I'll do that. Are you injured?"

"My head is bleeding. At least my hand came back with blood on it."

"Stay where you are until emergency services arrive unless you feel there is danger in staying in your car."

"No, I think I'll be okay here. The radiator seems to be blown, but I don't think there's any fire."

"I'll stay on the line until an ambulance arrives, and the police say it's all right to turn off StarLink."

"Thank you." Shannon sat back, suddenly exhausted. "I appreciate you hanging around."

Her mind wanted to go to sleep, rest, after this unexpected and unexplained crash, but her cell rang, bringing her back to the present. She'd placed the cell in the cup holder and the crash simply slid it across to the passenger seat, so it was easy to reach.

"Shannon! You all right? Your car emergency service just called!" Justin sounded like a scared kid.

"I'm alive though my poor SUV looks pretty dented. Head's bleeding, I think. I haven't tried to walk yet or anything. Still in the car. Ambulance and police are on the way. Where will they take me, Justin?" Shannon's voice cracked, and she realized she was crying.

"Hey, you'll be okay. I promise. I don't know where they'll take you, but tell me when they take you, and I'll meet you there."

"Okay, but—"

A siren sounded nearby, then another siren revved up.

"The ambulance is here, I think. Where—?"

"They may take you to Auburn Community Hospital but ask them to transport you to Saint Joseph's Health Center in Syracuse if they will. A little further but only if your injuries are not life-threatening. Otherwise the nearest ER you can get to…that okay?"

"Sure. Stay on till they take me?"

"You bet."

A man in blue pants and shirt with a medical logo on the pocket leaned over, facing the driver side window. "Can you open the door?" She managed that, and he swung the door fully open, then squatted beside her. "Ma'am, let's check you out." All the EMT found were bruises and a cut on Shannon's scalp. No broken bones. The EMT said she'd go to ER in order for them to check for any internal injuries.

A policeman hovered nearby, taking photos and writing information. As soon as Shannon was loaded on a stretcher but before entering the ambulance, he asked for her name and what happened. The EMT handed over her purse, and she offered to dig out insurance and such, but he said he'd do a follow-up at the hospital. At the moment she needed medical care.

At the last minute, Shannon realized she still held her

cell phone. "Justin? They're taking me to Syracuse. Is that okay?"

"You bet. I'll meet you there in the ER. Do you have your purse?"

"Yes."

"Good. That means you have all the information the hospital will need. Rest easy, and I'll see you there."

After that, the rest of the day turned into a blur. The only thing she remembered was Justin sliding his hand into hers at Saint Joseph's Hospital. She remained overnight, so they could get the test results back, but for the most part, the doctor said she was lucky to only have bruises. The cut quit bleeding on its own and would be sore and subject to re-opening if she forgot and combed or washed her hair for a few days.

By seven that evening, she lay in a private room with Justin on one side of her bed and Phillip on the other.

"Do you remember anything, Shannon?" Justin, the lawyer, sat up with his notepad out, ready to take down her answers. The police had asked the same things while she was in the ER.

"Uh, let me think. I was driving north of the city proper. Just taking in the area, you know. Thankfully, I wasn't on a major highway because..." She stopped and gazed out the window, trying to find pieces of the event that wanted to float away. "I think someone tried to run me off the road."

"What...what did you say?" Phillip went white and leaned forward, grasping her hand.

"I think...I remember someone coming up quickly behind me. I tried to move to the side, but it was a country road and not a lot of place to go, so I hoped he'd wait until there was a passing lane or at least no double yellow lines.

But he burst up behind me, made a quick cut around me, then like a flash, he drove right into me. Forced me off the road."

"Well, I'll be damned," Justin said as he scribbled notes.

"Why would someone do that to me?" The fear Shannon felt just after she woke up returned.

"I don't know, but we'll try to find the car. Was a man or woman driving?"

"A man, I think, but the driver wore a cap, so it could have been a woman with her hair tucked up."

"First impressions are usually the best, but I'll keep the woman/hair thing in mind. What kind of vehicle?"

"Brown. Big. Not a truck. Big SUV. Old looking."

"Any trim you can remember, like a logo?"

Shannon gave it a few seconds but shook her head. "I'm sorry. Everything about the crash is fuzzy."

"Not unusual. Most crash victims can't even remember as much as you do."

"And you think it was deliberate?"

"I got that impression. The driver didn't want to go around and ahead of me. He wanted to come even and push me off the road. He succeeded quite nicely too." It suddenly dawned on her that her ruby Subaru was definitely out of commission. "What about my car?"

"I talked to the insurance company, and they said it's totaled. The frame was bent when it slid into a big tree." Justin didn't look happy about delivering bad news. "I know how much you loved that SUV."

At Shannon's horrified expression, he added, "That tree was all that saved you from sliding off into a creek just past that stand of brush. The creek is running full right now from the rains we've had upstate. You're banged up, but you're lucky."

"I suppose, but what did the insurance people say about replacing my car? I've only made four payments on it," she sniffled. "That SUV and I have gone a lot of miles together."

"The company said they'd wait for the police report. I'll contact the officer that took your info in the ER and let him know this might have been an attempted murder."

"Murder! Who'd want to murder me?" Shannon sat up so fast her head spun. "Ow."

"Easy there. I have to call it like I see it, Shannon. Someone deliberately tried to hurt you. That is attempted murder in the eyes of the law. And whoever it was didn't stop to render assistance like he should if his car swerved to miss an animal for instance. The driver should have stopped and helped you. Not stopping, not innocent, in my book."

"I never thought of it like that." Shannon shook a little, from both reaction and fear. "Will I be all right at home? At Mon Coeur? Alone?"

"Humm, we'll come up with something. That idea of yours about roommates might be the best plan. Best we get someone there as soon as we can. In the meantime, you have an excellent alarm system. I think you forget about that." Justin rubbed his chin. "It might not be a bad idea to get someone private to check into this accident. The police will file the report and look for the SUV that rammed you, but short of putting a detective on it, I doubt they'll have time or man-power to really find who did this. I know someone though," Justin said as he read over his notes, not looking at his husband or Shannon.

"The doctor said I can go home tomorrow. It's Sunday. I don't want to be alone."

Before Justin could say anything, Phillip piped up with an idea. "How about I bring my sewing machine and some of my stash, and we have a one-day quilting retreat?"

"If my head's not aching, then you're on."

"Okay, that takes care of you two for the day. I have paperwork to do. I've got a court case Monday. But I'll contact that PI and send him over tomorrow if that's all right with you, Shannon?"

"Sure, but give me a call to let me know he's coming. Oh, and Phillip, bring food. I'm starving. As nice as Saint Joseph's is, I'd rather not indulge in hospital food if I can help it."

"How about a burger and fries with a Coke tonight?" Justin stuffed his notebook in his jacket pocket. "I'll get some for all of us and be right back. Phillip can stay. Good enough?"

"Perfect," Phillip and Shannon said at the same time.

———

"I think I'm going to cut these pieces into strips, sew them together, and make four-patches. That way I can use them in any kind of quilt. What do you think?" Shannon held up a dozen pieces of fabric. She'd already taken some pain pills, and her headache had subsided nicely. She and Phillip had set up their machines in the dining room, so they could use the big table to arrange their supplies and fabric.

"I like this color combination." Phillip took half of the pieces and laid them out on the table. "See, you could do this…or this." He moved the fabric around, showing her his ideas.

"Nice,"

He laid out a particularly attractive combination of colors.

"I'll work with this first."

Her cell rang just as Phillip returned to his machine, and she had a handful of fabric. "Hello? Oh, hi. Yes, we're good. Phillip brought a fantastic casserole. He told me he made it. Oh, I see." She cocked an eyebrow at her friend. "Well, whoever made it, it's wonderful. We had some for lunch, and he's leaving the rest for me. What? Okay, I'll send some home for you since you made it." She laughed as Phillip shrugged with a grin. "Michael Silver? What time? No, that's okay. Uh, Justin? What about tonight?"

She listened, nodding several times then said goodbye.

"Lovely casserole, Phillip, even if Justin did make it." She thumped his shoulder as she made her way to her chair.

"Hey, I tried."

"Yep, got caught too."

Phillip gave another shrug. "Justin's a better cook than me. I'm good, but he's creative. You'd think he'd be a quilter as artistic as he is, but he's a lawyer. How utterly boring," he groused, but she could tell he was proud of what his partner did. "So, who's coming?"

"A private detective named Michael Silver. He'll be here at three. We have plenty of time to be creative."

"Well, let's get to it."

For the next two hours, the pair sewed, compared, suggested, and laughed. At two-thirty, Shannon suggested they clean up their mess and put their projects away.

"Your head hurting again?"

"Yeah, a little. Probably from eye strain. Besides, I need to change clothes. I'm a bit *thready*." She pulled pieces of cut thread off her sweatshirt.

"Yeah, that's an occupational hazard for quilters." Phillip used a lint roller to remove the threads from his shirt and khakis.

Together they made short work of gathering Phillip's things near the front door and taking Shannon's fabric and machine upstairs in the elevator. While Phillip headed downstairs to prepare iced tea for their guest, Shannon changed.

"I hope this guy isn't some bulldog-like PI who thinks he knows everything and the client is a bubble-headed woman," Shannon said as she waited by the front door for Silver to arrive.

"We'll toss his ass out if he is." Phillip flexed a muscle and thrust his hands out, demonstrating his ability to get rid of annoying private investigators if necessary.

A few minutes before three, a car rounded the drive and pulled up behind Phillip's. A tall slender black man stood and adjusted his raincoat and small hat—like a golfer's hat. An easy rain fell, leaving the afternoon washed and cozy. He pulled out a narrow briefcase and moved up the front walk. Before he climbed the steps, however, he paused and looked around the place, noted the house and the surrounding forested property. A slight smile lifted his lips as he continued up the steps and approached the door.

Shannon saw him through the long glass window beside the door, saw him pause, then move forward. He appeared calm and assured, while exhibiting nothing she might call bulldog-like manners. She liked his approach. His demeanor reminded her of Justin—composed, alert, and personable.

Something about the man reassured her though she couldn't put her finger on just what that was or why. She waited though for him to ring the bell before opening the door.

"Mrs. Shannon Waller? I'm Michael Silver. Justin Black said he would call and let you know I was coming." Silver held out one hand as he introduced himself.

"Good afternoon, Mr. Silver. Yes, I'm Shannon Waller." She shook his hand, noting a firm but not crushing grip, then motioned him forward into the entryway. "This is my friend, Phillip Armean. We were working on projects today. Won't you come in? Would you like some iced tea? Let me take your coat and hat."

"Nice to meet you, Mr. Armean. Yes, I'd enjoy some tea. It's a bit humid-like outside. Nothing I can't handle though. I'm originally from the South. Humidity down there is thick enough to cut with a knife most times." He handed over his coat and hat, which Shannon hung up, then followed the two into the living room.

"I'll bring the tea, Shannon," Phillip nodded to Silver and headed for the kitchen.

"Thank you, Phillip. Won't you be seated, Mr. Silver?" She took a seat on the sofa and motioned him to the square wide arm chair where she often sat.

"I understand you just moved here, Mrs. Waller."

"Please, call me Shannon. Yes, I came from Montana. My uncle passed away and left his home—this place—to me. I plan on living here permanently after I travel a little."

"I'm sorry for your uncle's death. I knew Leon Jeffers. A...unique man." Silver spoke softly and lifted those thin lips again when he mentioned Leon.

"Thank you, sir."

Phillip entered the room with a tray of tea, glasses with

ice, spoons, sugar, and lemon. After each prepared their tea, Silver laid his briefcase across his knees and opened it. Taking out a legal pad and pen, he placed the case on the floor and rested the legal pad on the wide arm of the chair.

"I heard the report of your accident from Justin. If you hire me to look into the case, I'll also get the official police report. I understand from Justin that this might have been an attempted murder. Can you tell me why he might think that, Shannon?"

"Frankly, I didn't give it a thought. I figured this guy wanted more of the road than I could give him, and I wound up in the ditch. But Justin saw it from a legal angle, I guess. The guy intentionally ran up behind me, pulled around on a section of road with no extra space, then jerked his car over against mine hard enough to push me off the road. His SUV was old, but bigger and apparently heavier than my smaller one. The other driver never stopped. He might have. I wouldn't know… I blacked out for a few minutes. At any rate, no one was nearby when I woke up."

As she spoke, Silver made notes. "Most of us remember things once we get home and in our own surroundings and especially in our own beds. All sorts of things come to us just before we drift off to sleep. By any chance did you remember more about your accident once you got home?"

That wasn't something Shannon had considered…that her mind once relaxed might give up more details. However, she could think of nothing new.

Shaking her head, she admitted, "I can't remember anything else. I'm sorry."

"Don't be sorry, ma'am. You survived, and that's a miracle if this man was out to get rid of you for some reason."

Michael Silver and Shannon gave each other a slight smile, both aware how fortunate she was.

"Now let's look at motive. We've seen the results of the accident, but we need to back up and find out why someone might want to hurt or even kill you. We need a motive." His pen poised over his paper, he looked like calm in the middle of the tornado of her thoughts.

"That's just it, Mr. Silver—"

"Michael, please."

She nodded, that feeling of comfort coming again. "That's just it, Michael. I visited here a number of times for my vacation, but Leon and I never went into town, nor did we meet others. Leon and I enjoyed traveling around the country, going to garage sales and museums, or seeing lakes. Just being quiet here. That kind of thing. Before coming last week, I'd only been into Auburn proper once and that was for a few hours, just long enough to sign papers at the bank. Papers having to do with my inheritance, giving me access to finances. And I'd never met any of the people I met that day before when I visited Leon."

"I see. And who did you meet while you were here?"

"Justin picked me up at the airport. We drove to New York city and visited banks and investment firms there, then the bank in Auburn where I met Gerald Fergusson. He handled Uncle Leon's local finances though not his investments. Oh, and the financial analysts in Auburn. Then I met Phillip when Justin took me to lunch. We ate and talked, then Justin took me back to the airport."

"So, other than these gentlemen, investors and the bankers, you met no one else?"

"No, sir."

Michael Silver sat back in his chair and gazed off across

the living room. Shannon and Phillip gave each other raised eyebrows and shrugs. Silence settled for a good three or four minutes.

Finally Silver pulled his gaze back to the two in the room and sipped some of his sweetened tea. "I'm wondering if this accident had anything to do with Leon's death."

"How do you figure that?" Phillip asked but only seconds before Shannon could.

"Did you inherit a great deal from Leon? I understand he was something of a financial genius when it came to investments. Rumors are that he was worth mega-millions."

"Umm, those rumors are true. He was worth an unbelievable amount of money, and yes, it all came to me."

"And you have a beneficiary in case something happens to you?"

"Beneficiary?" The word hit Shannon like a brick. "I never gave it a thought. No one ever mentioned it."

"You've listed no one to inherit in the event of your death?"

"No. Justin never asked about it. I guess he thought it was something I took care of on my own. Do people really kill for money, Michael?" She sounded naïve even to herself.

"I assure you, killing for money is among the top reasons to murder someone though sex, domestic violence, and revenge are right up there with it."

"Oh, my." Shannon stood, her steps pacing across the room. "I guess I need to add a beneficiary to my will…just in case."

"Do you have someone in mind?" Michael asked.

"Honestly?"

"Yes."

"No. My husband disappeared fifteen years ago. We never found his car or body. No one suspected him of just leaving—like for another woman. He left for a trip in the dead of winter. Probably not the smartest thing to do, but the deal was a matter of timing. We had no children, and I'm the last of both his family lines and mine. Even our pets are dead now," she added bitterly. "I have no idea who I'd give my money to."

"I'm sorry for the loss of the life you probably wanted and were denied," Michael said softly.

Shannon stopped suddenly and focused on him, her thoughts settling on one thing. "You know something? In all these years, no one's ever said anything like that to me. Never saw it from my point of view like that." Still holding his steady gaze, she dropped her voice. "Thank you. That's insightful. And very kind."

Michael nodded, accepting her thanks without making a fanfare of what she said. "So money could be a motive. Domestic violence?"

"Well, there was this guy…"

"Tell me about him." Michael lowered his pen, poised to write down more notes.

Shannon told him about Charlie Hawkins, how he treated her in the office, how he wanted to come into her home one winter night, and how he did come into her godparents' home before she left.

"He's a narcissist. He's all great and wonderful, and everyone else should acknowledge that. He's always saying how he's the best at anything and everything." She finally returned to the sofa as she described Charlie's behavior. "He wanted total control of me like he thought he had when he was a salesman for the lumber company."

"Do you think he might be a threat to you now?"

She had to think about that. "He's got a good job, I understand, in Great Falls in Montana. He's making far more money than he ever did working for Waller Lumberyard. No one but Justin, his law firm, the investment advisors and Mr. Fergusson the banker are even aware of just how much Leon left to me. So, while I left the impression that I got several hundred thousand—without ever saying as much—I doubt Charlie would pursue me across the country just for money."

"Is there anyone else in that town where you lived who might have a grudge against you?"

"No."

"So, sex isn't an issue?"

"Sex?" Shannon sputtered. Phillip covered his mouth— whether to keep from laughing at her reaction or chastising the private investigator for embarrassing her—was hard to tell.

Michael Silver sat as calmly as ever, his pen held at the ready, his expression one of patient waiting.

"I assure you that the only one interested in sex with me was Charlie Hawkins, and after I called the police on his ass, he backed off. Though revenge might be up his alley." Shannon sat with a face still flushed red.

"Revenge. That would be another reason for someone to try to harm you."

"How do you figure that?" Phillip asked.

"What if she got something that someone else thought should be theirs?" Michael went off into that unfocused stare again. "Or what if she has something that someone else doesn't want her to see or have?" He returned his gaze to them. "All good reasons to murder someone."

"I'll be damned." Phillip went a bit pale. "I can't even imagine."

"Does anyone hate you, Shannon?"

"Hate? As in passionately?"

"Yes."

"I don't think so. Oh, my former boss, Mr. Leven wasn't happy with me when I made him take proper care of the employees he was about to abandon, but he isn't the kind to expend energy on hate, especially after he sold the lumberyard for a ton of money. He's probably taking a cruise and posting photos to Facebook. He's addicted to social media. That's the threat I used to make him do the right thing for the employees." Her grin this time was wide, full of satisfaction.

"Sounds like you had his number and used it against him." Michael gave her a nod of respect.

"I certainly did, and I'm damn glad of it. Nasty old man."

"So, he wouldn't try to seek revenge on you?"

"I didn't have to resort to posting the truth on Facebook, Instagram, or Twitter about what he planned on doing to the employees, so he'd have no reason to go after me."

"Fair enough, though I'm going to check into both men."

"Fair enough for peace of mind," Shannon said.

"So, any secrets? Anyone jealous of you or your new-found wealth? Any disputes with anyone?"

"Good Lord, is all this real? You really have to think of all these things in order to find out who wanted to hurt me?" The depth of his inquiry alarmed Shannon. Her pulse kicked up, and she grew agitated enough to start pacing again.

"This is overwhelming, I'm sure, Shannon, but yes, we

need to explore all possible reasons why someone might try to kill you. Not hurt. This person intended to push you off the road, probably into the stream. You might have drowned, or the wreckage might have pinned you there. No one might have missed you for days or known where to find you."

"Thank God for the car's emergency contact service then."

"Yes, ma'am."

"Michael, perhaps you can help with something else." Shannon suddenly had an idea.

"If I can." He put his pen down and leaned forward.

"I want roommates. Reliable people. Maybe a couple. Someone I can trust not to destroy my home or rob me blind. I want company that I enjoy being with. And no, I'm not looking for a husband." She added that with a twinkle in her eye and a hint of humor in her voice.

Michael's grin said he understood her perfectly. "Okay, so you want me to locate someone for you. Who?"

"Well, that's a good question, and I'd like you to find an answer." She confidently dumped her problem into his lap. She had a feeling he'd do right by her.

"A tall order, Shannon."

"I realize that, Michael, but I have a feeling you can handle that and an attempted murder investigation at the same time." Her answer sounded a bit sassy—something she'd not done in a long time.

"Is there anything else you want me to look into?" Michael raised an eyebrow and cocked his head to one side.

"No, no, I think that's plenty for the time being. Oh, other than who's paying your salary, sir?"

"Why, you are, ma'am. Through Justin's office. Standard salary per hour. I keep accurate accounts of time spent on the case."

"Are you working another case at the moment?"

"Just finished one, ma'am. Justin—and you—were lucky to catch me before I started a new one." Michael still sat, leaning forward, his face turned up to Shannon's as she stood near him.

"I think we'll do well together, Michael." She held out her hand to shake his.

"I think so, too, Shannon," Michael said, the two of them totally forgetting Phillip sitting in the rocker.

"One last question, Michael."

"Yes?"

"Do you have a gun?" Shannon asked, her hands clasped tightly across her waist.

"Yes."

"Are you carrying it right now?"

"Yes."

Shannon focused on Michael Silver but said nothing.

Almost thirty seconds passed before he spoke. "You didn't ask the most obvious question a client usually asks."

"And that would be?"

"Will you show it to me?"

"I have no need to see your weapon. It's enough to know you can protect yourself and your client if necessary."

"Good enough. So, let me ask you a question."

"Ask."

"Do *you* have a gun?"

"Yes. A woman alone and traveling. I'd be crazy not to have protection. I also have a double barrel shotgun as well as a rifle. And a license for each. I grew up in Montana where such things are necessary at times for protection against animals."

"Fair enough. So, we can both take care of ourselves—or each other—if needed."

"Like I said, Michael, I think we'll do well together." Shannon suddenly smiled, a true relieved smile. "Do you have a card in case I need to contact you?"

"Yes." He passed over a simple but elegantly printed card. "Now, if there's nothing else, I'll get back to my office and begin vetting these names you gave me. I'll contact you if and when I find out anything."

"That works."

He put the legal pad back into the briefcase and slipped the pen into his suit coat pocket.

"I'll show you out. Phillip, join us?"

The trio made their way to the door where Shannon returned Michael Silver's hat and raincoat. They stopped at the door, listening to the sounds of summer thunder and the pounding of a heavy downpour.

Before they got out of the door onto the porch, Justin's car pulled up by the garage, leaving Silver room to get out. "Hey, guys, it's wet out here," he yelled as he dashed up the walk and on to the porch.

"No shit, Sherlock." Phillip kissed his partner but refused a hug. "Yuck, you're all wet."

Justin leaned forward and shook his hair against Phillip. "Take that!"

Phillip thumped Justin on the head before slipping his arms around the man. "Ain't he something?" he asked Shannon and Michael.

"I agree, Phillip, but I'm not sure what *something* he is,"

Michael laughed as he shook Justin's hand. "Good to see you again."

Thunder cracked overhead.

"I best be on my way. Lots of notes to go over and plans to make. And Shannon, I'll take on that side job you asked me to." Michael slipped his golfer hat on, pulled his raincoat closed around him, ducked his head and cautiously made his way to his car. With a last wave he pulled out slowly and disappeared into the closing evening.

"What are you doing here, Justin?" Phillip led his wife/partner into the house. "Let me get you a towel before you ruin the furniture."

"Yes, dear." Justin laughed but remained standing.

"You're all wet," Shannon confirmed. "What brings you to Mon Coeur?"

"Here you go, sweetheart. Dry yourself up, and join us for an early dinner?" Phillip tossed a towel to Justin and motioned to the kitchen. "Okay by you, Shannon?"

"Absolutely."

They trooped into the kitchen, and while Phillip heated up the leftovers and Shannon opened some wine, both filled Justin in on what took place with Michael Silver.

"And he's going to look for someone to be a roommate here. Hopefully two people," Shannon concluded. "So, what about you?"

"I brought stuff to work on and clean clothes for both of us. I know you have a fabulous alarm system, but I thought you might sleep better, first day back after the accident if we were both here. That okay? And tomorrow you can go with Phillip to the shop."

"Oh, perfect!" She jumped up and hugged his neck.

"Hey, how about me? I might love him more than you,

but I'm not passing up a hug from anyone," Phillip whined.

"Oh, you!" Shannon raced around to give him a fierce hug as well.

"I'll pull the car into the garage after we eat and finish my notes for the case this evening. Quiet time?"

"Yes, please. I started a novel in Lancaster County and never got to finish it, what with the unpacking and all. So, I'm up for a quiet evening. What about you, Phillip?"

"I think I'll cook if that's okay with you. A casserole or two and you won't have to eat out or worry about cooking for one."

"You two are the best," Shannon sighed.

"Yeah, we know," the guys said at the same time with identical Cheshire grins.

———

Shannon spent several days in Phillip's shop, taking classes and just visiting. She had lunch with two of the ladies who frequented the shop. Phillip privately vouched for them. That made her feel safer.

By the end of the week, she chastised herself for being so paranoid. She took in a movie. Met Margie, one of Phillip's helpers, for lunch and generally began to settle into the town. In early mornings, she began walking the property, noting where she and Leon had gone. The lake was as beautiful as ever. The gardener had mowed but left the underbrush natural.

"Oh Leon, how generous you were to leave me this place. And such delightful friends," she spoke as a fish jumped and caught the sun, its scales flashing colors. In the middle of the lake sat Leon's folly, a bit of artistic madness is what he had called it. The structure stood about twelve feet tall and was probably that round. The tiny island it sat on in the middle of the lake couldn't have been more than fifteen feet across itself. The folly was made of slats that started at the bottom, gathered at the top, then the whole thing twisted, like a chocolate Hershey Kiss with vanilla strips in it. While Leon never took her to it, the thing looked like wooden slats interspersed with some sort of glass or plastic. Whatever was between the wood reflected the sunlight with an iridescent shimmer. She could see no way to moor a boat there even if one wanted to cross the water and investigate.

Shannon put Leon's folly off to a unique structure built who-knew-when, something to be admired or just to look at and wonder about. She gave it little thought other than to think it incongruous to have a Hershey Kiss sitting in the middle of a lake. With a grin and a shake of her head, she made her way back to the house.

Her cell rang as she settled on the front porch. "Hello?"

"Up for some bar fun tonight?"

"Hello, Justin. That bar you were telling me about a week or so ago?"

"That's the one."

"I don't want to stay out late or anything, please."

"Yes, Mother. I'll have you home before curfew," Justin teased.

"I'm not that bad." She moved inside and headed for her bedroom. "What time? Do you want me to meet you some-where, or will you pick me up?"

"We'll pick you up. That way we can make sure you get home safely."

"Sweet! Time?"

"Eight?"

"Works for me. See you then."

Despite a mild flutter of trepidation, Shannon showered and slipped into slacks and a pretty top. Justin and Phillip arrived at eight, and they drove off for a fun evening—that was Justin's description of the time ahead. The next few hours were fun but eye-opening as well, just not in the way Shannon expected.

———

"Auburn's a small town. You never know who's going to show up," Phillip pointed out when he saw Shannon's shocked expression. Nodding to the man sitting among what looked like body guards or acolytes, he scoffed. "Gerald Fergusson comes here on occasion, and he always attracts the kind I'd not associate with. Thankfully, they're just a small pool in the bigger ocean of fun."

"Yeah, fun. It's that all right, but it's just that…" Shannon sipped her rum and Coke and shook her head. "Will wonders never cease, I guess. I'd have never thought that man would hold court like that." She turned away from her banker, aware that the man did nothing wrong. He just seemed an odd contrast to his rigid appearance in the bank that day she flew in.

"Let me tell you about Gerry there." Justin leaned in to the other two. "He's not what you think. He's very…egotistical…self-important. His world revolves around himself."

"Narcissist is the word you're looking for, I think. I described a man I worked with when talking to Michael the other day using that word." Shannon shivered and cut a quick glance back at the man talking to a small group. He appeared to be the center and appeared to bask in the attention. "They're nasty people to deal with. Always wanting to make themselves a victim, the one who's always right. The person they dislike is *after* them. They have issues, as my father-in-law used to say about folks like him."

Several friends of Justin and Phillip stopped by to visit and meet Shannon, and a few hours passed before they returned to the topic of her banker.

"Do you think I should get another banker?"

"Why? Leon used him, and Fergusson handles the accounts well. I've kept track of them since Leon's death, and with your accounting background, you'd spot anything wonky in no time."

"True, but I'm not sure I want to deal with the man personally. The new strategy these days is not to deal with negative people. I know there are instances when you have no choice, and in the case of a narcissist, the best thing to do is remain silent." She put her hand over her glass when the waitress asked if she wanted another round. "The other thing you do is never turn your back on a person like that." She nodded toward Fergusson who still sat among friends, sipping his drink even slower than she had.

"Look, if he makes you uncomfortable tonight, we can go somewhere else. God knows, I can take you to a half dozen places that you'd love," Phillip offered.

"No, this bar is great. I like the people—well, excluding Fergusson there—and the music is great. The food's not bad either," she added as she finished off the fries with chili and cheese over the mound.

"Like I said, you never know who's going to show up, and speak of the devil—there's Margie." Phillip's banker frown suddenly turned into a grin. He waved over the woman who helped in his shop. The evening ended with the four plus four more as time went on. They had their own acolytes, and Shannon forgot about her weird banker.

———

Shannon spent most of the day sewing a quilt top together. Despite the fortune she'd inherited, quilting still seemed to be her sanity control. She loved creating her own designs or following patterns others made. But after hours of sewing and very little moving about, she needed to get out and move.

The rain of a week earlier had given way to summer heat. Beneath the thick canopy of oak and chestnuts on the five acres where Mon Coeur sat, she remained comfortable. Dressed in shorts, with a comfortable shirt and tennis shoes, she walked along, using a stick to mess up the grass or bend aside a branch. Mindless walking soothed stiff muscles. Sunlight flickered between branches as an errant breeze played among them.

A crack sounded behind Shannon...something that sounded like a branch breaking.

"Uuh." She moaned, then sank into darkness.

———

"Justin, where's Shannon?" Michael Silver asked. "She's not answering her cell. We talk every day. Even earlier this morning, but now nothing."

"That's odd. She's addicted to that thing now that she finally has one. And she knows how important it is to keep it close. Did you check with Phillip?"

"No, but I will. But Justin, if I can't get hold of her and Phillip has no idea where she is, then I'm headed to Mon Coeur."

"Better yet, we'll meet there. She might be hurt. Accidentally or not, she may need help."

"I'll call Phillip from the car, but I'm headed there now," Michael said.

All Justin heard was the sound of the cell call clicking off.

———

"What?" Shannon groaned and spat out a mouthful of leaves. "Ow." She moaned and put a hand to her head—the back this time. Too dizzy to think properly, she laid her face back on the path she'd been walking and closed her eyes. Sunlight kept her warm, but her stomach threatened to heave up her lunch.

"Shannon?"

In the distance she thought she heard voices. Too sick to answer, in fact, wondering if she imagined her name, she slipped in and out of consciousness.

"Do you see her?"

"Not yet, but she always walks on this path."

The voices came from off to one side. Not near enough to be distinct. She was dreaming. A heavy sigh escaped her, and a leaf swirled up to tickle her nose.

"Achoo!" She sneezed and slipped into a faint for a second as the action sent waves of nausea through her. The feeling built and swirled in her guts until she pulled her arms beneath her chest, lifted her body enough to open her mouth and vomited a long stream of nasty tasting bile.

Again, she heaved, and bile landed in an evil smelling puddle not six inches from her.

"Did you hear that?"

"Yeah, sounded like someone throwing up. Shannon?"

The voices came closer, amid the thrashing of brush and branches. Warm hard hands closed over her shoulders, laying her on her side, away from the mess she'd just created.

"Shannon, what happened?"

"Phillip?"

"At least she knows who I am."

"What happened to me?"

"I asked you first." Phillip ran his hands gently down her body, looking, she assumed, for broken bones. "Nothing broken but I don't like the look of that wound on her head."

"The wound looks deep." Justin touched her shoulder.

At least Shannon thought it was him.

"We really shouldn't move her in case she has internal injuries." Another voice, deeper than Justin's or Phillip's, moved closer.

"You're right, Michael. Look, she seems to be slipping in and out of consciousness." Justin reached for his cell. "Damn, I left my cell in the car. You two stay with her, and I'll run back to the house, call an ambulance, and bring them back here. Plan?"

Justin spoke with urgency in his voice. Shannon thought she ought to be worried, but she drifted away before she could.

"Plan, man. Go," Michael commended.

The sound of feet running along the ground faded. Hands moved her head just enough to keep it away from the wound, she reasoned. Other than that, both men sat with her.

Michael wore a suit; she could focus enough to see that. As she drifted back into waking, she realized he'd taken off the suit coat and draped it over her. A shiver ran through her; she was cold after all.

"It's going to be dark soon. Later than I thought." Michael knelt, still as a statue, on the ground beside her.

"Wonder what happened?" Phillip paced just to the other side of Michael.

"Don't know, but it looks like a branch snapped and hit her, though…"

"What are you thinking, Michael?"

"Nothing at the moment, but I want to check out something tomorrow."

Silence fell as Shannon slipped into a dark sleep.

———

"Who are you?" Shannon's head hurt so badly that the sound of her voice threatened to send her into a fetal position. "And who are you?" directing her second inquiry to the person sitting near her bed.

"I'm Dr. Patel, neurosurgeon. And no, you did not have surgery, but I thought you might need a procedure for a few minutes after I saw you in the ER."

"Where am I?"

"At Saint Joseph's in Syracuse…again," the doctor said without looking at her. He focused on the notes he had in hand.

"And who are you?" Shannon cut her eyes to a quiet woman sitting near her. She dared not move her head to look directly at the stranger.

"I'm Bea Slater. Michael Silver is my nephew and asked

me to sit with you so you'd not wake up alone." The black woman stood and impressed Shannon with her confidence and calm. Much like Michael. Bea wasn't tall and tended toward thick. However, Shannon could see that what she thought might be middle age fat was in fact muscle. The woman must work out. Bea wore a pair of heavy cotton sweat pants and a zip-up sweat shirt.

"You look comfortable. I'm freezing." As a demonstration of her statement, Shannon shivered.

"I can take care of that," Bea answered with a wink. "Be right back."

"Now, Mrs. Waller, you have a nasty concussion. Far worse than that accident injury you suffered a few weeks ago. I'd say you're accident prone, but Mr. Silver has informed me you're not, and he has proof. I'll take him at his word. The man inspires trust," Patel concluded.

"How long do I have to stay here?"

"At least another three days. You were unconscious for over twenty-four hours. Tests show no internal brain bleeds, but we want to monitor you for another few days. I expect you can go home then, but I'd feel better if someone stayed with you for at least two days afterwards."

"I'm sure I can find someone." Shannon knew she'd have to rely on the guys to find someone trustworthy.

"Here you go, sweetheart." Bea slipped back into the room, carrying a blanket. Turned out she had two, and they were straight from the blanket warmer.

"Oh, that's heaven." Shannon hummed in satisfaction as she closed her eyes and sank down into the warmth. "How did you know?"

"I've been in the hospital a few times. Used to volunteer too, so I'm familiar with how to keep people comfy. And a blanket warmer is tops on my ER list," she said with a grin that lit her dark face. Her short dark hair curled around her head and accented large dark eyes.

"You said Michael sent you?"

"Pardon me, ladies, but I need to check Mrs. Waller before I leave." He edged between Bea and the bed, his stethoscope out.

A few minutes later he left, and Bea pulled her chair up close to the bed. "You're tired, aren't you?"

"Yes." A yawn escaped Shannon before she could stop it. "Sorry."

"Not a worry, sweetheart. You rest, but you'll pardon me if I nudge you awake ever so often."

"Checking that I haven't died on you, huh," Shannon said as she closed her eyes. "See ya, Bea."

"You bet, sweetheart."

———

When Shannon woke up someone new sat by her side. "Margie! What are you doing here? Oh wait, don't tell me… Phillip asked you to sit with me."

Margie leaned over and gave Shannon a gentle hug and grinned as she patted the blankets over Shannon. "You bet. Phillip said you weren't to wake up alone."

"That must be the mantra of the day—don't let Shannon wake up alone."

"Not a bad mantra to have, considering so many people actually do wake up in hospitals, nursing homes, and rehab centers with no one there to say good morning or even hello."

"You make me feel selfish." Shannon winced as she

moved. "Sitting up is a challenge."

"Need some help?"

Together they raised the head of the bed and moved Shannon higher in it, so she rested against a mound of pillows.

"My head is killing me." Shannon laid her head back and closed her eyes, the steady beat of her heart resounding in her head.

"Shall I call the nurse?"

"Yes, please."

One Tylenol and two hours of rest later, Shannon spent two more hours visiting with Margie. Fortunately, her friend encouraged her to rest, and in no time, Shannon dropped off into sleep—not quite restful since her head hurt, but good enough.

Deep in the night, she woke, disoriented, and chilled again. Restless now, her urinary needs taken care of by a catheter, she thought of calling for a nurse. Rustling around among her covers for the call button, she woke someone napping in the chair tucked further into the shadows.

"Who's there?" Her heart rate jumped, and for a second she was scared.

"Hey, hey, it's only me." A tall black man stood slowly and stepped into what little light there was in the room.

"Oh, Michael, you scared me. Seems like every time I wake up, someone new is with me. Like a revolving door."

"I'm sorry, Shannon. I didn't mean to frighten you." Michael pulled the chair closer to the bed. "Actually, Phillip and Justin spent time with you, but that was early on. You probably don't remember."

"No, I don't. My head hurts, and that's pretty much all I can think of."

"Well, the doctor says you ought not to strain yourself. Take it easy on doing anything or stressing over anything. Did you know that your banker, Fergusson, sent word, asking about you?"

"Huh! Probably worried about his b…iggest client." She hoped she covered her near-boo boo. She almost said he was probably worried about her billions, though not all that money was in his bank by any means. But Fergusson would know how much she was worth. The B word wasn't something that normally popped up in her thoughts, but apparently it almost fell out of her mouth. Must be the headache, she reasoned.

"You don't think a lot of your banker?" Michael spoke softly as he sat and pulled a blanket over his lap.

"Not especially, since I saw him at a bar the other night, acting like a king surrounded by his court. But I've checked the accounts since Leon died, and they're all good. So, the man's not embezzling money from me. Still I find him a bit distasteful."

"Thankfully, you don't have to deal with him personally very often, right?"

"True. I'd rather surround myself with positive calm people…like you…and your Aunt Bea. She's so sweet. And buff. I've never seen a lady her age with muscles like that." Shannon yawned and apologized. "Sorry. I feel a nap coming on."

"No worries about the nap, and as for Aunt Bea, I hope you like her because she and her partner are two I wanted you to meet…want you to consider for your roommates."

"Really? That's wonderful." For the first time since she woke up, Shannon heard something positive. "When I get home and this headache passes, I'll invite them over."

"That may be a week or more because I understand your doctor doesn't want you making any big decisions or doing anything physical or even mental for at least two more weeks."

"Really? Well, dang. What am I supposed to do in the meantime? Patel probably won't let me read or quilt. Definitely not quilting. How about Aunt Bea and…who?"

"Oh, Susan McDonald. I call Bea and Susan *salt and pepper* if you get my drift."

"Oh yeah, that ought to make life interesting." Shannon tried to laugh, but she winced instead. "Damn headache."

"Before I shut up and urge you to get back to sleep, what were you going to say?" Michael kicked out the foot rest on the recliner.

"How about Aunt Bea and Susan come visit each day? They can do whatever they like and keep me company. By the time Patel releases me from home confinement, we'll know how we get along. What if they don't want to come live with me?" That thought sent urgency into her voice.

"Hey, calm down. The idea of them visiting is a good one. Anything else beyond that can wait until you're home and have enjoyed their company for awhile. How about we leave it at that?"

"Okay, but you promise they'll come visit each day?"

"On my honor." Michael crossed his heart.

"I'll hold you to that, tall man."

———

An entourage gathered outside Shannon's room the day Patel released her from the hospital. None of them knew she was awake; she slept so much. That's why she overheard a conversation between Justin and Michael that she knew they didn't want her to hear. The information they discussed also explained why someone remained with her at all times. Sure, they were all friends, but it was disconcerting to always have a visitor who sat with her for hours.

"What are we going to tell Shannon about that incident in the woods? You know she'll ask about how she got hurt. I'm surprised she hasn't asked before this." That was Justin, and he sounded concerned.

"Look, the branch that had blood on it—the one used to hit Shannon—was stout, and the person left her, thinking she was dead. But that branch didn't come from a nearby tree. The closest sugar maple tree is up by the house. Someone carried it back there, following her. That kind of concussion wouldn't happen from a branch that size simply falling. Someone used force to hit her. I'm telling you, Justin, between the car accident and this injury, someone wants to seriously hurt or kill Shannon Waller." Michael sounded slightly less calm but just as confident as ever.

Which worried Shannon. If Michael knew a mere branch falling didn't cause her injury, then that left them with the same mystery but bigger now. Who wanted to kill Shannon Waller and why?

Before she could puzzle out the information further, in trooped Margie, Justin, Phillip, Michael, Aunt Bea and a stranger whom Shannon assumed must be Susan, Bea's partner. She gave Justin a sharp glance, and he squirmed a little, but she said nothing to ease his guilty conscience.

Patel's nurse went over the instructions, and everyone nodded. Shannon would have laughed at the collective head bobs but after hearing the conversation from the hallway, having trusted friends around her made her feel better. Justin pushed her wheelchair, and Phillip opened the car door for her.

"When do I get a new car?"

"As soon as your head stops hurting…and don't lie about it. I know when you lie. You have a tell." Phillip gave her a serious look and nod.

"I do not," Shannon asserted though she had to think about that. She'd played poker with Immajean and her family enough times to know that her friend could beat her eighty percent of the time. "We're going to talk about that someday."

"No, we're not. I don't want to have to figure out a new tell when you stop doing what you do," Phillip informed her. "Bea, you and Susan are coming to the house, right?"

"Right behind you, Phillip." Bea waved as she and Susan headed to their car.

"Michael?" Shannon asked, as Justin clicked the seatbelt for her. "Seriously, I didn't die or anything. I can click my own seatbelt, thank you." She swatted weakly at his hands.

"Let me baby you for a while. When you get better you can go back to your usual independent self." Justin checked the strap, making sure it wasn't too loose or tight.

"Well, when you put it that way," Shannon conceded, "then baby on."

"Lord, I think you created a monster, my dear," Phillip said from the back seat.

"Yep," Shannon acknowledged. "Is Michael coming to the house?"

"Yes, and we've already got a meal there. Bea, Susan, and Margie have been cooking. Phillip, too. Your freezer is full, let me tell you." Justin put the car in gear and eased out of the spot in front of the hospital doors.

"Yum, sounds good to me. I hate cooking."

"Ready to go home?"

"Absolutely!"

———

"Enough is enough. My head doesn't hurt any more. Patel released me, and I'm a free woman again. So, it's time for me to put on my big girl panties, and get on with life," Shannon declared with her hand raised high, a glass of wine held ready to sip.

She'd invited her friends for a big Sunday dinner, cooked by most of them. She simply supplied the kitchen and fixings. No one groused, and laughter flowed as much as the wine.

"Here! Here!" Bea shouted. She'd already had a full glass of wine, but for all that, she still appeared as sober as a judge.

Glasses clinked as Justin added, "Thank goodness. We've spoiled the woman. She won't know how to get along without us."

Shannon gurgled at that, while Bea and Susan leaned against each other, laughing. Phillip rolled his eyes, Margie's eyes grew wide, and Michael hid a grin behind his hand.

"Okay, so now that you're back to being you, what's on the agenda?" Bea asked as they passed serving dishes around the table.

"First thing is to thank you all for being so wonderful to me while I was in the hospital and in confinement," Shannon raised her glass again and took a sip.

"Confinement, huh! Sounds like what the men used to

call it when they kept women stuffed in bedrooms for months before and after giving birth," Susan snorted. While both she and Bea were in a relationship and had been for decades, Bea had never married. But Susan had. When her only child died from abuse at the hands of her husband, she gave up men and found the love of her life with another woman, Beatrice Slater.

"Now, Susan, don't go off on one of your political rants today," soothed Bea.

"Yeah, okay, fine. I'll save my opinion for another day." Susan nodded to Shannon while patting Bea's hand.

"I look forward to it, Susan." Shannon passed two dishes, and when a bit of eating silence fell over her guests, she moved forward with the first part of her plans. "I'm looking forward to sharing views and opinions, suggestions and good as well as hard times with both of you, Bea and Susan. I hope you'll consider moving in with me as roommates."

Though Michael, Justin, and Phillip knew that Shannon planned on having roommates, only Michael was privy to the fact that she wanted to ask his aunt and her partner.

"Shannon, are you for real?" Her hands still and her eyes wide, Bea's dark skin paled a bit. "Do you know what you're asking?"

"Yes, I do. You and Susan are nice people. Honest and hard-working. I've seen you outside in the garden. Susan cooks like a chef and frankly could open her own restaurant if she wanted to work that hard. I've enjoyed having you here each day and frankly would love it if you moved in permanently."

That said, everyone broke out in chatter. No one

objected to the idea. Even Margie who'd only known the ladies for a few weeks seemed amenable to the idea.

"You had Michael vet us, didn't you?" Bea leaned over and asked quietly.

"Would it hurt your feelings if I said yes?" Shannon leaned into the conversation.

"No, it's the smart thing to do," Bea admitted, sitting upright and cutting her eyes to her partner. "But you know what we are. Someone might not like our kind living at Mon Coeur."

"Susan, Bea, listen to me. Michael vouched for you two before I even asked for the vetting procedure. That was simply formality. I would like to think I'm a decent judge of character. I like you both. I don't think you'd steal from Mon Coeur or allow anyone else to come in and steal or damage my home. Mon Coeur can be your home for as long as you like."

"We're not poor, you know. This isn't charity, is it?"

"I'm not poor either, and why would I offer two ladies like yourselves charity when it's obvious that you don't need it?" Shannon spoke as dinner conversation flowed around them. "I make the offer to you both and hope you accept it. If you'd like to think about it, don't think you're hurting my feelings. Just let me know what you decide." She picked up her fork once more and gestured to her plate. "Now finish this lovely meal, and we can enjoy coffee with Susan's salted honey pie that I understand two sisters make in New York City."

"Susan figured out how they made it and makes a slight variation of the pie. It's to die for," Bea told Shannon.

Beside her, quieter Susan beamed as she continued on

with her meal. "We'll let you know, Shannon. Don't you worry."

"Thank you, ladies. I look forward to your decision."

Later during dessert and coffee, Shannon brought up another part of her plans. "I'm ready to buy another SUV. I loved my Subaru and miss having my own wheels. So, no one's going to have to ferry me around for much longer."

"About time!" Phillip let out a gusty exaggerated sigh. "My tires are wearing out, hauling her around town."

Margie thumped him on the shoulder. "You're awful."

"Anything else?"

"Other than having a private conversation with Michael about an investigation I asked him to look into, the only thing else is me traveling to Texas to visit where my mom was born."

Michael nodded to let her know he was ready to give her his information about the car accident. He did shoot Justin a glance that Shannon interpreted as a question. Bet he wants to know if Justin thinks telling me about that branch is a good idea.

"Tell us about this place where your mom was born." Margie gathered empty plates as she waited for Shannon to answer. Susan hopped up and helped.

"Well, Mom was born in a city on an island south of Houston, a place called Galveston." And with that, she told them what she knew and what she'd like to see on the way to Texas. "I have no definite plans and would appreciate it if anything I mention stays here."

"After what's happened to you, sweetheart, I suspect we'd all best keep our mouths shut," Bea said as she sat down next to Shannon.

———

"I thought you'd get one the same color as the one that was wrecked," Justin said over the phone after seeing the photo Shannon sent in a text.

"Yeah, I thought so too, but my original plan had been to get a dark gray one, and the Subaru place had this one and not the ruby red one like I had before. Maybe going with a different color will change my luck."

"What do they call this color? It's a really dark gray."

"Magnetic gray metallic."

"Geez, what a mouthful. Okay, so it's dark gray. Looks good. The insurance paid, right?"

"They sent a check the other day. That's in the bank, and I'll follow the same game plan we used for the other SUV—make monthly payments for less than a year, then pay it off. I checked my credit rating, and it's coming up. As I use those credit cards for dinky things and pay off each month, I ought to have a top rating pretty soon."

"Sounds good."

"Uh, you do plan on joining me and Michael here later today for a conference, don't you?"

"I don't see why you want me there. I have nothing to do with that accident investigation."

"No, you don't, but you have things to share about other investigations." Shannon quickly ended the call. "See you at four. Later."

"But Shannon—"

Whatever Justin wanted to say was lost as she pushed the End button. "That'll teach you to keep information from me."

Several hours later, Shannon sat in the arm chair, her tea glass resting on the wide arm. Across from her in the recliner sat Justin. If his expression looked concerned, he should be, she thought. Michael sat on the sofa, his notes spread out on the coffee table.

"You found my roommates, Michael. Bea and Susan told me this afternoon. Thank you for that." She nodded his way, then continued on to the topic that interested her the most. "Now let's get to what I originally hired you to do—investigate that so-called accident. It wasn't an accident, was it?"

Michael cleared his throat softly, then shook his head. "Not really, no. I checked with the garage where the wrecker driver took your SUV. I got a sample of the brown paint left on the side of your car. I had it analyzed—don't ask me who or how much—"

"I got the bill for that, and I must say it was impressive by whatever stretch of the imagination you'd want to use. An average citizen couldn't afford that kind of thing." Shannon sat up and leaned forward, worries returning. "Go on."

"Yes, well, analysis isn't cheap, and it only proved that the paint came from a 1985 Ford Bronco. I then ran a vehicle check for all '85 Broncos and came up with thirty-five in the area. Just to be safe I got the number of those in the state of New York and Pennsylvania. I ran the names through my sources, and all have been recycled or destroyed by now. No vehicle with that color is still operating in this area. That we know of through data anyway."

Disappointment must have shown on Shannon's face.

Michael went on quickly. "I then used my sources to check those in the state. There are a lot of them, I'll tell you. Shannon, short of having a license plate number or finding the Bronco in a body repair shop, I've hit a brick wall. And before you ask, that was the first thing I did, check the body shops for a hundred miles around Auburn. If this guy drove that brown Bronco he either stashed it somewhere, or he drove it out of the state."

"What about traffic cameras? Don't they use that on TV all the time to find what they're looking for?"

"Yes, the authorities can do that, but a lot of time has passed, and those tapes would have been re-used. Besides, the accident happened in the countryside where there are no traffic cameras. I questioned the police when I started this investigation. Remember I said I would get an official copy of the report they filed. Seeing as no one was killed or seriously injured in the accident, they didn't investigate further."

"Damn, you'd think they might pursue the matter a bit more vigorously." Shannon slammed back in the cushions of the chair and scowled. The fingers of her hand beat a drum roll on the wooden arm.

With nothing else to add, Michael started gathering his notes. Shannon glanced at Justin who looked just a bit too relieved.

"What about my other accident? That was no random branch falling out of the tree and hitting me on the head, was it?"

This time Justin and Michael both looked guilty. Justin set the rocker to moving ever so slightly, while Michael took an inordinate interest in putting his notes back into his briefcase.

"Well, it's not like I slept *all* the time in the hospital. And some of us talk *louder* than others, especially when they're worried, like you two were the day I left the hospital." She gave them a hard stare and realized something: they were still worried. "Well?"

Justin put his foot down, stopping the rocker's motion. He leaned forward. His face worked as he tried to say what was on his mind. "I didn't think anything about the whole thing until Michael with his sneaky suspicious mind came to me while you were in the ER. When he mentioned certain details and said he was returning to Mon Coeur in order to find something, my lawyer mind kicked in."

"So, what did you go find?" Shannon turned to Michael and noted he was now quite calm. Almost too much so. *He's on familiar ground, knowing the facts and putting theory to them.*

"I thought it odd that you sustained such a severe injury after being hit by a branch that supposedly cracked and fell, coincidently as you passed under it. And in good weather. Phillip didn't notice when the EMTs finally gathered you onto a stretcher, and he was guiding them back to the house, but Justin saw me pick up that branch and carry it with me back to Mon Coeur. I laid it aside out of sight in case I wanted to check it out again. The more I thought of it on the drive to Syracuse, the more I thought that someone might have tried to kill you…again."

A soft gasp escaped Shannon. "But why? Why? I've never bothered anyone in my life…well, other than old man Leven and Charlie Hawkins. You checked them out, didn't you, when you looked into the car accident?"

"I checked out both men, and they're good with an alibi.

Their phone records don't show any connection to New York or areas close. So, I think we can rule them out."

"I've done nothing here to antagonize anyone," Shannon wailed. She covered her mouth and breathed heavily. "What else did you do in this investigation that you and Justin had no intentions of telling me about?"

"I'm sorry, Shannon, but you were hurt so badly that for a while we really thought you might need surgery. There was no reason to alarm you. At that point, it was all supposition." Justin held out a hand as if pleading for leniency.

"So now that I'm better and weeks have passed, you've still not told me what you found...if anything. So, now's a good time."

"Right." Michael relented, reached into his briefcase, and pulled out a different folder. Laying it open on the low table, he read for a few seconds, then turned to her. "I returned that night after we knew you were hurt but not fatally and didn't need surgery. I retrieved the stick of wood. I knew the blood would be yours, but I hoped that the other person might have scraped him or herself or at least left some DNA. The next morning I checked with the Agriculture Extension agent who's a friend as to what kind of wood it was. Turns out it was a maple just as I suspected. And the closest...the absolutely closest maple on your property is not far from your driveway. I checked. No sugar maples grow anywhere close to where you were. The other maples are on the far side of the lake. So, this branch didn't fall out of a tree and accidently hit you on the head. Someone carried it when he followed you. You're damn lucky the bastard didn't kill you." Michael viciously tossed the folder back into his briefcase. "There was no DNA on the branch other than yours, so the guy must have worn gloves. Your home security cameras picked up nothing so that tells me the guy was clever enough to either scope out the place or knows it. That could be who-knows-how-many people. I figure he parked somewhere along the road and walked to the house. How he knew you'd take a walk at that time I have no idea. Maybe he planned on waiting for you to step out of the house and then... Just a coincidence." He stopped. "I'm sorry we withheld that information. You deserved to know, but we just didn't want to scare you any more than you were after the car accident."

"So, someone wants me dead," Shannon said in a flat voice. Her mind suddenly swirled with sick images she'd often seen on the news and TV shows. "I've got to get my will in order. I forgot about that!"

Suddenly a fire lit in her brain, and a sense of urgency filled her. "Thank you, gentlemen, for trying to keep me from worrying, but I'd rather worry than live in ignorance. I don't want that old adage, *third times the charm*, to be me dying somewhere because I didn't have all the facts." She shot up from her chair and headed for the door. "I'll see you out, then I have work to do."

Neither man said a word about her ungracious invitation to leave. For that she was grateful because at the moment she didn't feel charitable toward either one though their intentions were honorable.

———

Once more alone, Shannon went to her bedroom and pulled out a lock box containing important papers, one being her will. She'd brought it with her but never gave a thought to updating it. No one ever mentioned it though, on second thought, Justin might have, but she had too much going on to catch the importance. She knew now that if she died, if someone succeeded in killing her, the state would get her entire estate, billions that it was. She knew some states put that kind of windfall into the state budget, while others gave any monies to the Education Department. She wasn't sure about New York State, but she had no intentions of letting any state get hold of Leon's fortune...her fortune.

Reading carefully and making notes, she revised her will. She'd make a copy later and take it to Justin's office to be put into safe keeping, but it would remain sealed until her death...which she hoped would be a long time from now and quite natural. Even her lawyer—Justin Black—wouldn't know what was in it. Just like Uncle Leon's will.

One million apiece to Todd and Emily Zimmer. Another million to Helen and Victor Bass, at Shannon's death. She included Immajean and her family as well as Martha and Wallace Ackerman, her godparents.

Like anyone else making a will, Shannon hoped to live a long and full life, so these inheritances might go to the off-springs of her friends except for the Ackerman's. Giving money away revived her spirits, made her feel just a little sorry for being nasty to Justin and Michael, but not sorry enough to apologize. Withholding information from her would just have to be a point they agreed to disagree on.

Over the years, she'd wanted to donate to several national charities. But her month-to-month financial exis-tence never allowed her to give. Now she could set aside a million apiece for three charities she was passionate about. That done, she looked online for the exact name of the first place. American College of the Building Arts specialized in teaching building arts the old fashion way—hands on but using the latest in technology and data as well. The school promoted excellence in craftsmanship. Jacob would have loved this place. She set aside a large sum of money in her will for the Charleston, South Carolina college.

She set aside a million apiece for several other charities, then re-read what she'd written to make sure there would be no trouble passing on the money.

Last of all, she named Justin Black as the executor of her will. He'd flip when he found out though he'd not know the details of what she put in the will.

No matter to whom she gave money or whom she put in charge of her will, she still had no one to list as a beneficiary. She was the last of her family, and Jacob was the last of his. When Leon died, that left her as last man standing, so to speak. She had the money, and she had the estate, but she had no one living with whom to share. This would be a problem she'd have to give more thought to.

Her pen left lying on the page of notes, she left the room and wandered downstairs to the glassed-in room on the first floor that she decided would be a perfect quilting room. A carpenter had built shelves up to the windows, and Phillip helped her organize the room with her stash of fabric and collection of threads. But tonight the room held no appeal for her.

Hitting a series of buttons built into the wall near the kitchen, she listened to the soft swishing of curtains closing over the banks of windows that she loved by day but covered at dark. Cozy behind a wall of fabric, she walked from room to room, thinking about who might benefit from receiving her wealth at her death. Again she hoped to live a long time, though current events pointed to the fact that someone wanted her gone sooner rather than later.

"Shannon, come look what we found!" Bea grabbed Shannon's hand while Susan danced down the hall before the two. The trio headed for the staircase leading to the tiny attic or what Leon called the third floor. Bea and Susan had moved in over the Labor Day holiday, and their few pieces of furniture and accessories blended well with Mon Coeur's style.

"There's nothing up here but two storage rooms, Bea." Shannon tried to catch her breath and not laugh at the pair.

"Just you wait and see, sweetheart. There's more up here than you think." Bea threw open the door to the second storage room.

Only it wasn't a storage room.

"Isn't this the most perfect place you've ever seen," Susan almost whispered.

"Good Lord!" Shannon stepped in a bright room, windows from the chair rail up on three walls. The wide roof jutted out, cutting off direct light so that the glorious colors of the area rug were less bright but not totally faded.

"This is Jo's garret." Susan glided over to a wing chair, in love with the reference to Little Women.

Bea stood by a narrow desk. "And look at this…a drop front desk. And the chair here…" she pulled a padded arm chair up to the desk, dropped the front panel and gestured as if presenting the lovely pieces of furniture. "fits perfectly. I can write here, or more importantly I can use my computer and do my genealogy work here. These cubby holes are perfect for keeping my notes and charts." With that she pulled out the chair, sat, scooted up to the desk, and started rummaging through the cubby holes, most of which were empty.

Shannon nodded and smiled, but the room dazed her. So bright and hidden away. Leon never mentioned it. If he had, she'd have been up here every day instead of reading in the wide window seat at the landing of the staircase. She moved over to sit in the other wingchair opposite Susan. Between the two chairs stood a table with two drawers and a marble top.

"Have you checked out the drawers?" Shannon settled in and closed her eyes for a moment. "I can see where you might think of this as Jo's garret—straight out of Little Women—but I don't think her attic was quite as nice as this one."

"For sure," Susan agreed as she pulled open the first drawer. "Look, checkers!"

"That explains this marble table top then. Two people could sit here and play checkers in comfort. That's neat." Shannon examined one of the pieces. "What about the second drawer?"

"Chess pieces. Quite lovely too."

"But there's no board. That's too bad," Shannon held out her hand for a knight made in exquisite pale marble.

"Humm." Susan sat for a few seconds, then whispered, "Ah hah!" She reached out, picked up the heavy piece of colored marble, and lifted it enough to see the bottom. "Get a load of this!" She turned the marble over to disclose a chest board.

"We have first dibs on this room, Shannon," Bea called out from her desk. "Of course, you can visit any time," she announced with an airy wave of her hand.

Shannon stood and moved to the door but stopped and

offered the ladies a small courtesy, "Thank you ever so much." She left two happy old ladies to an afternoon in a bright garret.

———

Summer passed with pleasant evenings on the porch, fun times in town with friends and the occasional squabble. Shannon and Phillip actually got into it one day about colors for a quilt of all things. She and Susan spent one afternoon walking around each other over the ingredients of a recipe. Justin came under fire for several days when he tried to be protective and stifle her activities. Even Michael—fast becoming part of her family circle—got into it with her as he tried backing up Justin's desire to keep her safe.

No word came back through Michael's investigation about the car that drove her off the road. Nothing came back from the limb used to whack her on the head.

Time settled all disagreements, everyone kept an eye on Shannon though she never actually caught them *protecting* her. The friends created a tight circle during those months.

———

"This is worse than leaving Cut Bank." Shannon gathered her purse and sweater, muttering under her breath the entire time. Her bags were packed and in the new *dark gray* Subaru Forester, as Justin insisted on calling the color. In the front seat lay her travel bag with books, snacks and wipes as well as several bottles of water.

Bea and Susan as well as Phillip and Justin hovered around her...they'd done that all morning since seven. She planned on leaving at eight, but considered leaving earlier if they didn't back off and give her a bit of breathing room.

They cared and would worry about her after she left. She understood that, but they acted as if she was going to the moon instead of touring the eastern seaboard and the Gulf coast.

"And don't forget to take pictures when you're in Hamilton. Maybe you can meet Jenny Doan." Phillip hovered at her elbow. Hamilton, Missouri had become a quilting Mecca in the last ten years. The Doan family had helped revitalize the small community with their quilting business. People made trips to the place like people planned trips to DC or Graceland. If you were a quilter, Hamilton was the place to go.

"I'll be doing that on the way home, Phillip. I'm sure you'll have to remind me a few weeks from now. I may forget." Shannon teased the man who lingered close to her side.

"Forget! Sacrilege! You won't forget! Huh!"

"Calm down, you'll blow a gasket, darling," Justin said as he embraced his husband. For a moment they lingered in each other's arms, giving Shannon time to slip away from the second floor to the first.

"You have enough food to last you for the day?" Susan caught her in the kitchen.

"I've got enough food in that cooler to probably last three days, Sus." Shannon tried to make her way unimpeded by well-meaning friends to the front door and her car.

"You have our numbers in that cell of yours, right?" Bea followed Shannon and Susan as they walked.

"I do and emergency numbers for the places I plan to visit."

"Check the weather every day. Don't drive into any storms. And watch out for hurricanes down there in Texas." Justin got in the last word over Bea's shoulder.

"Oh, for the love of…" Shannon grumbled—mentally so as not to hurt feelings— as the group followed close behind, still offering advice.

"I think you're going to do too much." Bea held up one hand, this being an old argument since Shannon announced her itinerary. "But hey, I'm not the one driving. Or paying the gasoline bill." Bea rolled her eyes at that.

"I'm not racing anywhere. Not like when I moved here from Montana. I'm going to take my time and enjoy the sights along the way." Shannon neared the door finally. The only one she had yet to see was Michael. He'd be close, but hovering wasn't his way.

"Can I please get to my car?" Shannon stopped at the door and turned to face two men and two women who'd become quite dear to her. "I love you all, and for your sake as well as my own, I promise to take all precautions." She held up her hand to forestall Justin's open mouth, coming question. "Yes, I have my gun and license to carry it concealed. I took those Krav Maga-style classes you told me about, Bea, and I feel confident I can handle myself in all but a dire situation. I'll fight like hell if I can't escape first. And we'll do a Zoom conference video every day. Satisfied?"

Four heads did the bobble bounce, but that didn't prevent them from stepping forward when she turned the door knob.

"Give me a few minutes to say goodbye to Michael? Alone? Then you can gather on the porch, so I can wave to you all at the same time." She phrased that carefully but meant that they could all wave to her at the same time. Again the bobble heads nodded. She held up one finger and promised, "Give me a few."

Stepping on to the shaded porch, she breathed deeply. The weather was cooler now in late September, a sign that winter might arrive sooner than expected. The sugar maple leaves glowed a bright array of reds and oranges, while most of the oak leaves were brown. Today the air was crisp, clean, and refreshing.

Michael sat in one of the Adirondack chairs, his hands tucked into the pockets of a padded sleeveless vest. Like her, he preferred long shirt sleeves when the temperature turned cooler. The dark green vest looked good on him, against the deep blue shirt.

"You manage to shake loose of that crowd?" He spoke without looking at her, a tiny hint of sarcasm in his tone.

"Don't make fun of them, Michael," Shannon said gently. "They mean well."

"They care for you, and that makes the difference." He relented and lifted a gentle smile her way.

"Yeah, it does. I have no one left in this world, so those four—well, five including you—are all I have. We've been through a lot together already, and I've known you all less than a year."

"It's quality, not quantity," Michael quipped as he moved to her side.

Shannon slipped an arm around his waist. "I'll miss you all, but I know you'll be here waiting when I return."

"You better believe it." Michael returned her embrace with a firm hug across her shoulders.

She could have sworn she felt a kiss touch the top of her head, but then...Nah, Michael wasn't... Not that she wished he had kissed… What confusing thoughts her mind could create here just as she was leaving.

"Now you better let that pack out of the door 'cause they're leaving nose prints on the window panes."

With a sudden burst of laughter, she gave him another quick hug, then yelled, "Are you lot going to see me off or hide inside all day?"

The four practically fell out of the door and rushed to hug Shannon.

"Take care."

"Check the weather!"

"Safe journey."

"Drive carefully."

Michael walked her to the car and closed the door, while the others spread out along the porch and steps. "Hurry home," he whispered.

"You better believe it." Shannon echoed back his words before she drove off, four of the five waving like crazy people, while one stood calmly with his hands tucked in his pockets, a slight lift of his lips making her smile.

———

Shannon kept a journal of her trip. Each evening she shared what she'd seen or done with the family, as she thought of them. They often had more questions than she had answers. Now and then she missed one of the group. Michael would be working a case. Justin was meeting a client. Phillip was at a quilt guild meeting. No one but those five knew her itinerary so whoever wanted to hurt her was out of luck. He or she would have to wait for Shannon to come home.

In Philadelphia she visited the Pennsylvania Academy of

Fine Arts and enjoyed a wonderful afternoon there. No visit to Philly would be complete without going to Independence Hall and seeing the Liberty Bell. She noticed a hush fell over the group as they entered the rooms filled with the history of the nation's beginnings. The last evening before she left, she walked along Penns Landing, laughed, ate, and had a great time with so much to do.

"Three days in Washington DC just aren't enough, guys," Shannon said one evening as she lay across her hotel bed, using her iPad for the evening video conference.

"Stay longer then," Justin advised.

"Or just see the things that are most important to you," Michael suggested.

"See as much as you want," Bea put in. "This time of year the place isn't so crowded though you missed a great show by the Marine band out by the Marine Memorial."

"I just got here, and I'm totally overwhelmed by the history of the place," Shannon sighed. "I thought it was over the top just visiting Independence Hall, but everywhere you turn here is something important."

"What would you like to see the most, Shannon," asked practical Susan.

"Well, I looked over a few lists of sites this afternoon after I checked in." Shannon shuffled several brochures before she found the list she made. She looked it over for a few seconds, then admitted, "I guess what I really want to see are the memorials like Lincoln's and the Vietnam Wall. I want to walk through the National Cathedral and the Library of Congress. How inspiring those must be." She pulled up another brochure and showed it to the group. "I could spend a week in the Smithsonian alone," she wailed. "I'll have to pick and choose there and only see what I think is most interesting, though to be honest, it all looks interesting." She paused to arrange the notes and brochures in a tidy stack. "I think I want to honor those who allowed me the freedom to drive through our nation and stop wherever I want. I'll for sure visit Arlington, the Marine Corp War memorial, the Three Soldiers statue commemorating the Vietnam War and the Women's Memorial statue there on the Mall."

"Hey, Shannon, a suggestion?"

"Sure Phillip, what's that?"

"You go see what you want to see, sweetheart, and don't worry about anything else. Make this trip about you."

"Thanks. Love you guys." Shannon closed the video connection and fanned out the brochures before her. "I think this is going to be a memorable stop."

———

Not every town got an extended visit, but Shannon did stop in Richmond, Virginia. She got there early in the day and made her way to the Lewis Ginter Botanical Gardens. A walk over the grounds eased her tired muscles and refreshed her fuzzy brain. Like her drive from Cut Bank to Auburn, you can only go so far before you have to do something outside. When she left the gardens, she hopped on a two hour trolley tour of the beautiful old city. By the time she returned to the car, she was ready to check in to the hotel and find dinner. Calling for a hotel room a day or two ahead of her arrival had worked out great so far.

She had booked a room at the historic Jefferson Hotel. The sight of the lobby took her breath away. When asked if she wanted to enjoy the Sunday Champagne buffet she jumped at the opportunity just to enjoy the facilities. As beautiful as the gardens and city tour was, this hotel blew her mind with its magnificence.

"Jacob, you'll never believe where I am now," Shannon muttered to her absent husband as a waiter ushered her to her seat on buffet Sunday.

Though she didn't take photos while in the buffet she did take discreet photos of the hotel to share with the family.

"Well, I never." Bea oohed and aahed over the photos Shannon texted. "Do people really live like that?"

"I don't know. I just passed through for a day or so and almost suffered from the extravagance," Shannon admitted. "This place is pretty spectacular. I suspect it's more of a *once in a life-time thing* for most folks."

"I'll say," Susan admitted.

"Onward to Charleston and Savannah. Talk about history!" Shannon shut down the iPad for the day, then took the elevator to the lobby where she sipped a drink and watched the world go by.

———

"That was so cool!" Shannon couldn't talk fast enough to tell the family about the walking tour she took that afternoon. "And I'm taking the other two. Walking lets you get right down on the ground level of Charleston."

"Now what kind of tour did you say you went on today?"

"I did the Ladies of Charleston today—women who were around the area like the pirate Anne Bonny and a ghost. The guide really knows her stuff."

"So, what kind of tour are you taking tomorrow?" Phillip asked.

"Another walking tour with this same woman—this time it's the Love Stories of Charleston. All about loooovvvee," she drawled.

"Oh, go on with you," Michael snorted. "You sound like my granny. She grew up in the South, and believe me, there's darn little romantic about hot weather, humidity, and mosquitoes big enough to carry off the family cat."

"Ignore him, will you. What's the last tour?"

Shannon suspected she'd caught Susan's romantic side. "Let's see—it's the High Society tour. With high tea and all. The guide said I could leave my hoop skirts at home."

While Bea gurgled in disbelief, Susan clapped her hands in delight. "What fun!"

———

"This is the coziest hotel I've ever seen. Well, not that I've seen a ton of them, but this is like being in a B&B and in Savannah, Georgia of all places. It's lovely. The Ballastone looks like a three story home from the sidewalk. But it's amazing. Old and lovely. The place reminds me of Mon Coeur. Oh, not in Mon Coeur's style or anything but just so welcoming." Shannon heaved a sigh and propped up on her elbows, her hands clasped under her chin. Tonight only Bea and Susan were on the video call. The guys had things to do. "Guess they're tired of me calling and gushing every night."

"Don't think that for a second, sweetheart. They're just busy this evening. They enjoy your calls as much as we do," Susan assured her.

"Some of them more than others," Bea quipped from somewhere out of sight.

"What did she say?"

"Nothing that needs to be or should be repeated." Susan made a fake slap at her partner.

"So, what's on the agenda for tomorrow?"

"I thought I'd do another historical tour. Those seem to do the best for me to get an overall view of the city. Then I'm going to Forsyth Park to see that famous fountain. I think there's a Farmers Market there tomorrow as well." She paused to check a brochure. "Yes, Saturday there's a Farmers Market, then a concert in the park that evening. I'll use Uber to get around. The streets in the older part of Savannah are a bit too narrow for me."

"Remember what we told you about Uber. Don't get in until you make the driver say who he's there to pick up, that his photo matches the one on your text notice and that the license plate number matches. I'd share the ride if I were you, but then you never know who you might be getting in a legal cab with." Susan gave one of Bea's airy queen waves and signed off. "See you tomorrow. Stay out of trouble, and have fun."

"Yes, Mother."

"Oh, you," followed by Susan's gentle laughter.

———

For the next few days, Shannon drove through Jacksonville, Florida and turned west through Pensacola. She did stop at Destin beach to admire the white sand. She'd read somewhere that the sand here was white, but the sand along the Texas coast was more tan. She had time to find out if that was true or not. Because she started so early in the day, she got to Natchez, Mississippi before dark, checked into her room and fell asleep right after she texted the family to say she was sorry, but she was too pooped to share that evening. For the next few minutes, texts returned telling her not to worry about it and get some rest.

By morning she rose refreshed and ready to enjoy the day. The first thing she wanted to do was tour the hotel…a small historical place called the Monmouth, a 19th century antebellum home turned hotel. The lush grounds impressed her, and she spent the morning outside. For the south, the later part of September remained warm. She'd shed her heavier clothes when she got to Savannah, so Capri pants and a light weight shirt were the dress of the day.

After consulting the front desk at the Monmouth, she took the Red morning home tour that included the Concorde Quarters and Sweet Auburn, saving Brandon Hall for after lunch. The next day she drove to Longwood, a most unusual, octagonal-shaped home. The home was unfinished, the craftsmen working just as the Civil War broke out. The men literally left their tools where they lay and made for the North where most of them came from. Shannon marveled at how workers in the mid-1800s could build such a structure that still stood well over a hundred years later.

For her final visit she toured Stanton Hall. The hall echoed of generations past. History weighed heavily in the halls and rooms.

Studying her digital map, she let the cell phone and Google plot a course to Baton Rouge on through to New Orleans. That afternoon she sent the family a text with a photo taken from the balcony outside her bedroom. The balcony overlooked the French Quarters.

"I can literally walk to the Quarters from my hotel, guys. It's really cool."

"Where are you this time?" Justin kept track of her trip

and the various hotels. "This one will have to be something special if it beats the Ballastone in Savannah."

"The Omni Royal Orleans. This is a great place, but so far the Ballastone has them all beat."

"A tour and then what?" Michael asked.

"Not sure. Just got here and took a Coke out on the balcony. Kicking back, you know?"

"I can understand that. Too many places. Too many faces. Too much of too much," he said in a quiet easy voice. "I've been in a similar situation. After awhile, you just want to sit alone and breathe."

"Yeah, that's about it," Shannon said with a hearty sigh. She took a last slurp of her Coke and propped her feet on the iron railing. "Okay, guys and girls, kicking back for the evening. I'll call tomorrow. Love you."

———

The drive from New Orleans along I10 wasn't interesting. Heavy traffic even in the morning hours often slowed traffic. Shannon always used her GPS to maneuver around central town traffic when she traveled. This time she set the GPS for New Orleans to Galveston and picked the route that did not go through Houston. The town was famous for its massive amount of traffic at all hours of the day and night.

She drove through a number of smaller towns, skirting along the edge of Galveston Bay. Somewhere south of Texas City she entered traffic on I45, almost directly across the causeway leading to the island. She wanted to look at the water but had to pay attention to her driving, being as she had never been there before…other than as a child.

The voice of her GPS took her along Broadway, then

turned off onto Sixty-First Street. As she topped the rise and turned on to Seawall Boulevard for the first time, the Gulf of Mexico spread out before her as far as she could see. She'd driven along Lake Erie and Lake Ontario on her way to Auburn, but that wasn't as impressive. Fearing she'd cause an accident while trying to take in the view, she pulled into a restaurant parking lot, locked the car and made her way carefully across the wide boulevard until she stood on what she knew was a seawall, a wide deep concrete barrier that protected the city behind her from rising water during storms. She'd read several books about the island before she came.

With wind blowing strong enough to twist her hair in several directions at once, she took several photos and texted them to the family. "In Galveston. Gulf is gorgeous. Tan sand. Not like Destin beach at all. Good breeze. Not hot. Glad I came."

She walked up and down the seawall for several blocks before returning to the car. When she did, she saw that she'd missed a call. "Probably never heard it because of the traffic and the wind." She hit re-dial. In the quiet of the car, Michael's voice almost boomed, it was so loud by comparison.

"So, it's all you expected?" He shuffled some papers as they spoke. She heard the rustle.

"So far. I didn't expect to be so awed by the sight of the Gulf. I mean, Ontario is wide enough that you can't see the other side. I think it's just the thought that this goes on for miles and miles. Being late September and a Monday morning there's not a great deal of traffic, so I can maneuver around without too much hassle. The Voice keeps me on track." *The Voice* was what she called the female voice on her GPS map.

"Wish I could see it again—the Gulf. I was born in Alabama north of Mobile. We used to go to the beach a lot."

"Bet you had that white sand like Destin. It's all brown or tan here."

"What's next now that you're there?"

"This time I'm not staying at a historical hotel. I wanted one that's tall and offers a great view. I booked a week at the San Luis. Besides there's an IHOP right near it, according to the map." She giggled because she'd become addicted to the restaurant's menu. "You'd think I'd order room service with champagne all the time, but that's not how I've lived. It's plain and simple for me. Fancy is a treat."

"More people with money should be like that."

"You're working a case?" She changed the subject, diverting the conversation away from her.

"Almost finished with a big one. Murder and kidnapping."

"Wow! Hope they paid you well."

"They did as a matter of fact."

She listened to the pleasant sound of his laughter and heard papers thump as if he were straightening them up. "I miss home. And all of you."

"You've been gone a long time. I'd say the feeling is mutual. We miss you, too, even if you call each evening." His chair squeaked as if he leaned back in it.

"I've still got things I want to do. I'll be home by mid-October and that includes my side trip to Hamilton. Phillip would kill me if I miss that."

"True. But he'd be happier to see you home once again."

"Home." Shannon sighed and adjusted her rear-view

mirror, so she could see the rolling water behind her. "I guess home is where you make it. Home is Mon Coeur and all that it entails now. Montana seems a million years ago."

"If you travel long enough, then when your heart finds a place it wants, you have to stick with it. Otherwise the heart won't be happy anywhere else."

"Sounds like you should know."

"The Army sent me a lot of places far from Alabama. Once detached, I never really wanted to return to the South. I met some former Army buddies, and they persuaded me to come north to New York. I set up shop— the PI work—with one of them, and we did a hell of a business."

"Where's your buddy now?"

"Did you know that even private investigators can be killed on the job," he asked softly.

"Oh, Michael, I'm sorry."

"It was a long time ago, but I never forget that I can die just as easily during an investigation as anywhere else. The odds of me dying in an accident might be greater than being shot, but there you are, the hazards of the job."

"You take good care of yourself. I'll be very angry with you if you die before I get home."

"Yes, ma'am. You and Aunt Bea are the few that I can say that, too. These folks around here think of *ma'am* and *sir* as insults."

"I've noticed that! I wasn't raised to say that necessarily, but I do once in awhile, and yes, they do look at you funny."

"I save things like that for those who don't get their feathers ruffled."

Shannon opened her mouth to continue the conversation, but Michael interrupted her.

"Sorry, Shannon, another call is coming in, and it's the client's lawyer. I have to take it."

"Go ahead. We can visit anytime. I'm so glad you called. Talk to you later."

"You bet. Bye now." A click and she was alone in the car.

———

"There are so many things to do here!" Shannon said that evening in her nightly conference call. She sat Indian style in the middle of a king size bed, pillows propped up behind her.

"Well, you can't do it all!" Bea was always one to insert reality. But she never passed up a good time.

"You can try though." Susan nudged her partner out of the way. Sweet Susan encouraged at every opportunity.

"Didn't you say you had a drink over the water this afternoon?" Phillip had several pins in his mouth, and Shannon had to interpret his question. He insisted on working on a quilt while talking.

"That was fun. Mom told me about this place. She didn't always talk about her childhood, but she mentioned a few places that were special to her. This is a huge souvenir shop called Murdocks. It's on stilts at the water's edge, and when you sit on the porch, you're over the water. It's a wide porch with chairs and those telescope things you can use to see ships or even some drilling platforms. Now and then birds fly by, but they don't come on to the porch often. I had to put on a jacket, the breeze going through that open area was chilly. Lots of humidity, the concierge said. Not something we dealt with in Montana."

"And you drank?" Justin wanted to know if drinks were the same all over the states.

"Schmirnoff Ice. Boy, it tasted good but only made me hungry. I decided to check in at that point if I could. I still had a few hours before *official* check-in, but they had my room ready. When I checked in, I moved everything out of the SUV and into the room since I'm staying for awhile. Then I changed, walked through the hotel and down the walk to IHOP. And I do mean *down*. The walk to the restaurant is way down. The San Luis sits high on top of some former military bunker from World War II if I remember correctly. Anyway, the view is fabulous. And I have a lot planned for the next few days."

"So everything is good? No troubles?" Michael asked.

She knew what he meant. Had anyone bothered her, such as trying to kill her? "All good, M."

"Well, I'll be damned." Shannon came out to get her car and discovered someone had jimmied the gas cap open. Something grainy lay around the bottom of the gas intake hole. She touched a finger to it and smelled, but the granules smelled like gas to her. The next step was getting the concierge to call a Subaru place and having the SUV towed to a dealership and repaired. The dealership could arrange a loaner car at the same time. Thankfully, she'd left nothing in the SUV that would tempt someone to break in.

The only thing this did, besides piss her off, was delay her exploration. Thankfully, she'd made no reservations to be anywhere that morning. Before she returned to the concierge though she called Michael on FaceTime.

"What's up?" Michael took one look at her face and changed the question, also snapping to attention. "What's wrong?"

"Someone pried open the gas cap on the SUV and poured something into the tank. At least I think they did. Looks like they did. Let me show you." She turned the phone away from her and showed him what the damage looked like. "I smelled those granules, but they just smell like gas. There's not a lot of them, and they might have melted in the liquid, so I'm thinking sugar and salt. Probably not sand. Whatever it is, it's going to cost a fortune to repair, and the insurance company is going to get tired of me filing claims."

"Piss on the insurance company," Michael said unexpectedly. "I'm more worried about why anyone would pick out your particular vehicle and do that kind of damage. It's not permanent, but it does detract you from any agenda. You'll have to rent a car now. This won't be a fast repair, I'm thinking."

"Why me?"

"Wealth. Revenge. Jealousy. The need to protect a secret...there are any number of reasons. We've gone over this. Do you want me to come down there?"

Shannon rubbed her head where a headache started. "Too early in the morning for this kind of shit. Gives me a headache. Look, I'm headed back to the concierge to get the help I need. I think things will be okay. I'll get a loaner and keep my eyes open and my gun handy. Will that do for now, M?"

Clearly Michael wasn't happy with her decision, but he didn't argue. "Call me if you need anything. File a police report, and take photos. Keep me in the loop on what they say about your car. Please."

"Sure thing. And for now we'll keep this between us. Can we do that? So the others won't worry?"

"I think we can, but they won't be happy if something happens to you as a result of your car being messed with."

"We'll handle it if that situation arises. I'll call you later and let you know what the dealership says."

Later that afternoon Shannon called Michael again. "This is a new one on me. I've heard of putting sugar or salt in a gas tank. Vandals do it quite often, but I've never heard of adding bleach. Bleach corrodes the engine while sugar simply clogs the filters. I suppose if you can't run the car 'cause of the blocked filters, that gives the bleach time enough to do its damage. Geez, what a mess."

"So, they're going to repair the car?"

"Replace the gas tank and filters and flush the entire system. And add a lock to the gas cap."

"Did you file a police report?"

"The concierge—a guy named Douglas—called them for me as well as the Subaru dealer on the mainland. The wrecker took it to a city called Clear Lake."

"You have a loaner?"

"Yes, a larger SUV—an Ascent. Too big for me, but I'll only have it a few days. I've still got lots of places to see before I head down the coast."

"What are you going to do about a hotel when you leave Galveston?"

"Oh, I think I'll wing it," Shannon said blithely, knowing he'd have a fit.

"Shannon—"

"Talk to you later, Michael."

Each day she toured the city, enjoyed a cool drink at Murdocks, and walked the beach, dancing with the tide at the water's edge.

One day she set out for the Strand, a section of the city on the bay side, rather than the Gulf side. The Strand consisted of several blocks, filled with interesting shops. She spent the day there, walking from the Railroad Museum with its life-like figurines positioned around the lobby down the blocks and into various shops. She bought little to nothing. For one thing, she simply didn't want to carry bags around with her. She wore her purse across her body and watched the people as they came toward her. She avoided crowded places.

Around two she returned to the car and made her way to the piers behind the Strand. First she'd have a late lunch at Willie G's, a restaurant the hotel waitress and concierge said served an excellent meal. Nearby was the Pier 21 Theater with its 1900 storm exhibit. She'd read about the storm—a huge hurricane—that practically wiped Galveston off the map just after the turn of the century. Nearby too was the sailing ship, Elissa.

She sent a number of texts with photos to the family, and the discussion that evening was lively. Shannon ticked off the places and things she still wanted to do, noting that she might finish up about the time her stay at the San Luis ended. By then she'd be ready to travel down the coast.

"And things are going well?" Michael asked a loaded question, knowing Shannon would pick up his meaning.

"Going well. Things should pick up tomorrow." Her

innocent sounding answer would let him know her SUV would be ready the next day.

"Take care, and sleep well then."

The others wished her a good night, and the conversation ended. However, Michael called back almost immediately, using FaceTime so they could see each other. "So, you'll pick up the car tomorrow? What time?"

"Late afternoon. They're also going to detail it. I understand that's important when you live along the coast. The salt can corrode the paint and parts."

"True. If you ever see some rust bucket of a car or truck go by, you'll know that driver doesn't visit the car wash often enough. Let me know when you have your wheels back."

"Will do."

The next day Shannon rode all the way to the end of Seawall Boulevard to where she could see the ship channel. The channel ran up to Houston. Galveston used to be the shipping magnet for the Gulf coast but now specialized in cruise ships, while Houston was now the port of choice for shipping. From there she headed back toward the island but turned north onto Ferry Road. Once she parked, she waited with others and several dozen cars for the next ferry to load. Aboard, she waited for the all clear before moving to the front of the ferry. The ferry carried passengers and vehicles from the island to Bolivar. A walk-on guest could stay on the ferry and return, a pleasant trip she discovered, especially after spotting a pod of dolphins keeping pace alongside the ferry.

Once she returned to her car, she drove down Seawall Boulevard to a German-looking restaurant called Millers where she enjoyed a delicious meal of shrimp and grits. She ordered the meal, hoping it wouldn't be nasty, but the dish turned out to be flavorful and not at all what she expected.

The last thing on her schedule that day before getting her SUV back was going on the Pleasure Pier, a long pier out over the water, filled with rides and entertainment. Though she didn't do any of the rides she did enjoy walking around, seeing what the vendors offered. She could imagine the summer months and this place packed with families. In the slight chill of an October afternoon, the less crowded pier suited her just fine, though a few times she imagined eyes on her. Then again security cameras abounded. Someone always watched those on the pier.

Ever so glad to get her ride back, she finished off the day with room service, so that she'd have time to read and update her journal. She'd done so many things in the last few days that she'd not written anything since her car required repairs. That still puzzled her. The police said vandalism wasn't all that common on the island, and whoever did it took a risk, as there are so many security cameras around the hotels. Still the damage was done, and Shannon took more precautions than usual.

She ventured to a small café and bakery called Sunflower near the Medical Center for a breakfast of bread pudding French toast the next morning. As she ate, she watched students come and go, one young doctor visiting with his parents who came from India to see him. Shannon couldn't help but overhear their conversation as the three sat at the table behind her.

This being her last full day on the island she wanted to visit a museum called The Bryan, eat lunch at the oldest drug store on the island called the Star Drug store—it was back toward the Strand. And finish off the afternoon by taking in Moody Gardens and its three pyramids.

Once again, she cut short the evening conference call. "Pooped."

Her last day on the island, she checked out after the concierge made arrangements for her car to be brought to the front entrance. A bellboy loaded her bags and totes, and she tipped him and the concierge well before driving away.

This morning she'd spend driving through the neighborhoods. Her mother never said much about where she grew up but said she lived in an area north of Broadway between 45th and 53rd. With no more information than that, she turned on to 45th street from Seawall Boulevard and drove slowly down until a block before Broadway, then she turned west and began slowly weaving her way along the streets from 45th to 53rd , back toward the seawall, just to get some sense of what the area was like. To her surprise, most of the homes were older ones. Any one of them could have been the house in which her mother lived. A few hours of this and she sighed in satisfaction. Galveston appealed to her; she'd look for a place here maybe. If nothing else she might snag an air B&B next time. Get more of a home feeling.

Knowing she'd seen all she wanted for the time being, she headed down the seawall until the road dropped lower, and she could see the Gulf. The seawall ended, and those who lived past that were subject to rising water and storm damage during hurricanes. That thought stayed with her as she drove past homes built on stilts but still beautiful and expensive looking. That made no sense to her, but then she wasn't raised within the sound of surf nor did she particularly crave being near the Gulf at all times. "It's a tourist thing, I guess," she muttered as she sang with the radio and rode with the windows down.

———

She drove down the Bluewater Highway that ran alongside the Gulf. Her video conference call came from a hotel in Lake Jackson that night.

"I'm stopping in a town called Palacios tomorrow, just to see what it's like. It might be fun to have a place on the coast to come to during the summer. Or even this time of year. It's not bad at all," she added with a coy smile, knowing the first cold front had just hit their area of the Northeast.

"Rub it in, why don't you," Phillip said as he pulled a sweater closer across his chest. He coughed and rubbed his nose with the sweater sleeve.

"Oh, good lord, Phil, that's just nasty," came Justin's voice. A hand with a Kleenex came into view before Justin showed up, practically standing on his head, looking at Shannon over the top of Phillip's iPad. "He's got a cold and has turned into a big baby."

"Will you be okay, Phillip?" Illness of any kind worried Shannon. And being so far from home and not being able to help worried her.

"I'll live, don't worry. Justin's taking good care of me." That hand once more came into view, but this time Phillip clasped it and kissed the palm.

"Take care, everyone. I miss you all."

THE TRUTH COMES OUT

"Palacios isn't a big place," Shannon muttered, correctly pronouncing the name of the town of less than five thousand. She'd embarrassed herself that morning when asking for the best way to get to 'Pal a shoos'. The desk clerk refrained from laughing, but it took effort, she could tell.

A gas fill-up and she set off along the road, but her car started jerking. A tire warning light came on. Thankfully, she wasn't up to road speed yet, but there were few places along the side of the road at this point where she could pull off. She drove a quarter mile and spotted a house with a realtor sign out front. It wasn't For Sale; it was a sales office. She pulled the SUV into the parking lot and rolled her eyes.

"At least this isn't a man-made accident." She thumped the steering wheel. "Humm, I better let those folks know I'm not here to buy but need help. Maybe they can call someone for me."

Another car pulled in and parked, and a man got out. He

moved to the steps as well, but he waited for her to go in before him.

On the small porch she straightened her clothes, then opened the door and stepped into a pleasant room that served as a reception area. The man followed and closed the door.

"May I help you, ma'am?" asked a pretty woman probably close to Shannon's age.

Before Shannon could explain her problem and ask for help, a man's voice came from another room, apparently headed toward the front room as it got louder.

"Della, can you call Mr. Hawes and ask him to come in. I think I—"

"Jacob?" Shannon didn't sink slowly into a faint. She collapsed like a ton of bricks right there in the reception room.

Images flashed in and out of her mind. A big Lab and Jacob coming across the back yard. The two of them—Shannon and Jacob—standing at her parents' graves, Jacob supporting her as she wept. Another moment of weeping at their wedding. Tears of joy. Images fresh but not...

"Should I call an ambulance, Josh?" Shannon wasn't all there yet, but she heard voices in the darkness of her mind.

"I don't think so. I think she just fainted. She didn't hit anything on the way down, but we'll wait until she comes around and see if we need to call for help."

Shannon heard a man's voice—one so familiar that her heart ached. A dear voice. A precious voice. But one that didn't know her, it seemed.

"Miss, wake up." Someone gently tapped her cheek. Her ears woke up fully before her eyes, but then she really didn't want to open her eyes and see that the man she thought was her long-lost husband was in fact a stranger that just looked and sounded a lot like Jacob. Her heart overruled her eyes, and she slid them open just enough to see a man leaning over her.

His eyes—they belonged to Jacob. The worried expression—that was Jacob. True, this man was fifteen years older than the last time she saw Jacob Waller, but if this wasn't her husband, then it was his twin. Either way, Shannon needed answers.

Her eyes opened enough, then opened so wide they seemed to dry out from staring. Visually checking the man beside her. Her heart straining to find the truth of the moment.

"You okay? You took a hard header to the floor." The Jacob-looking man knelt beside her, one hand on her arm. "Can you sit up? Let's get you to a chair, all right?" He stood and offered her a hand up, holding her elbow as she stared at him, never taking her eyes off his face.

Once settled into a chair in the front room, he gave the receptionist instructions. "Della, close the office for the day, and draw the shade. We've got a problem here. This lady may need help."

The man who followed Shannon in turned up both hands, palm forward. "I'll come back later. Hope you're okay, lady." He left and closed the door behind him, and Della turned the lock. She flipped the Welcome sign around and closed the blinds on the door and both windows facing the front porch and parking lot.

"Should I stay, Josh?" Della asked.

"I think it best if you do, please. And could you get a glass of water?" When she returned, he took the glass of water Della handed him and passed it on to Shannon, holding her hands, so she'd not spill any. Her hands shook like volcano tremors, and she only got a sip.

"Enough," she managed to say behind a hand that shook but wiped her chin. "Thank you." Still she stared at the man sitting to her left. "You look…" She shook her head, wondering if she only imagined this. Once again, she focused on the man, looked him over carefully from head to toe. Finally, she shook her head and tried to explain despite a pounding heart, hands that shook, and legs as limp as wet noodles.

She'd imagined Jacob returning—every night for fifteen years. She'd dreamed of him coming home. She'd prayed he'd return and explain away years of loneliness and dread.

"I have a flat tire. New tires but then who knows … I heard your voice, then saw you and…" She held up both hands and shrugged. "This makes no sense. It's unbelievable. Impossible."

The receptionist looked scared, took a step away from Shannon as if she were an escapee from a mental ward. Jacob, or Josh as the woman called him, certainly understood no better than his receptionist. Shannon sounded like a mad woman. She questioned whether she might have actually lost her senses and created a living nightmare.

But looking at the man across from her, she knew for certain he was Jacob Waller, no matter the years or what name he now used. But why? How?

She fumbled her words, halted, stared at the man, then staggered on with an explanation that would make sense to the other two. "I grew up in Montana. I married there, and my husband is Jacob Waller. I'm Shannon Waller. Fifteen years ago, Jacob set off for Bismarck but never made it to the hotel that night. The police searched for him, but in all this time, no one's ever found him or the Volkswagen he was driving. I've never given up hope that Jacob was alive —somewhere. And I've never asked that he be declared legally dead either. I've since moved to New York State and am down here visiting along the Gulf coast. So, I walk in here today, two thousand miles from Cut Bank, Montana and find a man who is *my husband*." One hand rested on her chest, above her heart and the other rubbed her pounding temple. With a dry mouth and hope, she gave him an inquisitive stare. "How do you explain that?"

"Your story is unique, I'll say that. Let me introduce myself," the man said cautiously. "My name is Joshua Caldwell. Everyone calls me Josh. I wasn't born in Texas. Mom told me I was born in North Dakota, but we moved to Texas after my dad died. Mom passed away a year ago."

Shannon's shoulders sagged. "I was so certain. I mean, how likely is it that I'd find my husband with all his little eccentricities this far away from home."

"What do you mean by *eccentricities*?" Della took the glass from Shannon and eased into the other chair.

"Jacob had a bad heart. One of the flaps over a heart valve leaked, so he had to rest now and then, but he stayed active otherwise. He had a scar that ran down the back of his leg from mid-thigh to mid-calf where he battled with barbed wire and lost. It took forever for his dad to cut that wire away from him. And then there's the tattoo." By now Shannon saw her memories and not the two nearby. But the loud silence and odd expression on the man's face caught her attention.

"What's wrong?" She feared she said something to make him think her some kind of nut case.

"What…kind…of…tattoo?"

"Uh, a dog. A tiny tattoo beneath his heart. The word *Trip* over it. He cried so when that Lab died. The next day he drove into Shelby and came back with that little tattoo. He mourned for the longest time, but he'd found a poor little kitty not long before the dog died and that helped. We named the cat Simon."

"Della, would you call Katie, and ask her to come to the office? When she gets here, you can go home. I'll explain things when I see you next."

"Sure thing, Josh." Della returned to her desk and dialed a landline. She spoke softly, then nodded to Josh. "She's on her way. She said she'd drop the kids off at her mom's house."

"Thanks, Della."

The receptionist remained at her desk but gathered up her jacket and purse and pulled the keys out, ready to leave.

Ten minutes by the clock behind her desk, a car pulled into the parking lot. A door closed, and Shannon heard the sound of running feet. Whoever was coming slammed into the locked door.

"Damn! Sorry, Katie, I forgot to unlock the door. Coming," Della called out as she hustled around the desk and threw the lock.

"Josh, what happened? Della said there was something important that couldn't wait. She sort of scared me," Katie Caldwell sank into the chair that Della used, without so much as acknowledging Shannon. The woman focused totally on her husband.

Josh rose, motioned Della toward the door, and locked it once she was outside. He returned to kiss his wife, then sat and introduced Shannon. "Katie, I seem to have a twin in this world. Or maybe not. This is Shannon…?"

"Waller, Mrs. Caldwell. Shannon Waller." She provided her name, but let the man finish whatever he planned on saying to his wife.

"Mrs. Waller," Katie said with a nod in her direction. Immediately she turned back to her husband. "What's this about a twin…or not?"

"First off, tell Shannon about me. About the things on my body."

"What? That's personal, Josh." Katie Caldwell protested as she cut a nasty glance at Shannon.

"I know, sweetheart, but just this one time, it's okay. And it's important."

Katie shook her head, but Josh asked her once more. "Please, Katie?"

"What do you want to know?"

"Why did the military refuse me when I wanted to enlist?"

She gave him an *are you crazy* kind of frown. "You have a bad heart."

"In what way?"

"Well, you'll need heart surgery sooner or later to replace an incomplete heart value that leaks. Leaves you short of breath once in awhile, so you have to sit down and rest."

One hand moved up to cover Shannon's mouth. The other bunched up into a fist, but she remained quiet. Once again, her heart pounded, but this time her chest hurt while sweat broke out across her face.

"Any distinguishing marks on my body?"

"Really, Josh, this is insane," Katie almost jumped up, but her husband reached out and caught her arm.

"It's important, Katie."

"You keep saying that, but I don't see how telling a stranger about you can be important."

"But it is, Mrs. Caldwell," Shannon said softly. "Very important, after so very long."

That caught Katie's attention, the sincerity with which Shannon spoke. She calmed and sat, holding her husband's hand and watching him, not Shannon, as she continued.

"Well, uh, Josh has a long scar down the back of his leg. Cut it on some tin, his mother said, when he was a kid. And there's that damn dog tattoo. Mary—that's Josh's mother— said he had a dog when he was a kid. Adored the thing. Back in those days, itinerant farm hands passed through during planting and picking seasons. One of them did tattoos and offered to put one on Josh's chest, so he'd always remember his favorite dog. Mary took one look at it and blew a gasket. Or so she said, but Josh wouldn't let her get it removed. He's had that under his heart since I've known him."

"And the dog's name tattooed there?"

"Trip."

Tears slid slowly from Shannon's eyes. Josh sat with an anguished expression, and poor Katie looked confused and scared.

"Tell me about your life in Montana," Josh asked quietly, reaching out to hold the hand of his confused wife while facing another, now certain of the facts.

Shannon sucked in her tears and a deep breath. She'd make the tale short but how to compress years into a few sentences? "I was born on Galveston Island, but Mom and Dad moved a lot when I was young. We wound up in Cut Bank, Montana. A guy showed up in elementary school one day. We became inseparable. Years later he told me he was going to marry me when we were old enough. My parents died in an accident. His mom was long dead. We got married. His dad died of a heart attack shortly afterwards. We wanted to live happily ever after as the last of our family lines." Shannon's breath hitched a little, and she swallowed. "Jacob had a dog named Trip, and just before it died, he found a cat. I named him Simon. Jacob worked in his dad's lumberyard. It went to his partner when Waller Senior died. Senior never changed his will to make Jacob a partner. I worked there for years as an accountant. Several years after we married Jacob took off for a meeting one winter. Bad timing all around. The weather turned foul unexpectedly. He never arrived at his destination. The police searched for him and his car that winter and the next spring after the thaw. No one reported seeing him, and we found nothing."

"I'm so sorry, Mrs. Waller," Katie whispered.

"I never asked the courts to declare him dead. I've always considered myself married until his body—dead or alive—showed up again. Through some strange circum-stances, I relocated to New York State and have a home there, though I've never given up looking for my husband. Until today." Shannon finished and sat back, her words gone, though tears still coursed in slow rivulets down her cheeks.

"What…what…do you mean *until today*?" Katie's face showed that she'd figured out the puzzle to the disappear-ance of Jacob Waller.

"I'm sorry, Mrs. Caldwell, but your husband Josh is my husband Jacob." Shannon said aloud what the other two suspected. She managed to stand and move across the room, away from the couple that had to absorb such a shock.

"That can't be," Katie yelled. She stood so fast her purse fell out of her lap.

"Please, honey, sit down, and let's talk this over." Josh tried to gather his wife into his embrace. Shannon moved aside to let him get to his wife easier.

Suddenly a loud shot went off, and the side window shattered. Josh cried out and collapsed. Shannon grabbed Katie and pulled her to the floor.

"Josh!"

"I'm okay, sweetheart, but I think I need an ambulance. The bullet hit low, and I bet it's still there." Josh moaned but tried to sound positive but sounding more like a man in pain.

"Katie, call 9-1-1. Josh, are you really okay, or are you trying to be a hero?" Shannon was both scared to death and mad as hell.

"No hero. I think I'll live, but this hurts like hell. Tell that ambulance to step on it, sweetheart."

Katie dialed the emergency number and gave directions while Shannon crawled into the bathroom Katie pointed out. She returned with towels that she pressed to Josh's side.

Before the ambulance arrived, he passed out.

While they waited, Shannon turned pressure duty over to Katie and scuttled to the side window. No sign of anyone. Marsh grass grew about four feet tall in the area next to the realtor office. Anyone could have been hiding there. The sales office sat along a fairly deserted road.

She reconstructed the scene in her mind, looking at the angles. She had to call Michael and get him down here. If her suspicions were correct, Josh Caldwell hadn't been the shooter's target. She was. By chance the guy with the gun missed her and hit Josh as he moved toward his wife and she took a step to one side so he could pass.

Drama abounds today, she thought, as the EMTs loaded Josh to rush him to the nearest hospital.

"He'll go by Life Flight to Corpus Christi Med Center in the Bay Area, ma'am," one man told Katie. "I understand that's where he goes for his heart checkups."

"Yes, we'll be right behind you," Katie said, her hands almost tied in knots she was twisting them so hard.

Together they watched the ambulance roar off, lights flashing.

Shannon turned to Katie and saw her head down in her hands, hard sobs wracking her body. She slipped an arm around the woman, terrified that this man they both loved might die before they could solve the puzzle of his identity.

"How can I help?"

"I need to let my mom know what happened, then I need to get to the hospital." Katie looked around as if she had no clue where to start, though she'd just outlined a good plan.

"My car has a flat tire. We'll use your car. Can you drive, or do you want me to?" Shannon guided Katie toward the cars.

"What? No, I'll drive."

"I'm coming with you. You'll need me, and there are questions that need answers."

"Okay. But let's get moving. It'll be dark before we get there. It's a good three hour drive, and we may hit traffic."

Katie turned into a whirlwind of determination. They sped to her mother's house where she offered quick introductions. She introduced the children, a boy age twelve, and a girl about ten. The boy resembled Waller Senior so much it was spooky. There was no denying who Josh Caldwell was anymore. Katie's mom said she'd take care of the kids, while Katie assured the two that their dad would be fine, but he might need that heart surgery the doctor had told him was coming.

"Those two live with the knowledge that their dad has a bum spot in his heart and will need heart surgery sooner or later. I bet with that hole just below his heart, the doctors will kill two birds with one stone and fix both the bullet hole and the bad heart value." Katie grabbed a sweater off her mom's coat rack and a jacket that she tossed to Shannon. "Hospitals are always cold. Germs don't like cold, therefore the place is always like a refrigerator. You'll need that."

"Okay if I text some information to a friend while you drive?"

"Sure, just don't bug me until I know Josh is going to be okay, then we can settle this who's-who thing. Okay?"

"Got it." By this time, Shannon figured Katie was working on auto-pilot. Her emotions would kick in when she stopped driving and found out about Jacob—Josh —whoever.

Her own emotions shredded by the discovery of her husband and now a severe if not fatal shooting left Shannon scared. Was that an accident? A hunting accident? Or did someone try to kill her and hit the man by mistake? Or was the shooter trying to kill Jacob? What a coincidence that this shooting happened just as she discovered her long-missing husband. Too many questions and no answers.

She sank into the passenger side of Katie's truck and pulled out her cell phone. She also pulled out the charging cord. Plugging it into the charger, she checked that Katie was doing okay, then pulled up Michael's number and started a series of texts, hoping he was available to get them tonight and come to help.

SW: 9-1-1 SOS-whatever gets ur attention. Found my husband! Need ur help here. Someone tried to shoot me and hit him. Going to hospital three hours away with his wife. Met his two kids.

Go to Mon Coeur. My bedroom. Get photo albums of me and Jacob in MT. Bring with you. Charter jet or whatever fastest way to get here. Will meet you at airport in Corpus Christi, Texas as soon as you get here. I'm scared, M.

Less than a minute later, Michael called. "Tell me you're all right?"

"I'm fine," Shannon said softly, wishing she'd added that she couldn't talk while in the truck with Josh Caldwell's wife.

"Tell me what happened?"

"Can't right now. Might disturb Josh's wife, Katie. She's driving. Understand?" Boy, she hoped he got the message.

"Oh…oh. Okay. Text me the details, and I'll get on to whatever you need. As long as you're okay." He sounded as scared as she felt.

"Yeah, that I can promise you. I'll send the info." The sound of Michael's voice helped steady her nerves. She wanted to borrow some of his calm so badly right then.

She pushed END on her cell and went back to texting, her hands still shaking bad enough that her fingers had trouble hitting the proper buttons.

SW: I had a flat and pulled into a realtor office lot. Deserted stretch of road along the coast. Man inside is Jacob. Have proof. His wife came. We were looking into details when a shot came through the side window

past me. I think the bullet was meant for me but hit this man instead. If he dies, this one is on me.

She hit the SEND button, then started a new text.

SW: Need investigators in Bismarck, ND checking a Mary Caldwell who lived there about fifteen years ago. Did she have a child? Living or dead? What about a husband? Alive? When did she leave? Did she take a child or older person with her? Follow that to Palacios, TX, and find out about her bk ground and everything you can about a man named Josh or Joshua Caldwell probably about thirty-two or thirty-three. Need info ASAP. Really need ur help.

Michael texted back immediately.

MS: Will get man I know in ND to check into Mary C. Will get another PI on Mary's trail in TX. Will arrive at CC airport tomorrow sometime. Will rent a jet—charge it to u Details to follow on flight when I know them. Rent a car. Better yet—stay at the hospital with lots of people around you. I'll rent car and come there. Deal?

The smiley face he added made Shannon smile, the only thing in hours that lifted her spirits.

SW: Deal

She hit SEND but immediately added:

SW: I really miss u rt now.

The back of her neck tightened with stress. Katie drove fast but not dangerously.

"How much longer?"

"At least another two hours."

"I'll pray for Jacob—I mean Josh. Sorry."

"I don't care what you call him right now as long as he lives," Katie said bitterly without taking her eyes off the road.

———

"Man, am I glad to see you!" Shannon fell into Michael's embrace in the hallway outside Josh Caldwell's ICU room. Emotions she didn't want to deal with flooded her as she stood within his warm firm hug. She wasn't alone, and that was more comfort right now than she'd had in hours. His calm presence and strength, his face…just Michael being there was enough for her.

"You're really okay?" Michael put his arm around her shoulder and led her to the small waiting room. No one sat there at the moment, so he dived into questions.

"Is this guy really your husband?"

"Yes, he has the heart value issue, the scar, and tattoo. He's Jacob Waller, all right. Did you bring the albums?"

"Yes. Bea wanted to come. Justin wanted to come. The whole damn family wanted to come. But I talked them into waiting, but you're going to have to call them soon, or they'll show up anyway."

"Hardheaded bunch, aren't they?"

"You could say that. But they care for you, and right

now they're worried you may never make it back home alive."

"I can agree with that. Frankly, M, I'm scared to death. Whoever went after me in Auburn must have a long reach. I honestly think I was the target of that shot. Jacob—Josh—got it when I moved so he could get to his wife." She propped an elbow on the arm of her padded chair and leaned her chin on her fist. Her body still shook now and then, whether from nerves or the chill of the place she didn't know or care. Slowly she leaned sideways until her head rested against Michael's shoulder. Comfort and safety, pure and simple, washed over her. Maybe other emotions she didn't want to deal with at the moment. Safe was good enough for now.

"When was the last time you ate or got some sleep?" Michael was ready to get whatever she wanted to eat. But all he got was a soft snort.

Leaning forward slightly he saw that she'd fallen asleep against his shoulder.

Pinned to the spot until she woke, he settled deeper into the seat. Shannon would have said he allowed his mind to rest. Things would work out.

———

"Shannon?" Someone shook her shoulder carefully. "Shannon?"

"Huh?" She woke slowly, her face resting against... Michael's shoulder. His head rested against the wall, and he slept. She eased up and patted his shoulder to work the crease out of it.

By way of introducing Michael to Katie, she touched his

shoulder to wake him. "This is my friend, Michael Silver. My partner in crime as they say."

Katie nodded and shook the hand Michael held out. She still looked distracted but not as frantic as the night before. "Josh is awake. Has been for awhile. We've been talking. Now he wants to talk to you."

Katie entered the room, and Shannon eased in quietly, not sure of her reception. If either of them figured out that Shannon was the target and not Josh, then they might try to bring some form of legal action against her. As it was, Shannon had already decided to pay whatever bill Josh might have after his insurance came through.

Michael stepped into the room with Shannon, introduced himself to Josh, and shook hands gently. "Nice to meet you but sorry about the circumstances." He eased back to stand next to Shannon.

"Josh, you look a lot better than the last time I saw you." Shannon spoke quietly as befitted a dim room and a man who just came through major surgery.

"Doctors did a jam-up job. Fixed that bullet hole in my side and the one in my heart. Doctor Foster said he was too close not to go in next door and do the job he knew I needed on my heart. Two birds—one stone, as they say." Josh sounded good, if weak.

"So, you'll be all right?" His health and well-being were Shannon's only concern right now.

"Doctor Foster says the nurses will have me up and walking tomorrow."

"You just had heart surgery!" Katie grabbed her husband's hand and squeezed his fingers hard enough that they turned white.

"Easy, Katie. That hurts."

"Sorry, love." Katie released her strangle hold on his fingers but kept hold of his hand.

"I need to get up. If I lay here too long, I might get pneumonia, and I'd rather hurt and walk than not be able to breathe." Josh clenched his wife's hand and laid it on the sheet. "And if I do well, I'll be home in less than ten days."

"Amazing." The miracles of medicine these days astonished Shannon. She thought Jacob/Josh would be in the hospital for several weeks if not a month. Who knew!

"Josh, how long will you be in ICU before you're moved to a private room?"

"Three days is the word I got. Josh was still asleep when the doctor told me." Katie answered for her husband.

"Okay, then let's do this. We've got to talk about this identity thing, but this isn't the best place. Or time with you right out of surgery. We'll meet you back here in three days in whatever room you're in, and we'll get this cleared up. In the meantime, M and I are going back to Palacios and get my car. We'll come back here, get a room, and meet up with you later. Before we leave though, have the police talked to you?"

"Standard procedure when a gunshot comes into the ER in Texas. We told them a shot came from the side of the office. We took cover and never saw the shooter or heard a vehicle leave," Katie said.

"Exactly. I suspect the police in your home town will have looked around the office just in case the shooter left any brass, foot or tire prints," Michael added.

"I guess." Katie shot M a confused look. Apparently, she wasn't sure how he fit into life with Shannon whom she'd met less than twenty-four hours earlier.

"We'll see you both in three days then. I'll call first to

make sure it's okay to visit." Shannon gathered her purse and motioned Michael out the door.

She didn't mention that Michael was a private investigator looking into Mary and Josh Caldwell's background. Or that other investigators were checking out the Caldwell's trail from North Dakota to Texas. Somewhere along the way, Jacob Waller became Josh Caldwell, and it wasn't by choice either, she'd bet.

———

"The shot came from that tall grass." Shannon pointed to the vacant lot when they arrived at the parking lot of Caldwell Realty in Palacios several hours later. She waited by the car while Michael reconnoitered the area, but he returned with no new information.

"Enough time's passed that even bent grass where he might have waited has straightened up. I found no casings, so this guy is smart. And I think he's a local. Our guy in New York must have contacts here too. Or else just hired muscle without giving any details."

"This is ridiculous, Michael. I can't go through life wondering when I'm going to be bushwhacked or someone takes a bullet for me."

Michael knelt by the car and examined the flat tire. "New tires don't usually have trouble unless someone sticks something in it, causing it to develop a slow leak. If you hadn't stopped for gas and weren't just getting up to speed afterwards, you'd have been cruising along at highway speed and had a blow-out, maybe sending you into a roll-over or something."

"So that tire isn't an accident."

"I can't be certain, but that's how I see it," Michael stood and dusted his hands. "Let's do what you were going to do the other day, go inside, and ask for help."

"Yeah, and I can let Della know that Josh is going to be all right."

———

Within forty-eight hours, Michael had gathered enough information from his associates to fill in the final picture of the Jacob-to-Joshua transformation. Part of what they knew was supposition, and only Mary Caldwell could have confirmed it. But Josh was truly Jacob Waller.

Nothing, however, got them any closer to knowing who wanted Shannon dead.

"Katie, how's Josh?" Shannon turned on the cell's speaker button so Michael could hear while he drove her car.

"Hi, Shannon. He's doing great. Hates getting up to walk using that tall walker, but after he's up he loves being able to move around. Of course, right now he can't go too far too fast, but he's getting stronger by the day."

"That's great news, Katie. Look, I need to speak to you both about what's going on. Can we visit you and Josh in his room?"

"We knew this was coming, Shannon. Yes, we need to figure this out. When will you be here?"

"Probably fifteen minutes? We just left the hotel, headed to the hospital. Good enough?"

"That works. See you in a few." Katie gave them the room number and disconnected.

"I'm not looking forward to this." Shannon fixed her

gaze out the front window but saw nothing in particular. Her mind's eye, however, saw her life with the man she was about to visit.

"How do you tell a man—and his wife—that his life is a lie?"

Michael drove with one hand on the steering wheel and the other resting on the console between them. He laid open his hand, and Shannon slipped hers into it. An easy squeeze to reassure her. She left her hand there.

"And where do I go from here?" Shannon could make or break the Caldwell's lives. But nothing she was about to do would solve the attempted murders.

———

Shannon assured herself of Josh's well-being after she and Michael arrived. He looked good and sounded positive. But she had questions that needed answers and answers to deliver. "Josh, tell me about your mother and what you remember growing up."

"Mother was a bitter woman, like she deserved better and never got it. She wasn't mean or nasty but sour. Not exactly the friendliest of women."

"She didn't mind us marrying but wasn't jumping for joy either. She never really took to the kids which I thought was odd. Like she just didn't care," Katie added, her hand snug in Josh's.

"So, what do you remember from your childhood?" Michael pulled Josh back to the original question.

"To be honest, nothing."

"How'd that happen?" His answer didn't surprise Shannon though.

"Mom told me that I was a good boy growing up. Not mischievous or anything. Not a trouble maker or anything. But when I was old enough to drive, Dad gave me an old car. I don't remember my dad at all. Only what Mom told me about him. Anyway, I wanted to drive it to school one day, and Mom said it was too icy. But Dad told me she was an old woman and a worry wart. He told me the roads were good enough to get to school and back. Turns out Mom was right, and he wasn't. That old car slipped off into the lake, and I was under the ice in freezing water for a long time. I managed to pull myself out and stagger back to the farmhouse, but I turned up sick and completely lost my memory after that night. Mom had to fill in the gaps for me."

What sounded perfectly normal to Josh sounded like a horror story to Shannon. Michael would feel the same because they both knew the truth.

"Mom said Dad had a heart attack when he found out I almost died from his bullheadedness. After his death, she decided it was time to leave the frozen states and get to warmer places. She had a bit of money inherited from her family. She'd never really liked living in North Dakota, but her family and Dad's family were there. By the time I came along and well before I almost drowned, all the relatives were dead. So, I was the last of the line.

We moved to Palacios. When we got here the place was only a blip on the Texas map. But we made a home, I married Katie, and we have two great kids. Mom died not long ago." Josh paused and admitted, "Frankly, she never took up a lot of space in our lives—her choice—so there wasn't a big hole left when she was gone. I was an adult when we came here. I'd lost all my childhood memories, so

I never really felt close to Mom. She was just the person who took care of me and lived close by."

Though talking so much tired Josh, Shannon knew they had to finish this and leave.

"Michael is a private investigator as well as my friend. When you were shot, Josh, I asked him to check into your background and that of your mother because I knew something was wrong. You're not Joshua Caldwell. You're Jacob Waller from Cut Bank, Montana."

Josh didn't look shocked.

But Katie looked surprised, then worried, then a bit angry. "And how do you know this?"

"I contacted people in North Dakota and here in Texas when I got the call from Shannon," Michael sat, pulled out a folder he'd been carrying in his coat jacket, and opened it on his knees. "They did some digging and found some interesting facts. They faxed everything they found to me. So, let me tell you the true story of Joshua Caldwell, who died thirty-four years ago."

Katie gasped, and Josh cried out, "What?"

"Dresden and Mary Caldwell had a child that they named Joshua. The Caldwells owned a farm just off a back water road, so few ever came to see them or bother them. They were as antisocial then as Mary was until the day she died, it seems. The PI interviewed people who knew Mary and Dresden. They confirmed much of this story. Seems Dresden Caldwell had a temper, and he took his anger out on his wife, Mary. Neighbors confirmed seeing Mary beat up. They had a child. More than one neighbor confirmed that. A little boy named Joshua. But something happened one night. Dresden lost the bid on some neighboring land, and those who knew him said he went home in a rage.

The next morning Dresden and Josh were gone. No one in that area ever saw the two again. But years later the man who finally paid the back taxes and took ownership of the Caldwell place discovered a grave with a tiny pile of bones buried in it. No one's ever found where Mary might have buried Dresden, but one older woman said she suspected that Dresden killed the boy, and Mary killed Dresden. For all anyone knows, Mary might have left the body outside for the wolves to take.

Mary stayed on the farm for almost twenty years alone. Then one night an unexpected blizzard came along. The next morning a stranger staggered up to her house, half dead from near drowning. He babbled about his car skidding off the road into a frozen lake and being caught under the ice. He had stopped at another house and tried to tell the folks there the same story, but they feared the man was there to rob them. A Mrs. Merriweather told my investigator that story. She remembers it clear as day because she also recalls that within a few weeks, Mary Caldwell left. The stranger they turned away stumbled off in Mary's direction. The man scared her. Mrs. Merriweather never reported the stranger nor was she aware of a missing person later when the police searched. She and her husband read no papers or had a TV. Was it possible that Mary took in the stranger, then took him with her when she left? She certainly never reported a stranger showing up at her door, half dead from near drowning. We found no police record of any calls notifying them of this man's presence."

Michael stopped and consulted his notes. "The next part of the story comes here in Texas. Seems Mary's best friend, Frieda Green, married a man from the coast of Texas and moved to a small community called Palacios. Frieda was the town clerk, in charge of all records. Mary contacted Frieda and told her what happened. That she had her son back. Joshua was alive."

"No, that can't be," Josh said softly, but Shannon could see that he was starting to believe what Michael said.

"Mary showed up in Palacios with her *grown* son, Joshua. Frieda finagled the records to show that Josh lost his wallet in a near-drowning accident and got a new driver's license and Social Security card. Miss Frieda created that one too. Years passed. Your mother never returned to the Dakotas. She remained quiet and never bothered anyone. Her only saving grace was her son. All thoughts of that tiny body buried in the Dakota plains went out of her mind, it seems, when you showed up. And you looked enough like Dresden Caldwell for the lie to hold."

"So, my life is a lie?" Josh was having trouble accepting Michael's story after all.

Shannon knew the best way to solve this predicament. "Your life is a wonderful one, Josh. You have a son to carry on your family name. He looks enough like your father— Waller Sr.—that I would have known the truth immediately." Shannon held out a photo of Jacob Waller Sr. for Katie to pass over to Josh. "You have a beautiful daughter who'll marry one day. You and Katie will be blessed with grand-children who will love you as much as their parents do. You are not what you were before, that's true. At least Mary made you part of the permanent records of government even if the way she did it wasn't exactly legal. But you're a happy man. I can't take that away from you."

"What do you mean?" Katie passed the photo back to Shannon and sat forward, hope glowing on her face.

"We'll declare Jacob Waller legally dead due to his

long absence. I've hunted for years but never found you. So, I give you to Katie and your kids. I loved you then, but I've changed. So have you. I'll send you a copy of the papers as soon as we can get them through the judge's court. You can burn them or whatever. But then you truly will be who you've been for the past fifteen years—Joshua Caldwell."

"You don't want your husband back or sue us for money or anything like that?" Katie sat with disbelief plain to see on her face.

"I have no need for money, and I lost Jacob Waller a long time ago. We don't know each other now other than the medical things we both know. He's your husband, Katie. Love him and your kids. If there's someone to take the blame here, it's Mary Caldwell, and even she's gone now. Let's let things lie as they are. Deal?"

Josh and Katie sat in silence, focused on each other.

"Before we decide, I have something that may belong to you," Josh said. "Hand over my wallet, would you, Katie?"

"The key?"

"Uh, huh."

She passed over his wallet, and he fumbled through it for a second or two, then came up with a key, an old wide faded gold key. "Does this belong to you? To the house we shared?"

He handed the key to Katie who passed it to Shannon. She rubbed the key and covered her mouth for a moment with a hand that shook. No one spoke as she dug into her purse and came up with a small coin purse. Digging among the change, she pulled out a key that looked similar.

"I gave a key to the new owners—a new one, but saved this one...just for memory's sake," she whispered. She handed them both to Michael. He moved to the strong light near the sink and held the keys up, side by side.

"They match."

He started to hand one back to Josh, but he waved it off. "Give it to Shannon…for closure."

———

"Things worked out well for them, don't you think?" Shannon moved to a more comfortable position in the cushioned chair aboard the jet taking her and Michael home.

"It did, but where does that leave you?"

"Huh?"

"You just gave up your husband."

"Not really," she admitted. "I think I knew all along that Jacob would never come back, and if he did, the same thing would happen. He'd be a different person. We'd both be different. With a death certificate, I'm no longer *married*—even though Jacob lives. Well, sort of." She waved her hand about in a dizzy circle. "You know what I mean. No." She stopped to straighten out her thoughts. "Jacob Waller is truly dead. I think sometimes that it's best to let the past go and move on. You can't bring back the love after that long. Why try when that man's heart clearly belongs to another?"

"You are a generous and loving woman, Shannon Waller," Michael clasped her hand gently, then laid it back on the arm of her chair. He closed his eyes as if going to sleep, but Shannon brought him awake with a touch on his arm and an intriguing question.

"Michael, what if that shot really *was* meant for Josh?"

———

They discussed Shannon's question all the way back to Syracuse. Michael gave her good reasons to believe his theory about the shooting, but Shannon still had doubts.

Justin picked them up. "How are you getting your car home?"

"I hired a friend of Michael's to fly down and drive it back."

"You look beat, Shannon. We need to get you home." Justin opened the car door and closed it, then he and Michael loaded the luggage. "Family conference when we get home?" he asked Michael.

"Despite what Shannon might think, that's a good idea. Everyone on the same page. Everyone looking out for each other. The family could be targets if my theory is wrong."

"That sounds ominous." Justin spoke quietly enough that he hoped Shannon didn't hear.

The drive home was a silent one.

———

If the hugs were extra hard and a bit long, no one objected. The family sat around the large dining table. The dinner plates were gone. The wine glasses were empty and gone. Now it was time for sharing—about what happened in Texas.

A half hour later...

"And that's what happened. I had a great time in Galveston, but someone damaged my car. Whether that had anything to do with the accident and getting hit on the head here, I have no idea. The shooting in Palacios damn near killed Joshua Caldwell. I thought it was meant for me, but then I got to thinking, what if the shooter meant to take out Josh?"

"And here's what I told her." Michael jumped in before anyone added a new theory. "Josh is about four inches taller than Shannon. If the shot had hit her, it would have been a kill shot through the heart. As it was, he moved, she moved, and the shot hit Josh. Level with where it might have hit Shannon. Only it wasn't a kill shot. And he was lucky his heart didn't decide to play out at that particular moment."

"So, evidence points to a shooter going after Shannon and not Josh. Just an odd stroke of fate or a really weird coincidence that she met up with her long-lost husband at that precise moment." Phillip, gentle soul that he was, was having a hard time getting his head wrapped around intentional killings.

"What made you think the shooter might have been after Josh?" Bea spoke up for the first time with a question not one of them had yet to ask.

"If someone found out or suspected that Josh was related to me—might be the beneficiary to my will—then wouldn't it make sense to take him out while still going after me?"

"That sounds good, sweetheart, but you're forgetting that the slow leaking tire seemed planned for you. Meeting Josh and taking him out within an hour of you two meeting is asking just a little too much of coincidence. I mean, if you just discovered that this man was your long-lost husband, then that means someone else would have had reason to track down Jacob long before you. This seems like too random a thing for Josh to be a target. I'm with Michael on this one. The guy shot at you, missed, and hit Josh. An accident. A twist of fate with dramatic consequences." Bea patted Shannon's hand as she offered her thoughts.

"You think Josh and his family are safe?" Shannon didn't sit at the head of the table. Justin did. Michael sat to his right. "Michael?"

"I think Josh getting shot was him taking a bullet meant for you. I think now that you're gone, he and his family are safe."

"Then that just leaves me on the hot seat like it was before." Shannon drew lines with her finger through some water still on the table top.

"Looks like it. But you're not alone, you know. You have a family whether you want us or not," Susan said quietly. The bobble head thing happened again. Five heads nodded like wildflowers in the wind.

"Okay then, I have a family. But you're not going to the bathroom with me. That's just too weird."

"Oooh." Phillip scrunched up his face. "Don't leave me with that mental image. Someone pour me a glass of wine."

Life returned to normal, or at least the *normal* the family established. Keeping tabs on each other, especially Shannon. She finally put a stop to the hovering.

"Enough!" She cast a fierce glare at Bea one afternoon. "I'll be okay. Really. I love you, but you guys are driving me crazy, hovering over me all the time. I'm lucky to go to the bathroom by myself."

Bea didn't respond, a bad sign. Her shoulders drooped, and she shuffled off toward the front door.

"Bea! Bea! Wait, I'm sorry. I didn't mean to hurt your feelings," Shannon rushed after the woman.

"You're right, though, Shannon. We love you and want

to keep you safe, but we're getting kind of weird about it, aren't we?"

"Yeah, a bit. And I truly do understand why you all sort of cling to me, but I need a bit of breathing space now and then. Is that too much to ask?"

"No. Space you can have, and I'll pass the word on, but that doesn't mean you don't be safe, and take care of yourself."

"Thanks, Aunt Bea."

"Ah, go on with you now." Bea gave Shannon a bear hug that threatened to break the younger woman's ribs.

"So where are you off to this time?" Shannon asked only when she could breathe again.

"It's my turn at the library this afternoon. Susan got a call earlier to come help at the soup kitchen. Seems the lady who does the cooking is sick this week. Naturally, they wait until the last minute to call." Bea snorted in disgust as she made her way down the sidewalk to her car. "Check you later."

"Bye. Drive careful."

Suddenly it dawned on her that she had an entire free afternoon. It wasn't even twelve-thirty yet. "Free! Yea!" Ready for some fresh air, she slipped on a coat and headed for the lake. In her free moments she often thought about Leon's folly. How was it made? What was its purpose? Who made it? How the heck did they get it on to that tiny island?

Halfway to the lake she stopped. If she wanted to check out the folly, she would have to do it up close and personal, and to do that she needed to get to the island. No boat lay available so she'd have to get something. "A kayak!"

She ran back to the house, grabbed her key and locked up, then headed to town. The closest sporting goods store handled a variety of kayak, so she bought one built for one. One of the store clerks helped her fasten the kayak to the roof rack of her SUV, and she headed back to Mon Coeur, having used up less than an hour of her free afternoon.

Thankfully, the kayak wasn't too heavy. She balanced it on her head, the paddle strapped into the kayak. Carrying her transportation, she headed for the lake and Leon's folly.

Splat! The kayak didn't slide so graciously into the water as it slid off her head and smacked the cold water. She had a cord tied to her wrist that connected her to the kayak, an idea one of the clerk suggested.

Her tennis shoes got wet as she maneuvered into the wobbly thing, but after a few minutes of getting the feel of paddling, she headed off to the tiny structure. She paddled around it several times before she decided that there was more solid ground than obvious from the lake's shore.

Keeping the kayak tied to her, she stepped out and onto dry land. As she walked around the structure, she pulled the boat. She found a tiny hook under the edge on the back side. That would hold the rope while she explored. She shook out her arm as she ran her fingers along the weathered wooden slats that ran up and twisted. The shiny pieces between the wood really were made of glass—something tinted that probably sent prisms of light on the inside.

"Whoa!" she yelled and grabbed for anything to hold on to when her feet hit a patch of mud. She grabbed a wooden rib and saved herself from sliding into the lake. As she pulled herself up again, she heard a click. A tiny piece of wooden slat popped open about two feet above her head. She had to hold on to the wood by her fingertips in order to lean back and see what was inside that opening. Excitement bubbled up when she saw an old fashioned lock. All it needed was a key to open whatever door was hidden, then she could explore the insides of the folly.

Her excitement dropped like a lead balloon. "No key, damn it."

That doomed excitement took a rollercoaster rise when she realized she actually had the answer. "That old key—the last key on the ring. I bet it fits this lock. It's the answer to Leon's folly! Yippee!" She pushed the lock cover closed and crab crawled her way back to the kayak. "I gotta get that key!"

She ran back to the house and grabbed the key ring, but before she could head back to the folly, her phone rang. Caller ID showed it was Gerald Fergusson. *Talk about throwing cold water on your hot enthusiasm.*

"Hello, Mr. Fergusson."

"I'd like to speak to you, Mrs. Waller, about some of your expenses during your trip...that you neglected to tell me you were taking."

"Now?"

"Yes, please."

Damn, that meant she'd have to change clothes and go to town. The only upside was that she could get one or more of the family to share dinner with her while in town. "I can be there in thirty minutes."

"That will do," Fergusson said and immediately hung up on her.

"That man reminds me more and more of Leven every day." But she rushed through her change. "The sooner I get there, the sooner I can leave." The reflection in the mirror nodded in agreement.

The banker's secretary ushered Shannon into his office. She spoke as she advanced toward him. "Mr. Fergusson, what is it you want?" She extended her hand to shake and he stood, but reluctantly, she thought. His attitude seemed at odds for a banker entrusted with a client's moneys. *He'd have preferred not to shake hands. His problem, not mine.*

"I'd like to confirm that some of these purchases are legitimate." He scanned the pages before him.

Shannon could read documents lying upside down and saw that he had a printout of her bank statement. "May I ask what business it is of yours to check into my purchases when I have a fraud detector app attached to my debit and credit card accounts?"

The man looked shocked, as if a mouse had roared in the face of a lion.

"You doubt my ability to handle your accounts accurately?" Fergusson's face grew red, and his lips drew tight.

"Did I say that? Exactly that?" His personality suddenly mirrored Mr. Leven—a controlling narcissist. Shannon knew this man would try to bully her into believing she caused him personal harm by questioning his judgment. Charlie Hawkins and Leven tried that, and she learned from experience. Her emotions shut down, and her logic rose to the top, ready for whatever he threw at her.

"Not in those words, but you imply that I cannot handle your affairs properly." His hands grasped the sides of his desk as if he prepared to stand...or jump over the furniture at her. "Perhaps you're not as good an accountant as your lawyer makes you out to be. Fear of being debunked can make one irrational." His words turned her questions around, his way of making her look the victim here. "I take my job very seriously and do perfect work for my customers."

His sanctimonious reasoning disgusted Shannon. "I believe that you're meddling into things that aren't your affair, questioning my spending when it's minimal and innocent." Shannon spoke quietly, her head cocked to one side, as if examining him for worthiness. She was pushing his buttons but didn't care. At this point, he was no longer her banker. She'd find another bank. Even another person within this bank would always be under scrutiny or harassment from Fergusson.

"You poor woman, all alone for so long. I'm surprised no one ever took advantage of your financial situation," Fergusson crooned, sitting back in his chair, apparently thinking her cowed and ready to leave him alone. "Let me handle these purchases for you. You'll make wiser choices with my guidance."

Shannon gasped, held her breath, then burst out laughing. Long and hard. "Seriously? You'll guide me—a grown woman who's lived alone and managed okay? You...you... can't be serious." Before he could answer—and his red face said that might be a few seconds—she held up a hand and stood. He would come back at her with either the strong silent parental disapproval treatment or fly into a throwing-objects fit. She wanted no part of either one.

"You, sir, act more like a child than a lot of the children I knew back in Montana. You are self-centered and egotistical. In fact, there's a commonly used word floating around these days that perfectly describes you—narcissistic. You have no idea how to deal with others, and I have no intentions of dealing with you further. I have better things to do...like explore Leon's folly that I just unlocked. Good day."

She turned her back on him but felt the daggers of his stare along her spine as she pulled the door open, crossed the threshold without haste and calmly closed the door. She anticipated silence but heard something fragile like glass shatter behind the door.

"I'd take a break right now if I were you," she told the secretary. "He's a bit upset."

THE ANSWER KEY

S hannon returned home rather than wait in town until the
others finished their jobs. She gunned her SUV back to
the house. With everyone gone for the afternoon and that
distasteful interview with Fergusson over, she wanted to get
out and breathe fresh air. She'd deal with a new bank tomorrow. A typical Scarlett O'Hara attitude but one she'd live
with for at least one afternoon.

Like a mad woman, she threw off her good clothes and
pulled on her jeans and long-sleeved flannel shirt. She
hopped on first one foot then the other as she made her way
precariously down the staircase. Grabbing her key ring and
coat, Shannon raced to the folly.

Common sense returned as she seated herself in the
kayak. She reached for her cell phone and dialed Justin.

"Hey, what's up?" The sound of papers shuffling and
thumping into place came clear in the afternoon quiet.

"I found a way into the folly. Leon's folly. I think that
old key opens a door. I'm headed there now. Call Phillip,
and let him know. I'll see you guys in a bit." Immediately

she hit END and called Michael. She repeated the same message about the oldest key and the folly.

Ending her call, she zipped the cell in her coat pocket and took up the paddle. Rowing slowly, as she was still new at the whole kayak and paddling thing, she edged around to the back side of the folly and stepped out—getting her tennis shoes wet again. She secured the rope to the small hook, then stopped to scrutinize the folly. Five minutes passed before she found the hidden cover for the key hole. She only found it after she looked for the skid marks where she almost went off into the lake. Cold water that sent an image of Jacob—now Josh—in freezing water, almost drowning. She shook off the mental image, knowing he lived a wonderful fulfilling life now.

Inserting the antique key, she heard a click, then a slow screeching as a narrow section of the folly wall slid open. Not a lot but enough for a slender person to go through. The air coming through the open door smelled musty, so she gave it a few minutes so fresh air could circulate inside.

Thinking she'd only find the bone-like structure of the tiny building, she entered the doorway and stopped, her jaw literally hanging slack.

Prism glass threw narrow bands of multi-colored light across an old-fashioned bedroom, the whole folly being less than twelve feet round. A double bed with tall posts and bed curtains stood in the middle of the tiny room. Small tables hugged the bed's sides, a lamp and cup and saucer on the table farthest from Shannon. On the table nearest her stood another lamp with a bouquet of flowers, long dried, covered with dust. A ruby-colored plush chaise lounge stood next to the folly's wall, the bed mere feet away. The bed covers lay as if someone had just left, the sheet and rose-decorated comforter thrown back on one side. At the foot of the bed lay what looked like a painter's traveling box of colors and paper.

Shannon slipped off her wet muddy tennis shoes and made her way across the room.

It's beautiful. She ran a hand over the paint box's smooth top. Standing in the middle of this unexpected room with its faded glory she had to ask the powers-that-be just what went on here. Sudden inspiration, a flash of insight, caused her to collapse on the side of the bed.

"This was Uncle Leon's trysting place." Her uncle used that word a lot, and it came to her that he meant it for its true meaning. *Meeting his lover in secret.* Once she remembered that Leon was gay long before the world acknowledged people as such, then this secret place made sense. *Leon met someone here, and they spent afternoons…making love.*

One hand ran over the bed covers. So soft but cold. Once upon a time, they would have lain warm from the heat of passionate bodies. How sad that Leon's love wasn't someone with whom he could share his world. At least not in public.

Her hand brushed the painter's box, and she pulled it to her. A scrolled-work handle hid a small catch that held the box closed. Similar scrolled hinges held the top to the bottom. She could image someone taking out paper and watercolor, laying the paper on the slanted top and producing the delicate drawings so common during the early twentieth century.

What the…? Inside the box lay a pen made of gold, an inkwell, and a book. *Not for a painter. I bet this is Leon's journal.* She pulled the small leather-bound book from the case and gently lowered the top.

Fascinated by the thought she might have discovered more of her uncle's writings—they'd shared letters for years before she started actually spending her vacations with him —she carefully pushed the box further down on the bed. Rather than bother the bed and its sad display of mussed covers, she took several steps and sat on the lounge. Untying the leather thong that held the journal closed, she carefully opened the cover to the first page.

"Property of L Jeffers and ..." Where the second name should have been, Leon had drawn a heart.

You old dog, you. Let's see if you mention your lover...by name.

Careful not to tear pages that appeared quite old, she turned page by page, scanning the tight handwriting for names. But Leon was a crafty lover. Never once in the lines she read did he mention his lover's name. Frustrated by the lack of disclosure, she actually read bits of Leon's writing aloud.

"Oooh, Uncle, you could be a porn novelist these days with this kind of writing." The man wrote in explicit detail. "I bet you wrote this, then read it to your partner." A shudder went down her back again, this time one of distaste. "You did your thing, and I did mine, Uncle, but we sure had different tastes," she commented aloud. "So how did this end?"

She flipped to the back of the journal, to the last page, read, blinked, and backed up a few pages. Alone in the dusty silence, she read aloud, then shook her head, unable to believe her uncle could be so heartless. "Oh, that's cold, Leon. Cold! You were going to leave him as a lover, and you weren't working with him anymore? And you changed your will. That's pretty heartless. Wonder who you were talking about?" She flipped back through the book, reading pages here and there, looking for a name, but Leon carefully never identified his lover.

Shannon stopped, her heart racing. *Motive.* Michael always said there was motive for what happened. *She* was the motive! Leon ended his journal, writing that he was leaving his lover. He wanted no competition between that man and his niece. The last few sentences were the real reason someone wanted to kill her. Leon not only planned to end his affair with his mysterious lover but before he did, he changed his will, cutting out the lover in favor of Shannon, his last surviving relative. The lover never found out their affair ended or the will was changed; the man died first.

A shudder ran down her back. Not repugnance at her uncle's proclivity, but the thought that someone else knew of this place. Leon's lover. She had no idea who; she'd only told a few people that she just now found a way in.

"It took no time for the lover to learn he was getting nothing from Leon's estate or finances, losing billions when I showed up."

"Years of devotion and nothing to show for it," came a voice from the doorway.

Shannon jumped up and back, bumped into the bedside table, jostling the flowers and rocking the lamp. "What the hell are you doing here?" Her mouth went dry. Her body shook and went cold. Her heart beat so fast her chest hurt.

Gerald Fergusson stood in the doorway. "Kayak, my dear. I'm an avid kayaker. How the hell do you think Leon and I got over here? I carry that thing on top of my SUV all the time." His smug grin faded when Shannon didn't cower.

"Get out of here!" Shannon took a step forward. Her

progress came to an immediate halt when Fergusson pulled a gun from his coat pocket and calmly pointed it at her.

"I think not. Leon played me for a fool. We loved each other. I should have inherited when he died. How did I know he changed his will to leave his fortune to some nobody little niece in no-where USA? He sent me a letter…a letter of all things! Said he was changing his account to a different bank to avoid conflict of interest between us. Huh! No one will ever see that letter because I burned it. And you, missy, you're going to mysteriously disappear, and I'll arrange for the bank to manage the estate. No one will question what I do."

"You can't do that!" Shannon's shout produced that cold silence he exhibited when she left his office earlier.

"Watch me." He edged into the small room and motioned her back. "Let's see. First kill you. Find that damn key, lock up this place, then toss the key into the lake. No one will ever think to check this place. After all, it's been here for decades, and no one's discovered that door. Lucky you." He shrugged, his words sarcastic.

"But he loved you. How could you hurt him like this by killing me?" Shannon hoped he'd keep talking. After all, she'd called Michael and Justin. Both of them would be dying of curiosity to learn what she found in the middle of the lake. And even if Fergusson did manage to hurt her, they knew the folly was more than it appeared. That would be the first place they'd look.

"I loved Leon with passion. With all my heart. If that bed could talk it would tell stories of endless hours of loving. We shared that cup of tea. Smelled the flowers and used them in our love play. We read poetry and talked about our lives now and into the future."

Fergusson stood lost in memories, while his gun hand remained clearly in the here and now, quite steady. One could almost feel sorry for what the man lost. Almost…

Shannon miscalculated by bringing him back to the present. "Someone will miss me. They'll look all over the place. They'll question everyone when I don't show up. You being in control of the money—you're the first person they'll suspect. And you're the last person who saw me today. Your secretary can testify that you weren't happy when I left. I bet the pieces of whatever you threw and broke are still in your office."

Whatever control Gerald Fergusson had on his emotions shattered. His mouth worked. Shannon sensed he was trying to order his thoughts. "You should have stayed gone. You survived that crash and even came back from that wallop I delivered in the woods. You should have died! You're such a creature of habit…walking those paths all the time. Paths Leon and I walked, hand in hand. Lovers! And that damn Texan couldn't even shoot you. I even told him where you'd be most vulnerable along that isolated stretch of road. Really —I tracked your credit card charges like a bloodhound while you traveled. You should have died!" His words came out in bellows. "You need to die." His rant sent words scattering like leaves before a winter wind. The gun in his hand waved in mad circles now, first pointed at Shannon, then the ceiling, then the floor. Spittle formed around his mouth. His eyes roved wildly, as if looking for Leon. His gun hand moved too erratically, giving Shannon little opportunity to escape past him.

Her hand rested against the nightstand. In desperation she scooped up the bouquet off the table and sent them flying across the room. Fergusson's gaze automatically followed the small wad of flowers. One second of distraction and she grabbed the lamp, stepped forward, and smashed the glass over his hand. The gun went off with a roar, shattering one of the glass slats. Using self-defense techniques she'd learned before her trip south, she slugged him, and the man went down hard, dazed. His body still blocked her exit though. He raised up onto his hands and knees, but she kicked him in the ribs hard enough to send him flat to the floor again. Before she realized his intentions, he reached for the gun, just beyond his reach. But she dived for it as well.

Fergusson had at least a hundred pounds on Shannon, but she fought for her life. They struggled, and the gun went off again. This time the bullet hit the door frame. Shannon raised her arm, the gun in her hand and brought it down with all her might on Fergusson's head. He slumped unconscious beneath her. She rolled to one side, sides heaving, heart pounding, adrenaline surging. She glanced over to make sure the man still lay unconscious. Her glance caught movement. Michael and Justin stood at the door, the gouge of that last bullet's path next to Michael's shoulder.

Gun in hand, she rushed to the tall black man, unmindful of the water that dripped off him. "Oh my god, M, I could have killed you!" She embraced him desperately, her heart racing, her legs wobbly. "Hold me. Hold me." He pulled her tighter, but then she pushed away, using both hands to pat him down, frantically searching for a bullet hole though the hole was in the door frame and not in his arm.

"I'm good, Shannon. See, I'm okay." Michael showed her his shoulder and the bullet that still lay buried in the door frame. "Come here, woman. You need another hug." While Michael embraced Shannon, he nodded to Justin, then the gun she still held. "Take that damn gun away from her, will you, before she kills one of us."

"Gladly. And you might want to tie him up."

"Here." Michael handed over Shannon who fell willingly into Justin's embrace. "This is one crazy old coot." He used a rope that held back the bed curtains to tie up Fergusson. The man groaned but didn't open his eyes.

"What's that?" Justin nodded to a crumpled piece of paper that Michael's foot dislodged when he jostled the bed covers.

Michael picked it up with two fingers and brought it to Shannon. "Maybe you better read this. We're a bit wet right now."

"Comes from swimming out here to the folly. No rowboat." Justin shivered after his sarcasm as Shannon took the paper. While she read aloud, the men looked over her shoulder.

"My dear Gerry, though I love you, we shall not meet again. Times were good for us, but they're over now. I'm withdrawing my accounts from your bank, but don't throw a tantrum. And you do toss some spectacular tantrums. I love you still, but I've found someone else that's closer than a lover. Take care."

"It's a practice letter. See the mark outs? Like he couldn't exactly figure out what he wanted to say or how to say it. Leon sent a letter to Fergusson. He told me just now. Said he burned it. Fergusson was furious. I think he expected to inherit when Leon passed away." Shannon smoothed out the wrinkles and folded the paper before sticking it in her pocket. "Boy, this whole inheriting thing must have come as a shock!"

———

"And that's the story. The police know everything as well." Shannon rattled the key ring that lay on the table in front of her. "All the keys accounted for. The final key being the one for the folly. You can imagine the authorities' reaction when they had to boat over to the folly, and we showed them the whole layout while they gathered up Fergusson. I'm sure his lawyer will put a more delicate spin on what happened if anyone even cares. I was going to change banks, but now I'll have to think about it. That man was one despicable character."

"So you're safe now?" Bea clung to Susan's hand.

"As far as I know."

"Are you staying at Mon Coeur?" Phillip leaned closer to his wife, while Justin leaned forward, anxious to hear her answer.

"Of course. My family is here." Shannon graced each with a smile and blown kiss.

"Damn, woman, I'm going to stick around even closer and make darn sure you're safe," Michael said. He had paced the floor the entire time Shannon told the story to the family. Now he put one hand on her shoulder and squeezed it. "Think you can handle me around all the time...keeping you safe?"

The family cast looks at each other, their grins giving him their answer, while all waited to hear what Shannon Waller would say.

"Humm, I can do pretty well on my own, but I think I can handle you being around all the time." She gave him a sassy wink and teasing grin.

Michael bent over her. The long tender kiss they shared drew sighs of contentment from their entire family.

———

Don't miss out on your next favorite book!

Join the Satin Romance mailing list
www.satinromance.com/mail.html

THANK YOU FOR READING

———

Did you enjoy this book?

We invite you to leave a review at your favorite book site, such as Goodreads, Amazon, Barnes & Noble, etc.

DID YOU KNOW THAT LEAVING A REVIEW...

- Helps other readers find books they may enjoy.
- Gives you a chance to let your voice be heard.
- Gives authors recognition for their hard work.
- Doesn't have to be long. A sentence or two about why you liked the book will do.

ABOUT THE AUTHOR

My love of writing dates back to when I taught. I wrote during the summer. Then I wrote during my breaks at school. The time came when I could write full time. I love words. They go together in such fascinating ways. Just like my love of quilting—fabric goes together in such intriguing patterns. Both writing and quilting challenge my creative side. When I write, I listen to the voices in my head. They lead me to the most captivating stories. That sound odd? Maybe, but that's my story and I'm sticking to it.

janer.carver@gmail.com